Praise

BECAUSE SHE CAN

"Bridie Clark's book world novel is stirring mirth with its story of an overbearing literary diva."
—*New York Daily News*

"Entertaining . . . devilishly funny . . . Vivian's vitriolic tantrums are laugh-out-loud funny."
—*Booklist*

"She nails the idea of the badder-than-bad lady boss, and she should know."
—*Hartford Courant*

"Clark's tale of a young editor who goes to work for the publisher from hell is laugh-out-loud funny, outrageous, and all too true to the world it portrays."
—Amy Sohn, author of *My Old Man* and *Run Catch Kiss*

"A devilish read . . . nails the dark side of the vulgar, spiteful boss archetype."
—*Publishers Weekly*

"Funny . . . especially in the gleeful anarchy of some of Vivian's more sociopathic rants."
—*Kirkus Reviews*

BECAUSE SHE CAN

BRIDIE CLARK

GC

GRAND CENTRAL
PUBLISHING

NEW YORK   BOSTON

This book is a work of fiction. Names, characters, places, and incidents are the product of the author's imagination or are used fictitiously. Any resemblance to actual events, locales, or persons, living or dead, is coincidental.

Grand Central Publishing
Hachette Book Group USA
237 Park Avenue
New York, NY 10017

Visit our Web site at www.HachetteBookGroupUSA.com.

Printed in the United States of America

Originally published in hardcover by Hachette Book Group USA.

First Trade Edition: February 2008

10 9 8 7 6 5 4 3 2 1

Grand Central Publishing is a division of Hachette Book Group USA, Inc.
The Grand Central Publishing name and logo is a trademark of Hachette Book Group USA, Inc.

The Library of Congress has cataloged the hardcover edition as follows:

Clark, Bridie.
  Because she can / Bridie Clark. — 1st ed.
     p. cm.
   ISBN-13: 978-0-446-57924-7
   ISBN-10: 0-446-57924-6
 1. Chick lit. I. Title.
   PS3603.L3565B43 2007
   813'.6—dc22   2006019191
 ISBN 978-0-446-69757-6 (pbk.)

Dedicated to my family

BECAUSE
SHE CAN

PROLOGUE

 POSTCARDS FROM THE EDGE

I t's my wedding day. T minus two hours until I'm supposed to be walking down the aisle.

My best friend, Beatrice, helps me pull my dress over my head, smiling as it rustles down around me, fastening the small row of delicate buttons in the back. *Thank God for Bea*, I think for the millionth time that day. We both look at the bride in the mirror. She looks just the way brides are supposed to look: dark mahogany hair pulled back into an elegant twist at the nape of her neck, flawless makeup, porcelain skin, diamonds dripping off each earlobe.

I spin a little to see if the Perfect Bride in the mirror will follow my lead—and she does, of course. Then she examines her spectacular train, custom-designed by Vera herself, onto which a dozen seamstresses at the House of Lesage have sewn the finest little diamonds to look like fairy dust.

"You're stunning, Claire," says Bea, because what else can you really say to a woman wearing this kind of masterpiece. We stare at me in the gilded mirror. Neither of us bothers to smile.

A bony knock on the door of my bridal suite snaps us out of the fog.

"It's open," Bea calls out, and in charges Lucille Cox, my mother-in-law-to-be—face taut as a Doberman pinscher's, body the size of a scrawny eight-year-old boy.

"I come bearing a gift from the groom!" Lucille booms exuberantly to neither of us in particular—what Lucille lacks in stature, she tends to make up for in decibels. Today she is smaller and louder than usual, drowning in a crimson Oscar de la Renta gown that cost three times more than my mother's car. Prewedding jitters have reduced Lucille's diet from Spartan to Ethiopian. The pigeons in Central Park are better fed.

"Oh, Claire, *darling*, you look…" Lucille ends her sentence by pressing a jewel-encrusted hand to her freckled, skeletal décolletage—a gesture in lieu, I have to assume, of kind adjectives. Then she finishes her thought: "You look *just* like your mother."

Stop the presses—has Lucille actually said the right thing? Shockingly, Lucille—a woman whose most frequent meal is her own foot—has paid me my all-time favorite compliment, and one that I know is highest praise coming from her. Lucille has always idolized my mother, ever since their roommate days at Vassar.

I feel a rush of gratitude toward her. Lucille, as if sensing softer emotions in the air, awkwardly thrusts a velvet box into my hands to dispel them.

"Open it!" she commands.

I do as I'm told, as has become my bad habit. I undo the little clasp and crack open the box's stiff hinge. On a pillow of plush black velvet rests a spectacular necklace, loaded with diamonds—the most expensive piece of jewelry I've ever seen, let alone held.

"Oh, my *dear*," purrs Lucille, gazing with adoration at the necklace as if it were her first grandchild. "Vintage Bulgari. *Stunning.*" I fasten it around my neck, and the three of us turn to the mirror once more. It's perfect. Absolutely spectacular. My fiancé's secretary has exquisite taste.

"*And* I got my hands on an advance copy of the Sunday edition," Lucille trills, unclasping her Judith Leiber and pulling out a newspaper clip, which she hands to me.

Claire Truman,
Randall Pearson Cox III

Claire Truman, the daughter of Patricia and the late Charles Truman of Iowa City, Iowa, and Randall Pearson Cox III, the son of Lucille and Randall Cox II of Palm Beach, Florida, are to be married today at St. James' Episcopal Church in New York City.

Miss Truman, 27, is an editor at Grant Books. She graduated summa cum laude from Princeton with a degree in English literature and language. Her mother is a painter, and her late father was a poet-in-residence and professor at the University of Iowa.

Mr. Cox, 31, is a Managing Director at Goldman Sachs, an investment bank in New York. He also received his bachelor's degree from Princeton, as well as an M.B.A from Harvard. His mother is on the board of the Flagler Museum and the Palm Beach Historical Society. His grandfather was the former CEO and Chairman of McCowan Trust, where his father retired as Senior Vice President last year.

"Are you all right, Claire?" asks Lucille, looking down. I follow her gaze. My hands are shaking violently, as if they're gripping an invisible sledgehammer. Thankfully, Lucille has the attention span of a baby gnat and is diverted by the entrance of our makeup artist, Jacques, who pulls her into a chair for a touch-up.

"Where is that mother of yours, anyway?" she calls out to me over her shoulder, scanning Jacques's tool kit for the right shade of burgundy lipstick.

"She'll be here any moment." I check my watch, silently willing time to stop for just a second to let me catch my breath. Doesn't work. Hasn't worked all month.

"I need her advice on earrings," Lucille whines.

Bea looks up, incredulous. Well, it *is* pretty laughable, the thought of Lucille—society matron, with several walk-in closets full of unworn couture—asking my aging hippie of a mother for her advice on which arrangement of Harry Winston diamonds works better with a straight-off-the-Paris-runway gown. Mom, whose only adornment since I've known her has been her plain gold wedding band. Mom, whose idea of decadent pampering is a hot bath and some organic aromatherapy given to her by her best friend in Iowa—a lesbian farmer/fellow artist who makes her own soap. Mom, whose wardrobe consists of flannel, denim, tie-dye.

It's hard to imagine, but apparently Mom and Lucille had been as close as sisters at Vassar. Lucille (who grew up in a one-horse Kansas town that drifts closer to Chicago every time she's asked) spent four years peppering Mom (who hails from Boston Brahmin) with pointed questions about etiquette, style, refinement. I suppose Mom found Lucille's aggressive social climbing benign and even somewhat amusing—she didn't care enough about the world into which she'd been born to feel possessive of it or object to anyone's desperate desire for access. And Lucille's secondary education paid off richly when she landed Randall Cox II, a debonair, blue-blooded polo player. He'd been dating five Vassar girls at once, but he'd chosen Lucille to be his wife. Quite the campus coup, or so she's informed me.

Lucille's snared husband, aka my future father-in-law, turned out to be as unfaithful as he was successful (wildly, both counts). But as far as I know, Lucille's never minded her husband's flagrant transgressions—so content has she been with the mansion in Palm Beach, the private jets, the jewelry, the seven-bedroom "cottage" in Southampton, the fashion shows in Paris and Milan, the peripatetic cook and masseuse and secretary, the town house in Manhattan. The lifestyle of Mrs. Randall Cox II.

Mom, on the other hand, traded her family's life of privilege for my incomparably wonderful father—the love of her life, a close to penniless poet who nonetheless provided us with the richest life imaginable. Money was always a bit tight—Dad taught classes at the university, Mom sold her watercolors in local boutiques to subsidize his income, and I worked hard to gain my scholarship to Princeton—but looking back on my childhood, I wouldn't have changed a thing.

I grew up in a small, picture-perfect white farmhouse in the emerald cornfields of Iowa, an only child surrounded by a brilliant coterie of poets, students, playwrights, novelists—all of whom had gravitated to the university's famous Writers' Workshop. Starting at around age ten, I was often asked to read and give my input on the work of this extended family circle. Having my opinion valued was a thrill for a burgeoning bookworm (okay, burgeoning nerd) like me, and I would spend afternoons holed up in my bedroom writing detailed letters with my thoughts and suggestions. Maybe our friends were just humoring me, but working with such brilliant writers, penning my first "editorial letters," getting my first taste of creative collaboration—these were the unusual childhood delights that led me to major in English in college and then into a career in book publishing.

Maybe that's my problem: My life has been a series of easy, clear choices. I've never appreciated it until today. Unlike almost everyone else I know, I've never had to grapple with which path to take.

I look down at the *Times* announcement again, my eyes suddenly stinging with tears.

"You okay?" Bea rests her hand on my shoulder. Then she grips my hand, which is still shaking.

"Cigarette," I whisper urgently. She nods like a dutiful soldier. *Thank God for Bea.*

Ten minutes later, Bea and I crouch in the stairwell, sharing our second contraband Marlboro Light and swilling Veuve Clicquot straight from the bottle, a blanket underneath us so my dress won't get soiled. I feel like a fugitive and know I'm on borrowed time.

"Mandy'll have a search party out in about two minutes," Bea snorts. Mandy is the de rigueur neurotic wedding planner whom Lucille forced upon me the day after Randall and I got engaged. (Here's some advice: Never trust an unmarried wedding planner over the age of thirty-five. Mandy's single and forty-two.)

Combined, Mandy and Lucille have the diplomatic skills of a bulldozer. At first, I put up a halfhearted fight about the wedding plans, but they quickly broke me—and the intimate gathering on my parents' farm exploded into a white-tie soiree at the St. Regis Hotel with 600 of our "closest friends." Otherwise known as 300 of Lucille's crusty Palm Beach set, 250 of Randall's business associates, and a handful of my friends and family.

I shouldn't complain—the Coxes are picking up every tab. There was no way Mom could afford the kind of wedding Lucille had her heart set on.

"Here," says Bea, handing me the champagne. I chug, and the fizz goes straight to my head. She refills. I chug again.

The past two months have been grueling. My boss—the notorious sociopath Vivian Grant—has been on a particularly ruthless rampage. I've been working around the clock... barely an exaggeration. If Mandy and Lucille hadn't stepped in, I wouldn't have had a free minute to deal with the wedding details. I've barely had time to see Randall since we got engaged three months ago.

Lucille even set the date for us, a shockingly early date at that—she hadn't wanted our wedding to get "lost" in the lineup of society weddings planned for the following fall.

A door crashes open down the hall, some distant floorboards creak, and Bea and I exchange furtive glances.

"Claire," starts Bea, biting her pinkie nail as she always does when she's not sure how to phrase something gently. (After a decade of best friendship, we've developed an awareness of each other's body language that sometimes borders on telepathy.)

"Okay, don't," I interrupt. "All brides get cold feet." I can't back out now. Maybe Julia Roberts can dodge the altar a few times and still seem adorable, but this isn't some Hollywood movie. This is my life. Deposits have been paid... *What am I thinking?* I can't back out now because Randall is a good man—no, he's a *great* man—and I'd be pretty much insane not to marry him.

As I take the last drag of our cigarette, a memory involuntarily pops into my head—an increasingly frequent problem—of the night before Beatrice's wedding to Harry, now three years ago. She'd been one of the first of our circle to get married, and they'd opted for a simple ceremony in the garden of Bea's family's home. We'd stayed up the night before trying to bake something remotely akin to a wedding cake, sitting around the big table in their kitchen and dipping our fingers into the spilled batter.

"Getting nervous, Bea?" one of the bridesmaids had asked.

I remember how Bea had just shrugged, taking another swipe of the batter. "Excited, yes. Nervous, no," she'd answered honestly.

I think of my own wedding cake. How could any bride *not* get excited about a statuesque twelve-tiered cake with sugar-spun, botanically correct rosebuds and irises (a dusting of colored sugar on each one to look like pollen), not to mention a background pattern in the frosting that's consistent with the beading on my dress *and* the china? So what if this skyscraper of a cake costs roughly the same as a year of tuition at a private college? It is literally perfect. A Sylvia Weinstock masterpiece. What more could I ask for? What more could I possibly want?

The heavy door to the stairwell slams open, and Bea and I both jump two inches. The bloodhounds have found us.

"Claire, darling! Sweet pea! I've been looking high and low for you! Just an hour until we have to leave for the church!" Mandy, flushed and badly in need of a Xanax, rushes over to pull me to my feet and smooth out my dress. "I'll get hair and makeup to come do a touch-up."

"Unbelievable," I distinctly hear her whisper as she herds us back to the bridal HQ. I shuffle wordlessly behind her like a prisoner called in from the yard.

"Claire!" Mom sprints toward me as we turn the corner to the suite, pulling me away from Mandy and into just the kind of hug I desperately need. I feel my shoulders drop, my neck relax. It feels so good to be held—*really* held. I take a deep breath, inhaling the faint eucalyptus scent of her shampoo. Mom squeezes me tighter.

"I have something for you, sweetie," she says, pulling a small velvet pouch out of her handbag. "Your grandmother's pearl necklace. I know you've always loved it, so I thought it could be your 'something old.'"

"Oh, Mom," I gasp, running my fingers over the cool, lustrous pearls. As a girl, it had been such a special treat to try on my grandmother's necklace during our summer visits. "It's beautiful, Mom. Thank you so—"

"The pearls are lovely, Tish-Tish," interrupts Lucille, "but Randall just surprised Claire with *this* necklace. Fabulous, isn't it?"

Mom steps back, taking in the sparkling rope of diamonds around my neck. "Well, my goodness!" she says, "It's...it's gorgeous. How generous of Randall. Well, Claire, you can wear Grandma's pearls another time. They're yours now." Mom slides the pearls into the velvet bag. It hurts to see the effort in her smile.

"Or, um, maybe I could wear Randall's necklace some other time?" I ask tentatively, knowing it's a long shot.

And sure enough, Lucille explodes immediately. "What's this? *Not* wear Randall's necklace? Why, Claire, he'd be *crushed*! It was his special wedding-day gift to you! You must wear it, you just *must*!

Mom nods in agreement. Then she stretches out her arms to give me another hug.

Please don't let me go, I think, burying myself in her arms, twenty years melting off me. With Mom's arms around me, I feel the pit in my stomach dissolve just a little.

"Tish-Tish, please, I'm desperate for your help with earrings," whimpers Lucille, wresting Mom away from me. The feeling of Mom's arms pulling away is worse than the sound of a blaring alarm clock after a night of insomnia. I watch helplessly. I'm too old to dive for my mother's knees and hold on tight, but it takes every ounce of restraint not to do that.

And then, just when I couldn't feel any worse, I do.

Because I hear her. The unmistakable voice: deep, throaty, powerful, *cruel*. The voice that's ricocheted off the walls of my nightmares for the past eleven months.

And the dreaded voice seems to be walking very briskly down the hallway toward me.

"Claire!...*Claire!* There you are!"

If I were a deer, that voice would be the headlights. Freezes me in my tracks every time.

Is it actually possible?! It seems too horrible to imagine—

"Jesus, Claire, I've left you a dozen fucking messages on your cell and home phones! Finally I got through to some pea-brained, inbred relative of yours—and after *much* hemming and hawing, she finally managed to tell me where you were. *Un*acceptable, Claire. I need to be able to reach you 25/8, we've been *over* this—"

Breathe, I think frantically, not turning around, palms starting to sweat. *This* must *be another nightmare. It just can't be real.*

I force myself to turn around. She's really here. The afore-mentioned boss from hell: the merciless, glamorous, one-and-only Vivian Grant. At five feet one, a tiny terror. Hip jutting out impatiently, face flushed with rage, legal pad in hand.

No, no, no! I scream silently. There is *no way* that Vivian is really crashing into my bridal suite with a look in her eyes that can mean only one thing—

"I need ten minutes to give you some of my ideas for next week."

Bea crosses her arms and glares. She looks ready to rip Vivian limb from limb. Mom and Lucille reappear in the doorway, dumbstruck. Vivian's audacity has even managed to silence old Luce.

"Vivian," I say very slowly, "I'm getting married in one hour. I'm postponing my honeymoon so that I can stay on top of my work responsibilities. Can this wait until Monday?"

Vivian glowers at me, brow knit. This is *exactly* what she'd been hoping I'd say. It allows her to segue seamlessly into one of her favorite tirades.

"I'm so glad you think *my* schedule should revolve around *yours*, Claire! All I'm asking for is a measly fucking ten minutes. Do you think you can tear yourself away from all this"— she sweeps a hand dismissively around the room, where Mom, Lucille, and Bea are now staring with jaws open—"for something so frivolous, so insignificant, as your *career*?"

Briefly, I consider running over to the window of the bridal suite, prying it open, and...

"I thought you were made of stronger stuff, Claire," Vivian sneers derisively, "I thought you had it in you. But I guess now that you're getting *married*..."

I know she's crazy. Her elevator doesn't go up to the top floor. Still, the woman has a powerful, pathological effect on me—as she does on most of her employees.

"I'll give you five," I tell her (brazenly, for me), taking a big slug of champagne as I grab the notepad and a pen.

"This is really nuts," Bea hisses after Vivian has swept past her. "You're a book editor, Claire, not the leader of the free world. What could possibly be so urgent that she needs to barge in on your wedding day? It's insane! Why is she doing this to you?"

Why does Vivian do *any* of the things she does? I think about the question.

"Because she can," I tell Bea.

I have a chilling epiphany: As ludicrous as it is that my boss won't leave me alone on my wedding day, part of me is grateful for something to take my mind off the impending event.

For a few moments more, I won't have to think about that long walk down the aisle. I won't have to think about the life I'm stepping into or the life I'm leaving behind. I won't have to think about the man who'll be waiting for me at the altar, or why I'm not overjoyed to be marrying someone so undeniably great.

And most of all, I won't have to think about the man I kissed six weeks before.

_____ ONE YEAR EARLIER

CHAPTER ONE

 A GOOD MAN IS HARD
TO FIND

Exactly one year before my June 26 wedding day, I was curled up on my couch with a large pepperoni pizza, a half-empty pack of Marlboro Lights, the world's most comfortable blanket, and several hours of TiVO ahead of me.

Under normal circumstances, this lineup would've thrilled me. On another night, my pack of cigarettes would have been half-full. But tonight, even the prospect of watching Kiefer Sutherland save the world for six straight hours was of little solace.

For starters, I was still fresh on the heels of an ugly breakup with my wannabe rock-star boyfriend, James. (In the interest of full disclosure, it was the final of four breakups, each one more obviously necessary than the last.) That had me down.

But what had me *out* was a crisis of a professional nature. Just that afternoon, I'd gotten the crushing news that Jackson Mayville, my beloved boss at Peters and Pomfret (the top-tier New York book publishing house), my professional mentor during the five years since I'd graduated from college, would be hanging up his cleats this summer. He and his wife were moving down to Virginia to be closer to their grandkids.

I probably should've guessed it was coming, but I've always been pretty bad at doing that. So, when Jackson gave me the news, I immediately misted up—embarrassing but very genuine tears.

"Aw, now. Don't do that. We'll still be in touch, my dear," Jackson had consoled me in his gentle Clintonian drawl, patting my head gently and offering me his handkerchief. He pulled me into an awkward half hug, his forehead wrinkling with paternal concern.

All of which, perhaps needless to say, did nothing to dry my tears. I tried to smile and act somewhat professional, but I couldn't pull it off. I was devastated. Jackson had been much more than a boss—he'd been a father figure for me since Dad passed away five years ago. Like Dad, Jackson radiated kindness and intelligence. Both men were tall, lanky, dashing (if not precisely handsome), with a thick shock of silver hair and a tendency to rail against the Way Things Were. Both had approached their work with unwavering devotion. Both were generous, emotional, sincere. Both adored their wives.

And both men made me feel...well, loved. Many a Friday night, Jackson would find me working late and wave me into family dinners with his wife, Carie, and their teenage sons, Michael and Edward, the youngest of their brood of five. Sitting around the table in the kitchen—warm and toasty from the oven in which Carie had almost invariably burned the roast or the lasagna—made me feel I'd found a real home in New York City.

"I'll be okay," I gulped, my face still muffled by Jackson's Harris Tweed blazer.

Jackson and I first met at the tail end of my senior year of college. I'd stepped nervously into his office, crisp résumé in hand, and perched on the same worn leather couch that I'd cried on this afternoon. Graduation loomed just weeks away. I'd been able to nab a job offer from another big publisher—the result of many trips to New York City in Bea's beat-up station wagon—but when I managed to get a meeting with the legendary Jackson Mayville, I told the HR representative at the other company that I needed more time to consider my options. After all, it was Jackson Mayville. He'd edited some of the century's most important literary voices and was truly in a league of his own.

I'd known since girlhood that I wanted to be a book editor. By high school, I'd pore over the acknowledgments section of novels I loved, daydreaming that someday a brilliant talent might see me as the person who "made her book possible" or "enhanced every page with editorial wisdom and insight." Could I be the Maxwell Perkins to some future Hemingway, Fitzgerald, Wolfe? Learning the ropes from Jackson Mayville seemed like a great first step.

And, as it turned out, it had been. Five years with Jackson had flown by, and I'd learned more from him than I'd ever imagined I would.

Sure, it hadn't always been a bed of roses—professionally or personally. It'd been five years of struggling to make ends meet, weathering one failed relationship after another, watching friends settle into domestic bliss while I was still heating up Campbell's soup for one most nights of the week. But it'd also been five years of learning the ropes from a talented and generous mentor, kicking up my heels, savoring my independence. So it all evened out.

But now that balance was about to shift. No more Jackson.

And frankly, my heels were beginning to get tired from so much kicking. James had been an exhausting experience, but then so had most of my recent flings. Lately it seemed I was always trying to convince myself that the guy I was dating wasn't A) a moron (*So what if he isn't into opera? Or museums... or newspapers... or reading without moving his lips?*); B) a slacker (*So what if he's been unemployed for a decade? He's nonmaterialistic. And so secure with his manhood that he lets me pay for everything*); C) an inconsiderate prick (*So what if he's left me waiting in this restaurant for nearly an hour? He's Latin*).

I cued up another episode of *24*. *You know what?* I thought. *A day like this calls for a double pie.* I called Mimi's for backup. Some people practice yoga, some people run to therapy—when life gets me down, I prefer to cope by eating my own weight in pepperoni pizza.

Of course, it wasn't just the emotional loss of not seeing Jackson every day that was upsetting me. I had my practical concerns, too. Jackson had gone to bat for me countless times—making sure that Gordon Haas, the publisher, paid attention to *some* of the proposals I brought to the table, fighting for my promotions, haggling with HR for a few much-needed bumps in salary. What would his retirement mean for my prospects at P and P? I'd still have my job, or so I'd been immediately reassured, but there was no doubt that the absence of a strong ally like Jackson would slow my trajectory. Not a cheering thought, given that it'd taken me five years to climb the editorial ladder to become an associate editor—a rate that the company considered fast.

I lit up my eighth cigarette of the evening and tried to focus my attention on Kiefer—but it was uncharacteristically difficult.

The thing was, I already had a tough time lining up meetings with Gordon—meaning it was hard to get his approval and financial support to bid on books. How could I get promoted to editor if I couldn't show my ability to make good buys and edit well? I knew there were many of us on the junior staff who grappled with this catch-22. With so many talented senior editors laying claim to Gordon's attention and budget, it seemed nearly impossible to break into the starting lineup as a junior staffer—even *with* Jackson pushing for me.

During the past few months, I'd watched several promising books fly out of my fingers because I'd been unable to get an answer in time from Gordon. I couldn't fault him for the bottleneck—not only was he a nice, well-intentioned guy, but he was clearly working at full capacity and trying his best to get to everyone.

Still, it was frustrating. I was hungry for more responsibility. I'd entered the business because I was drawn to the conceptual, collaborative, creative work of an editor—not because I loved to photocopy manuscripts for five hours a day.

And this is where I was one year before my wedding day: no romantic prospects and a career that seemed stuck in a holding pattern. I was in a rut roughly the size of the Grand Canyon.

As soon as I'd dug into my second pizza, the phone rang: Beatrice, asking if I'd meet her for the opening of some new art gallery.

Not a chance, I thought—and, come to think of it, might have said out loud. I could guess the kind of party it'd be. A sea of laughing, reaching, swilling, flirting, posing New Yorkers. Socialites who'd spent the entire afternoon choosing their outfits. Slick-haired men who scanned the room while you answered their questions. Young fogies with farcically WASPy first names and platinum blond girlfriends. Trustafarians who'd been born on third base but bragged as though they'd hit a triple. The flashing bulbs of society rag photographers. Cheap chardonnay. Watered-down conversation. Small talk was the only language spoken, and even the most interesting characters went bland after spending too much time on the circuit.

I was cynical, yes. But also pretty well-informed. I'd been a peripheral part of the scene for five years—mainly because Bea, an interior designer, worked these parties to expand her clientele—and I knew what to expect from it by now.

Recently, for example, she'd dragged me to a cocktail party at Soho House for a budding young writer who'd just published her first collection of short stories. I watched as a cluster of A-list party girls, all clad head to toe in white (the season's new gray, which was last season's new black), positioned themselves in a corner by some bookshelves. Society shutterbug Patrick McMullan hovered nearby; the girls coyly pretended not to be aware of the enormous camera hanging from his neck. And then Patrick began to click away. One of the girls, an ex-model, pulled a book at random from the shelf and pretended to read it. Another followed suit. One by one, the girls each adopted expressions of academic seriousness, their eyes narrowed as if absorbing some deep point, their ever-so-slightly furrowed brows a caricature of scholarly intensity. Patrick loved it. One of the girls held her book upside down, but nobody cared. It was a completely harmless photo op, I knew that, but it still made me put down my drink and say my good-byes.

Anyway, I just wasn't in the mood. Not tonight. My mind was stuck on my work situation, plus I still had a solid week of moping over James left in me. (Who doesn't secretly relish a breakup—or at least the guiltless freedom it provides to smoke way too many cigarettes, eat buckets of ice cream, not move from the couch, and indulge in every other possible cliché? I wasn't about to cut this short.)

I explained to Bea that my sweatpants had developed a terrible case of separation anxiety, but she persisted. Then she begged.

Still I wasn't budging. And so she moved on: "I wonder if James is sulking on his couch right now."

"I'll meet you in an hour," I muttered, getting up. Had to give her credit, she'd played her hand well. As we both knew, odds were high that James was at that moment chatting up some indie-rock chick who'd been throwing herself at him during his opening set. His weakness for these types had been a precipitating factor in our breakup.

"You won't regret it, Claire," Bea said excitedly. "And wear your red dress, okay?"

My red dress? She hung up before I could renege, having caught the unmistakable whiff of a setup.

Walking into the crowded gallery at 8:20, I spotted Bea by the bar and made a straight shot for her. "All right, where is he?" I smiled wearily, kissing her hello and snagging a miniquiche from a meandering cater-waiter.

Harry ambled up behind me, smoking an illicit cigar that only he could get away with. He laid his hand affectionately on Bea's shoulder and gave me a wolf whistle. "Watch out, men of New York"—he leaned in for a kiss—"Miss Truman is back in circulation."

Side note: I love, love, love Harry. He's one of the most self-effacing, smart, funny human beings I've ever known, one of those men who make you grin by sheer proximity. He's also a bad-ass assistant district attorney, always full of real-life *Sopranos* stories, and he's been a steady part of my life since Bea finally agreed to go on a date with him during our sophomore year of college. Thank God she saw the light, because you've never seen a college boy work so hard. And that's what it is, really—apart from his considerable charms, what I really love about Harry is how much he loves my best friend. Bea's a goddess among women in his eyes, a perspective I agree with wholeheartedly.

Not a perspective that's uniquely ours, I realize. Bea is stand-out fabulous. Naturally thin, despite a lifelong aversion to "healthy" food that prevents her from eating vegetables—she subsists on steak frites and KFC, but you'd never know it to look at her. Classic, fresh-faced, straight-off-the-Miss-Porter's-lacrosse-field good looks. Thick cascades of flaxen hair that would make a Breck girl weep with envy, enormous eyes the color of sea glass. In the looks department, Beatrice could give Charlize Theron a run for her money—a fact of which everyone is aware but her.

Then there's her blissful marriage to a man who still pens spontaneous love letters, who took a year between college and law school to study French cooking, who brings her home violets (Bea's favorite) every single Friday. Plus she's got her thriving career as an interior decorator—the creative work she's always loved, with great flexibility in her hours.

Yeah. If I didn't love Bea like the sister I'd never had, I'd probably have to hate her.

But I do love her. Always have, ever since she sat a few rows ahead of me during one of the placement tests we were forced to take during our first week at Princeton. She and I had each happened to wear a brightly colored grosgrain ribbon tied around our ponytails for luck—one of those random details that one takes notice of while scanning the room during a mind-numbingly dull, four-hour-long quantitative reasoning test. Leaving the test room, we struck up a light-hearted conversation over our shared, if misguided, fashion superstitions—a shallow dive into what would become a deep friendship.

"You are going to thank me for dragging you out tonight," Bea whispered now, grabbing my elbow hard to get my undivided attention. Her knuckles were white. "You're never going to guess who's here. Guess!"

I glanced around the party, not really seeing anyone who'd merit her level of excitement.

"Pabst Blue Ribbon," Bea pronounced the words slowly, solemnly.

My eyes grew as wide as hers. "You're *joking.*"

"Would I joke? He's here. And I think he's gotten even more gorgeous since college, if that's possible." She jerked her head slightly to the left, and I looked over nonchalantly.

Randall Cox.

There he was, across the room. I almost couldn't believe my eyes, but there was no mistaking the tall, lean rower's build, the wavy auburn locks and piercing blue eyes, the air of absolute confidence.

"Catch me if I faint," I instructed Bea, only half-joking.

A little background: Randall Cox was the most desirable man that anyone I knew knew. The gold standard in hotness. During our freshman year, Bea and I would walk ever so slowly by Randall's off-campus apartment building, hoping for just a glimpse. He was a senior, a Princeton icon with an equally gorgeous girlfriend.

By second semester, Bea and I had developed an intricate underground network of spies to keep us informed of Randall's public appearances at parties or local bars. Then we'd plant ourselves wherever he'd been with hopes that lightning would strike twice in the same week. If by chance we were so blessed, we'd pretend not to notice him—such were our highly mature mating rituals as eighteen-year-olds.

Once, Bea saw Randall coming out of McCosh Hall and pretended to take a picture of me in front of the building. That framed photo, with Randall's slightly blurry figure in the background, rested on our dorm-room mantel for years.

In other words, we stalked him. Hard.

"You have got to talk to him," said Bea, squinting to check if any miniquiche had gotten stuck in my teeth. "You *must*. I'll never speak to you again if you don't." Harry raised his eyebrows and wisely took that as his cue to hit the bar.

Déjà vu. Two weeks before Randall's graduation (a very traumatic event in our young lives, needless to say), Bea and I had spotted him through the window of the Annex, the local watering hole. Hearts aflutter, we'd emptied out our piddling student bank accounts to grease the bouncer.

"This is your last chance," Bea coached as we made our way to the bar where Randall was waiting for a refill of his pitcher of beer. Our crush had really become my crush; Bea was slowly starting to warm up to Harry, who'd been pursuing her relentlessly all year.

Standing at the bar with our backs to Randall, trying desperately to look cool, we struggled for a plan, some entrance ramp into talking to him. Say hello? Too unoriginal. A girl couldn't be so pedestrian when starting a conversation with a Greek god.

Twenty seconds of awkward vacillation later, Bea did the unthinkable. Pretending to trip on an uneven floorboard, she checked me hard with her right shoulder and sent me careening backward into Randall. He steadied my arms with his strong hands, and for one sweet, golden moment, I could feel his strong chest pressing against my back.

I peered up to find Randall looking down at me, amused. I was awestruck. And dumbstruck. I couldn't move or breathe. He smiled—graciously, I might add, considering that I'd caused him to spill some of his freshly refilled pitcher down the front of his rugby shirt.

"Can I get you another pitcher?" I offered, shocked and proud that I'd been able to form words in his presence.

"Hmm. I don't know, can you?" he asked, fingering the laminated ID I was holding in my hand. He grinned. It was as bad as fake IDs got. The girl in the picture had long, stringy white blond hair and freckles. I have my father's olive skin and light brown eyes, and like most of my peers at the time, I was wearing my dark hair in the ubiquitous "Rachel" cut. Instead of freckles, I had a spotty, scarlet blush spreading like wildfire across my cheeks and down my chest...very alluring.

I stared at Randall. Forget witty banter—I was suddenly unable to connect syllables to form words.

"Hey, no worries," Randall said finally, perhaps realizing that I'd exhausted myself with my first sentence. He asked the bartender to top off his pitcher and ordered a Pabst Blue Ribbon, which he handed to me. I mumbled my thanks, and he nodded good-bye, joining a group of his crew buddies at the pool table nearby.

No contest, this was the most exciting moment I'd ever experienced in my eighteen years of life. I felt dizzy and exhilarated—still too giddy, in fact, to start kicking myself for my nonexistent conversational skills. After I'd savored every precious drop of the beer he'd bought me (smuggling the empty bottle out in my purse, natch), Bea and I walked home in a daze, collapsed on her futon, and analyzed the entire encounter.

"I really think he liked you," she murmured before dropping off to sleep—further cementing the bond of our friendship.

Weeks later, back home in Iowa, I gave the play-by-play to my mother at our kitchen table. "Randall Cox?" she repeated innocently. Then she proceeded to tell me about her old friendship with his mother, Lucille—what would have been the *perfect fodder* for conversation. Why hadn't I mentioned my crush to her a few weeks earlier?

History could've been rewritten; the string of failed relationships and love-life disappointments that I'd go on to endure throughout my twenties could've been sidestepped. At age eighteen, I could've started living happily ever after.

So anyway, here was the second chance I'd been waiting a decade for. Hadn't I evolved from that tongue-tied teenager into a confident, articulate woman? *Yes*, I thought, *I'm going to talk to him—*

I was still giving myself a pep talk when I saw Bea's expression change.

"Hi, girls," said a sonorous voice behind me. I turned around. There was Randall—staggeringly gorgeous Randall—extending his hand. I could hear my heart thudding like a bass drum.

"I think we were at Princeton together. Randall Cox," he said. Beatrice shook his hand and introduced herself.

"Claire Truman," I answered in a surprisingly calm voice that belied my inner percussion. "I think you were a senior when we were freshmen, right?" *Hmm, yes, the memory is vague*, my tone of voice implied. Little did he know I'd once saved an empty detergent bottle he'd used for three weeks. And I still remembered the color of the window curtains in his room, visible from the outside courtyard. And I knew his shoe size. And if I spent ten minutes looking for it, I was pretty confident that I could find that blurry snapshot of him outside of McCosh.

"Right. You're both looking very grown up." Randall kept his eyes on me as he said it. Wow. *This dress.* Men generally zoom right in on Beatrice, and she has to deflect them back to me. I was never going to take this dress off—well, unless Randall himself happened to ask me to.

"I'm going to refresh my drink," said Bea with a twinkle in her eye. "Can I get either of you something?"

"I'm fine, thanks," Randall and I said at the same time. Then we laughed. Talking in unison? We were freaking adorable!

After Bea headed off, Randall and I moved seamlessly into the two staples of New York cocktail party chitchat: where we lived, where we worked. Even small talk with Randall was riveting—or maybe it was just the thrill of being able to stare directly at him while standing three feet apart.

"I went back to Goldman after getting my MBA," he told me after I'd given my far less impressive synopsis, "and I live all the way uptown—Fifth Avenue and Eighty-second Street."

"Right by the Met?"

Randall smiled modestly. "My terrace looks out over the Met, yeah. I wish I were home more to enjoy it, but the view from my office is all I've been seeing lately."

Forget crazy real estate: My mind burned feverishly with the most important but as yet unanswered question. Was he single? Could a guy who looked so fabulous on paper and in person be unattached?

Of course not, I told myself. *There's got to be a Molly Simms doppelgänger lurking in the wings.*

Not wanting to come right out and ask him, I took a roundabout route. "Didn't you date Alexandra Dixon back in college?" I asked. Alexandra was the femme fatale.

"I did, you've got a great memory. Did you know Alex?"

"We took a few English classes together. She was *such* a nice girl." Okay, so these were not exactly true statements: Alex Dixon and I had taken one class together, and she'd never looked at me once. I had no hard evidence that she was *nice*—only that she was stunning, brilliant, poised, and multilingual. I swear I never heard her speaking the same language twice. Since I didn't necessarily want to remind

Randall of *those* attributes, I'd pulled a more banal adjective out of thin air. Nice.

"Well, she's doing amazingly well. Spent a year modeling in Milan, and then came back to the States for med school. Now she's a neurosurgeon, if you can believe that!"

Of course I believed it.

"Wow," I said lamely, "I bet not many models can make that transition. Are you guys still in touch?"

"No, we're not. Haven't been for years, unfortunately. She's living in Chicago now, with her husband and two kids. Crazy, huh?"

"Two kids?" I repeated, mood brightening. At least his model-neurosurgeon ex sounded pretty tied down.

"So how about you?" he asked, his eyes focusing on me intensely. "Married? Kids?"

"Nope, not yet"—I could feel myself blushing—"I've been pretty focused on my career."

"I hear that." Randall looked at me again in a way that made my knees wobbly. "I ended something long term last year. My ex was a terrific girl, but I just couldn't see myself marrying her. It didn't seem fair to keep her hanging."

My heart did secret backflips at the poor girl's misfortune. "Well, I'm sure you have no problem meeting women."

"Meeting women like *you* is much harder than you think," he answered. "You know...smart, successful women who also happen to be beautiful?"

Had I just received the triple crown of compliments from Randall Cox? Smart? Successful? Beautiful? Was this actually happening?

"Listen, Claire, I know the party's just getting going, but is there any chance you'd feel like grabbing dinner? The cheese puffs aren't doing it for me."

Remain calm. Remain cool. Do not dork out.

"I'd love that," I squeaked.

Randall smiled. The next thing I knew, we were gliding together toward the door, Randall's strong hand on the small of
my back. I waved to Bea over my shoulder, and she gave me a
discreet thumbs-up.

∽

"You're quiet, Claire. I'm talking too much about work,"
Randall apologized, refilling my wineglass.

It was a slightly out-of-body experience, having a date with
my biggest crush of the past decade. It might be comparable to
sitting down to dine with some mega-watt celebrity and having
to gracefully overcome the shock of being so close to a face
you'd seen on billboards, on movie screens, on *E! True Hollywood Story*. Randall's face had starred in my daydreams for so
many years, replaced temporarily by lesser crushes but never
completely retired. So, naturally, I was a little overwhelmed to
find myself sitting across a small candlelit table from him at Il
Cantinori—a perpetually hot date spot that Harry referred to
as Il Can't-Afford-Me.

"Not at all," I answered, "It's really amazing how much
you've accomplished in such a short amount of time." It
was true, even if it did sound as though I were laying it on
thick—Randall had a phenomenal résumé for such a young
guy. Besides picking up his MBA from Harvard, he'd become
the youngest managing director in the history of Goldman
Sachs—an investment bank not exactly known for employing
noncompetitive slackers. And he'd done it in one of the tough-
est economic climates imaginable.

"Well, I like to feel challenged," Randall deferred humbly.
His BlackBerry went off and he glanced at the screen. "I'm
sorry, Claire, it's Greg again. Really busy time at the office. I've
got to take this quickly."

Greg had called three times since we left the gallery. I

checked my watch. It was now 10:45. Did Randall *ever* get a break from work? Poor guy! Although I often gave Bea a hard time about gabbing on her phone when we were together, I waited patiently as Randall gave his associate a series of indecipherable commands.

Actually, I was impressed by Randall's work ethic, especially given that he could've coasted through life without lifting a finger. I knew from Mom that the Coxes lived large and that Randall could've chosen a far less arduous career path—as an ancient compass collector, say, or an unemployed actor—if he'd been so inclined. That he'd instead opted for the rigors and challenges of a fast-paced career said a lot about the kind of guy Randall was.

"Where were we?" he said a moment later, after the crisis had been averted. "Tell me more about *your* job. What kinds of books do you work on?"

"Well, I have a feeling it might be changing. Jackson Mayville—my boss since college—just announced his retirement, and it's a bit unclear how his departure will affect my track at Peters and Pomfret."

"I know Jackson. He's a member at the Racquet Club. Nice guy. Lousy squash player, but a nice guy."

I giggled, unable to imagine Jackson doing anything more athletic than tying his shoes. "He's the best. I've learned a lot from him. I actually just found out about his retirement today. Pretty crushing news, although it's great that he'll get to spend more time with his grandkids."

Randall chewed thoughtfully. "I don't have much time to read these days. Actually—I really shouldn't admit this to you, you'll think I'm a complete cretin—but I did just finish a book that Vivian Grant published. It was a *New York Times* best seller, I think—about the nun who left her order to become a stripper? The title was really bad...what was it? It's right on my bedside table, I can see the cover—"

"*Naughty Habits?*" I asked. Gordon had made a few cracks about it during last week's editorial meeting. *Naughty Habits* had been on the *Times* Best Sellers list for six weeks already, which was a little depressing. Randall had read that?

"Exactly, *Naughty Habits*." He bobbed his head, a thick lock of hair falling across his forehead. "Not great literature, I realize. Probably not even literature." He looked at me with a sheepish grin. "I just ruined any shot at a second date, didn't I?"

"Of course not," I said, heart racing. Who cared if he wasn't the literary type? Working as hard as he did, Randall probably had zero desire to dive into a book that felt like more work at the end of the day.

"You know, I've met Vivian Grant a few times," Randall continued, "she's a friend of my father's. Smart woman. I know she's always looking for good editors. I'd be happy to give her a call on your behalf, if you think you might be ready for a change. It can't hurt to meet with her."

Meet with Vivian Grant?

Grant was a big hitter who was widely known as the most hotheaded, ruthless woman in the industry. Her name seemed to be often met with eye rolling. Grant had her own imprint at Mather-Hollinger, another major publishing house, and she'd made her name and fortune by producing tabloid-inspired blockbusters and crass market stuff, including authors such as underage porn queen Mindi Murray, a despicable serial killer who'd terrorized Chicago for an entire year, and a roster of loudmouthed pundits from the furthest extremes of the political spectrum.

To be fair, these high-profile, lowbrow authors obfuscated some of the very intelligent, quality books she published. Grant had also thrown her weight behind some great novels, garnering a stratospheric level of success and recognition for a few previously unknown authors. I'd read one interview in which she'd complained—justifiably—that nobody ever seemed to give her kudos when she published a book of literary merit and that people were only interested in associating her with smuttier fare.

Whether people liked her or not, Vivian Grant was widely considered to be one of the most fascinating characters in the business—as well as one of the most successful. Meeting with a woman who'd single-handedly forged a huge publishing empire? It wasn't an opportunity I should pass up, regardless of whether Grant Books was a place at which I wanted to work.

"That'd be really nice of you, Randall, thanks," I answered. How sweet of him to take such an immediate interest in my career.

"My pleasure." He typed himself a reminder in his BlackBerry.

A molten chocolate cake—sent over by the owner of the restaurant—arrived at the table, and I actually felt relaxed enough to enjoy it. I speared my fork in, letting the chocolate ooze out like lava.

"Couldn't eat another bite." Randall smiled, sitting back and patting his rock hard stomach. I put down my fork. Randall was probably used to dating models who considered dry watercress a hearty meal (and then spent two hours on a treadmill burning it off). Even though the chocolate cake was spectacular, there was no need to reveal—on our first date, at least—what a little piglet I could be.

"I'm so glad we bumped into each other at that party." Randall reached across the table and laid his hand gently on mine.

With my other hand, I discreetly pinched my thigh. Had I actually been moping over James three hours earlier? And now I was gazing into the eyes of the most perfect man I'd ever encountered?

"To old acquaintances and new beginnings," Randall said, raising his glass.

I lifted mine to meet his. Life was *really* looking up.

CHAPTER TWO

 GREEN EXPECTATIONS

Y ou're chipper this morning!" observed Mara, my friend
and fellow associate editor with whom I shared a cubicle wall.

"*Amazing* night."

Mara Mendelson and I knew nitty-gritty details about each
other's love life that we'd be embarrassed to share with a diary.
Last night's date with Randall wouldn't feel real until I'd down-
loaded it to her.

"Uh-oh. You look kind of goofy, Claire. You didn't relapse
with James again, did you?"

"I said *amazing*, Mara, not stupid. It's a new guy. Actually,
an old crush. His name is Randall, and—"

"Randall?! You mean the hottie you went to college with
Randall? The really gorgeous one who looks kind of like Pat-
rick Dempsey? Pabst Blue Ribbon Randall? Moms went to
Vassar together Randall? Demigod Randall?"

"Okay," I muttered, embarrassed, "I've mentioned him
before?"

"Do you still have that blurry snapshot of him?" Mara
laughed.

Resounding confirmation that I was the Queen of Over-share. Sure, she and I were really close—but that was just a sad level of detail to share about an adolescent crush that never went anywhere.

"So tell me absolutely everything." Mara settled back in her swivel chair for the play-by-play. She twirled one of her flaming red corkscrew curls around her finger.

Mara and I had kept up a steady dialogue for the past five years, starting as assistants at P and P the same month and inching our way up the ranks together. She'd become one of my closest friends. Mara seemed immediately to know everything there was to know about the company and its players, instantly tapping into a huge network of friends within the industry—all drawn to her dry humor, booming laugh, and generous spirit. I thanked my lucky stars for our shared cubicle wall—not only had it allowed us to forge a great friendship, but it also gave me daily access to Mara's smart, informed opinions about...well, everything.

"Hang on a sec, let me settle in first." I waltzed around the corner to Jackson's office to drop off the sticky bun and coffee I brought in for him every Friday morning (my little way of saying thank you for all the times he brought me home for family dinners). He wasn't in yet.

I plopped down at my desk again and turned on my computer. Jackson and I had a few meetings scheduled for the day with prospective authors, and in the afternoon we were meeting with a novelist to review our notes on her manuscript. Jackson preferred to talk through his editorial letters in person so that there could be no misunderstanding with the author about the revisions he was looking for. It was an old school approach, and maybe not the most time-efficient one, but I'd benefited enormously from being part of these discussions.

You have new mail, my Outlook told me.

Thursday, 8:23 pm

To: Claire Truman
(ctruman@petersandpomfret.com)

From: Courtney Ronald
(cronald@nyagent.com)

Subject: Sorry

Hey, Claire—
    You know how much I was hoping to pair
you up with Nicholas for his next novel.
He'd love to work with you, and I know
you've got a lot of passion for his work.
Unfortunately, I just don't feel we can
continue to string along these other
offers. I know you're doing your best to
get an answer asap from Gordon, but this
editor at Random House is chomping at the
bit and we're under pressure to accept
his very generous advance. I've got to do
what's best for my client, and that means
taking what we've got on the table. So
sorry that we won't be working together
on this project, but hopefully we can
find one very soon.

Best,
C.

Ugh. I'd put a lot of work into helping Nicholas develop his
story line, and it was disappointing to think that I wouldn't have

the pleasure of seeing it through to the finish. But I understood Courtney's decision. They'd given me more than enough time to come up with a counteroffer, but unfortunately, I couldn't seem to get the project onto Gordon's radar screen.

My phone rang and I instantly—if irrationally—thought of Randall. "Peters and Pomfret, this is Claire Truman," I said in my most professional voice.

"Claire?" It was Mr. Lew, landlord of my West Village apartment building. *Shit.* I knew immediately why he was calling—it had happened once before, last Christmas, when I just couldn't make my paycheck stretch in all the directions it had to.

"Hi, Mr. Lew," I answered gloomily.

"Claire, I am sorry, but your rent check? It bounced like nobody's business. It's no problem, Claire, I just need to know when you can pay."

I apologized and promised to drop off a new check for him next week. *Double ugh.* I had been working too long to be still struggling on my current salary. Sure it would have provided a very decent lifestyle in Iowa, but in New York the rent on my shoe-box studio ate up three-quarters of my take-home pay every month.

The only thing to do was to focus on the day ahead. I was glad it was heavily scheduled. Things had been pretty slow during the first weeks of summer, and I was ready for more action. I dialed into my voice mail while my nearly antique computer woke itself up...two new messages were waiting for me.

The first was from Jackson, saying that he'd be working from home and that I should reschedule the day's meetings and feel free to take off early. I sighed. Maybe not the normal reaction to hearing that the day would be slow and relaxed, but I wasn't in the mood for a leisurely pace. I was already on top of my own workload, and I'd read and written reader's reports for all the submissions that had come in for Jackson. There wasn't much I could do to forge ahead without him—at least, there wasn't enough to keep me busy all day.

"Jackson's not coming in," I lamented to Mara over the wall. She scrunched her freckled nose in sympathy, knowing that I'd been feeling underchallenged lately.

"Claire, this is Vivian Grant," said a sultry woman's voice on the second message. I sat up straight at the sound of her name. "I've just spoken to Randall Cox, who tells me that you're an up-and-coming young editor. I'm in the market for one of those. You must be getting bored to tears over there at P and P. Call my office. Ciao."

I took a gulp of my coffee, pulse racing. Randall had wasted no time—he must have called first thing this morning! How incredibly thoughtful! And now Vivian Grant wanted to speak with me?

Despite a few not-so-stellar preconceptions I had about Vivian, I was tremendously flattered. I did a quick Google to refresh my memory: Ten years earlier, Vivian had left Peters and Pomfret herself and struck a distribution deal with Mather-Hollinger. She'd knocked the ball out of the park time and time again, mainly with the bottom-feeding books for which she was famous, but also with some great novels and really solid books about politics, history, and finance. Two years later, the execs at Mather-Hollinger were so bowled over by her performance that they offered Vivian her eponymous imprint, which had since flourished during an industrywide downturn in sales. According to an article in last month's *Publishers Weekly*, Vivian was the most financially successful publisher in the industry— during the past year alone, she'd managed to land fifteen titles on *The New York Times* Best Sellers list.

The woman was doing *something* very right. And she wanted to speak with me?

Before I could get nervous, I punched in the number at her office.

"Grant Books, how may I help you?" a weary-sounding assistant answered flatly.

"May I speak to Vivian Grant, please?"

Mara's head rose slowly above the divider, one eyebrow raised artfully.

"Who should I say is calling?" the assistant asked.

"Claire Truman. I'm a friend of—"

I heard the click of someone picking up the line at another extension. "Can you be here in half an hour?" Vivian asked. I recognized her deep, slightly gravelly voice from the message she'd left.

"S-sure, that'd be fine, I—"

"See you then." The line went dead.

Half an hour? That was sudden. Thankfully, I'd thrown on a suit this morning, thinking that Jackson and I would be in meetings all afternoon.

"Vivian Grant? What's going on?" asked Mara, sounding concerned.

"Can't talk now. Sorry, I promise I'll fill you in later," I mumbled, clicking open my résumé—last updated two years ago—and frantically making amendments. A few minutes later, I hit print. Mara just watched me with wide, unblinking eyes.

"I'm just going to meet with her, Mar," I whispered, despite the fact that at 9:30 a.m. we were still the only two people in editorial row.

"*What!?*" Mara shrieked under her breath.

After stuffing a few copies of my résumé into my bag, I headed for the door. "I'll be back," I promised.

"You better be!" she called after me.

It was an unseasonably cool June day, but I still felt a slow trickle of sweat slide its way down the left side of my body as I walked quickly up Fifth Avenue, weaving through tourists.

Not only did this interview represent a chance to accelerate my career, but it was also strangely tied to my personal life, as the introduction had been made by Randall. If I won over Vivian, maybe she'd give me a great job offer and him a glowing report—a winning double punch. On the other hand, what if I really screwed it up? Not only would I have squandered a potential opportunity, but I'd look like a loser with Randall. The pressure was palpable! Another trickle snaked its way down my right side.

"Claire Truman to see Vivian Grant," I told the white-haired security guard behind the desk in the Mather-Hollinger lobby, hoping to exude an air of professional confidence. He looked up sharply when he heard Vivian's name and gave me a long once-over.

"Good luck, sweetheart." He nodded encouragingly, handing over my temporary access card.

The elevator was already crowded when I stepped inside, and I asked a man in suspenders and a bow tie standing next to the panel of buttons if he wouldn't mind hitting twelve for me. This, for some reason, made everyone in the elevator pause in their conversations and look at me in a strange way. Was asking someone to hit the button for you considered to be a rude request? I made a mental note to be more self-sufficient on the elevator next time.

"Good luck," said Bow Tie when I stepped out onto the twelfth floor. Could he tell that I was here for an interview? Another woman glanced at me and shook her head sadly. What did that mean? *Very* disconcerting. Was I trailing toilet paper? Was my skirt tucked into my underwear? I did a quick head-to-toe check but couldn't find anything obviously amiss.

Taking a deep breath, I pushed open the heavy glass doors and entered the sitting area.

"You Claire?" A kid who looked about sixteen years old immediately appeared in the doorway to greet me. He also looked as though he'd just woken up from a nap. One side of his hair was flat and pressed to his head, the other was fluffed up—like a mix between a Johnny Rotten and a down-covered baby chicken.

"Yes, I am," I said, smiling and extending my hand. He wagged it limply.

"I'm Milton. Vivian's assistant," he mumbled. "Follow me."

"Nice to meet you, Milton," I said to his retreating back.

Milton didn't answer—instead, he opened the door of a conference room and gestured toward an empty seat. "Vivian will be out to see you in a few minutes. Can I get you some water or something?"

"That's okay, thanks. I—"

Before I had a chance to finish my sentence, Milton had lurched off down the hallway. I cleared my throat and laid my résumé on the table, aligning the corners with the edge of the table, scanning the list of books I'd worked on so they'd be fresh in my mind during the interview.

The Grant Books conference room itself was pretty bland, except that the walls were covered with hardcover editions of the imprint's best-selling titles. I scanned the display. Vivian had published some really great books—as well as some really lousy ones. The range was exceptional. A trashy tell-all written by a washed-up soap opera star who'd once had a steamy dalliance with the wife of a well-known European tycoon was perched next to a weighty tome about military operations in Iraq, penned by a top homeland security adviser. A phenomenally successful diet book series—with glowing quotes from devotees such as Gwyneth Paltrow jumping out from the cover—shared a shelf with a whimsical, clever novel that had been adapted into a Broadway musical. More chick lit than the eye could take in, all arrayed in a candy store collection of tangy pastels. Three award-winning cookbooks that Mara—who specialized in cookbooks—used as her model for design inspiration. A series of quickie paperbacks written by reality show stars during their fifteen minutes of fame. Up on the walls were some fiercely polarized political books, too—there was oversize, frothing-at-the-mouth, mega-best-selling neoconservative Samuel Sloane at one end of the seesaw and a slew of die-hard liberals balancing him on the other side.

The only common thread among the dozens of books on display was humongous sales numbers. Vivian clearly had the Midas touch, no matter what kind of book she published.

I could learn a lot from someone like her, I thought, taking a deep breath.

Angry voices suddenly clashed just feet away from the conference room. I sat forward and strained to hear, but all I could catch was "a fucking baboon, you know that?" More yelling, and then I heard a door slam so hard that it made the wall shake. It was unnerving, hearing that kind of unmitigated rage within the confines of an office, and my whole body tensed when the conference room door swung open abruptly.

In swept a beautiful woman, calm and composed, a dead ringer for Isabella Rossellini but with strawberry blond hair and green, almond-shaped eyes.

"Claire?" she asked with a captivating smile, shaking my hand firmly. "Vivian Grant."

This was Vivian Grant? In all I'd heard about Vivian, nobody had done justice to how movie-star gorgeous she was. She looked much younger than her fifty years. With her hair pulled back into a loose bun, her skin a perfect alabaster, she was stunning.

Vivian Grant settled into a chair at the head of the conference table. "Randall speaks highly of you," she said, reaching for my résumé and skimming it momentarily.

"Does he? That's nice." I wished I could pump her for details.

"So, you thinking about having babies anytime soon?" Vivian wore a black power suit and an impressive emerald necklace, but her sprawled pose—a leg hooked over the chair next to her, an arm draped across its back, finger twirling her hair—evoked a woman of leisure, not a powerhouse publisher. It was as if we were two girlfriends out for a relaxed Sunday brunch.

"Hmm?" I responded eloquently, figuring I must have misheard her.

"Babies," she repeated, as if it were the most natural question with which to open an interview. "So many of my female editors tell me they're waiting for kids—waiting to meet Mr. Right, waiting to get to a certain place in their careers. One of my editors must be, like, thirty-six? Thirty-seven? She's married, but waiting for God knows what. I don't know *what* she's thinking. I tell her all the time to *get on the program*! If I'd taken that approach, I wouldn't have my sons. Women are supposed to get pregnant in their early teens, you know. We make such a big fucking deal about preventing teenage pregnancy, but that's what nature intended. Girls are really *supposed* to get knocked-up at thirteen."

"Um, how many kids do you have?" I asked, evading the question.

"Two boys. Marcus is twenty-six and gorgeous. How old are you? You should meet him. Oh, right, but you're with Randall. *Are* you with Randall? I used to doink Randall's father, you know. That's how Randall and I first met. I strolled out of his parents' bedroom one morning wearing nothing but his father's button-down and a smile, and there was little Randall, eating his Lucky Charms with the nanny. *Anyway*, inseminator number one, my son Marcus's father, was this super hot one-night stand I had in the seventies. And my son Simon's twelve. Inseminator number two was a perverted fuck-all whom I made the grave mistake of marrying. He kept me in litigation for years. But my kids turned out great, really great. God knows how. I was starting my imprint when Simon was born. I'll never forget it. I was in a meeting with Clive Aldrich"—the megapowerful CEO of Mather-Hollinger's parent company—"when I happened to glance down at my watch. Thank God I remembered that I had a C-section scheduled in an hour! Even back then my assistants couldn't organize my schedule for shit." Vivian rolled her eyes in utter exasperation. "Anyway, two hours later I was reading submissions and taking calls. Morphine shmorphine. It never slowed *me* down, honey. Back to work! I didn't have a single diaper, I didn't have a crib. Simon slept in a duffel bag for the first four months of his life." Vivian smiled nostalgically at the memory. "That was the first year I broke into the double digits in number of best sellers published."

I felt as if I'd just fallen down a rabbit hole. The little monologue I'd rehearsed on the walk over—about why I loved book publishing, what I'd learned in the past five years, why I'd be excited to work for someone like Vivian—now seemed too young, dull, naive, and...well, a little too sane for the conversation we were having.

Thankfully, it didn't seem that I was expected to talk during the interview. Vivian forged ahead.

"So, are you just about ready to chew your leg off to escape P and P? What do you think of the place?"

I paused. I could sense that Vivian wanted me to rip my current employer to shreds, that this would somehow make her feel I was on her wavelength, but I couldn't lie. Not to mention, based on the first five minutes of our interview, I was pretty sure I didn't want the job.

"Well, I've learned a great deal," I started. "I've been able to acquire some interesting books, although I'm hungry to take on much more. And the people are—"

"Oh, God, the *people*," she groaned, flashing me a conspiratorial look as if she were finishing my sentence for me. "Everybody's a zombie over there—if Gordon fucking Haas had the instincts I have in my baby finger, he'd be printing money. I hated it there. I was sexually harassed by not one— not two—but *four* of my colleagues. I'd walk into work every morning expecting a gang bang. You know what I mean? It's a fucked-up place. And they don't understand the new direction of book publishing. They're still selling to the baby boomers, still publishing the same old books. Bo-ring."

I had no idea which part of her monologue I should respond to—or how. Had she actually been harassed by that many people? I couldn't imagine who—

"So, how's your line editing?" she asked, changing the subject. I exhaled for what seemed like the first time since she'd entered the conference room. Finally, she'd lobbed me a question related to the job.

"Well, strong, I think. I've had a chance to work on all of Jackson's titles, as well as many of—"

"Good, good. You'll be doing a lot of heavy line editing. I'm looking for someone who can take initiative, who wants to bring in lots of books and really run with the ball. Are you ambitious?"

"Yes, I—"

"Good. Because that's what I'm looking for, someone who's

really passionate about the work. Someone who gets it, you know? Between you and me, I don't have a single person on this staff who gets it. Maybe Lulu, some of the time. But other than her—and she's got plenty of flaws, too, believe me—I need to spell everything out to these people. There's no intuition, no initiative! I need someone with instincts about what fucking *works* and what doesn't! You know what I mean?"

I nodded, not bothering with an attempt to squeeze words in edgewise.

"What kind of books would you be interested in working on?" she asked.

I told her that my background at P and P was in literary fiction, mainly because that was how Jackson filled his plate, but that I liked the variety at Grant. It was true. As I spoke, however, Vivian's mind seemed to drift off and her eyes glazed over. In less than ten seconds, I'd completely lost her interest. I stopped talking. Thankfully, in the silence, she sprang back to life.

"That's right," she said, nodding emphatically. "Right, I'm doing something that nobody else does. That nobody else *can* do. So when can you start?"

I blinked. "You're offering me a job?"

"Oh yeah. An offer. What're they paying you at P and P?"

I told her. It was a number all too close to my age.

"God, that's really pathetic. I'll triple that and give you the editor title. You'll be expected to carry a lot of books here, but it's an exciting, fast-paced environment. That work for you?"

I told her I'd think about it and get back to her quickly. She smiled at me with amusement. "I hope you'll say yes," she said, standing up. "I could use someone like you here. Someone smart, ambitious, ready to take on the world."

I wondered briefly how she'd been able to forge such a generous opinion of me from the three sentences I'd uttered during our interview, but I decided to accept the compliment. My head was spinning as Vivian shook my hand and vanished down the hallway. A beleaguered Milton rematerialized—still scowling, looking even more dejected than he had before— and ushered me out to the lobby.

I have a lot to think about, I mused as the golden elevator doors squeezed shut and I was carried back down to the lobby.

When I got back to the office, Mara was grinning maniacally at me. "You have an admirer," she sang.

I looked at my desk. An enormous bouquet of bright pink peonies had overtaken it completely. I raced over to read the note: "Can't wait to see you again. Hope it went well today with Vivian. —R."

I pinched myself. *Ouch*—same place I'd pinched the night before, apparently.

"You have *got* to fill me in!" Mara squealed. "C'mon, let's go to lunch. I need to know everything that led up to those flowers. And Vivian Grant! Are you seriously entertaining the thought of working for that dreadful woman?"

"How 'bout sushi? My treat. And keep your voice down," I shushed, although our editorial department still looked pretty much like a ghost town. I guess a handful of people had decided, like Jackson, that it wasn't worth coming in on a summer Friday, opting instead to work from home.

As we walked the block to the restaurant and I filled Mara in, I felt myself growing more and more excited. By the time we plopped down into a big red booth at Hana Sushi, I could barely restrain myself from pumping my fist victoriously in the air. Work and love were finally clicking into place! The perfect man had reentered my life after a decade of daydreams, *and*

I was finally going to be an editor! Vivian might be eccentric, but she would give me the reins to acquire books that I'd long dreamed of editing. She'd teach me to approach books with her true marketing genius, she'd show me how to lift a book over the flooded marketplace. I'd be challenged to reach my full potential! And I could finally stop worrying about making ends meet. Mr. Lew would be happy.

All in all, I thought, *days don't get much better than this.*

"So can I tell you what I think?" Mara asked as we popped edamame in our mouths.

"Shoot."

"I know the money's great, and the title, but Claire, this Grant woman is an absolute *horror*. I know a girl who worked there for six weeks after working for four years at Little, Brown. She was so traumatized by Vivian's tantrums that she moved to Wyoming and took up macramé, tossing her whole publishing career down the drain. Another friend of a friend was in double sessions of therapy every week and still coming apart at the seams. She developed this *nasty* skin rash from all the stress—" Mara shuddered at the memory. "You probably don't want to hear about it while you're eating. Anyway, Vivian is brutal, Claire. Nobody wants to work for her. She looks for green, eager-to-please young editors and basically piles crazy amounts of work on them, without any support, until they burn out in a few months. There are reasons why she's not going after senior people, experienced editors. They wouldn't put up with her crap."

I winced, ego bruised. Suddenly I didn't feel so much like doing my victory dance. Was Mara suggesting that Vivian hadn't offered me the job because she thought I had great potential—but, rather, because she couldn't find anyone else who'd work for her?

"Don't get me wrong," Mara backpedaled, realizing that

she'd hurt my feelings, "she clearly recognized that you're a rising star. And who knows, you might learn a ton by being thrown in the deep end without a life jacket. But I don't know anyone who hasn't been miserable working for her, and I'd just hate to see that happen to you."

We ate our shrimp shumai in silence as I ran my options through my head. I thought about what Mara had said. So what if Vivian was looking for a workhorse? Maybe drive and work ethic meant more to her than experience. And so what if I did burn out a little at Grant Books—I could handle anything for at least a year, I reasoned, and by then I'd have a much improved résumé and track record.

One year of hard labor in exchange for a major breakthrough in my career. It seemed like a worthwhile trade-off, all things considered.

"But enough about work stuff," Mara piped up. "For God's sake, Claire, please tell me why Randall Cox is sending you flowers!"

I gave her the rundown on the night before, which had ended with the perfect good-night kiss in his town car before he dropped me off. It had been just right—not too dry, too wet, too long, or too short. And most miraculously, I'd found the strength to pull away first. I, Claire Truman, had left Randall Cox wanting more.

Mara gazed across the table, loving every word.

After lunch, the workday over, I walked to my apartment from the Christopher Street subway station. I'd lived in the same tiny studio apartment on the same block for the past five years—and even though my street was crawling with hustlers and crowded with kinky sex shops, it felt like home.

I fished out the business card that Randall had given me the night before and took a deep breath. *I'm not eighteen years old anymore*, I reminded myself, trying to calm my jitters. *I shouldn't be this nervous about calling a boy.* Another deep breath. I dialed his office number.

"Randall Cox's office."

"Oh, hi—is Randall in? This is his friend Claire."

"I'm sorry, Claire, he's tied up in a meeting. I'm Deirdre, Randall's secretary." Deirdre sounded reassuringly middle-aged and professional. "Actually, Randall had asked me to call you. He wanted me to check your availability for dinner on Monday night. Unfortunately, he'll be away on business this weekend, so that's his first opportunity to see you. Are you free?"

"My availability for . . . oh, yes, Monday works for me." That was a little strange. I'd never been asked out by anyone's secretary before. But then I'd never dated anyone as successful and important as Randall before.

"Lovely. Randall was hoping you could meet him at Bouley at eight-thirty p.m."

"Sure, that sounds great."

"Lovely. And did you receive your flowers?"

"I did, actually, that's really why I was calling—to thank Randall for connecting me with Vivian Grant, and for the beautiful peonies. They're absolutely—"

"Lovely," Deirdre cut me off. "I'll let Randall know you called, dear, and he'll see you Monday at eight-thirty p.m."

"Lovely," I echoed. Uh-oh. Maybe Deirdre's one-word vocabulary was contagious.

I swung open the door to my apartment, dropped my bag on the floor, took two steps, and collapsed like a 1940s film siren on the couch.

I was grateful to have the afternoon off. Lots to think about. Lots to mull over. Big decisions. Would taking the job with Vivian be selling my soul to the devil, as Mara seemed to think, or would it be the booster shot my career desperately needed?

But the truth was, I already knew my answer. Vivian Grant had me at "editor" and "triple the salary." How could I possibly say no?

CHAPTER THREE

 THE AGE OF INNOCENCE

Waiter! A bottle of '82 Lafite Rothschild. We're celebrating!" Randall called out rather grandly, steering me toward the back of Bouley.

Exactly what I needed: a *drink*. What a day. Between telling Jackson about my job offer and then telling Vivian that I would accept it, I'd run the emotional gamut. On the bright side, all that drama hadn't left me much time to get nervous for my second date with Randall.

But now I was making up for lost time. Taking a deep breath, I straightened the black Calvin Klein pencil skirt that Bea had convinced me to buy at the Barney's warehouse sale two years ago. Thank goodness she had, as it was the only thing in my closet— save the red dress, which had already made the rounds—that seemed adequately sophisticated for a date with Randall Cox.

And I'd paired off the skirt with my first ever pair of Jimmy Choos, purchased during a panicked sprint around Saks's shoe department that day. I'd planned to wear my usual black heels—Nine West, slightly scuffed but still professional—but during my lunch break, it suddenly struck me that a date with

Randall Cox practically *required* Choos. Even if they maxed out my credit card.

As beautiful as the Choos were—and they were, truly, with delicate stilettos and a thin silver strap around the ankle—they were also precarious. As Randall propelled us briskly toward a small candlelit table, the combination of my snug skirt and four-inch stilts made me feel as if I were walking a tightrope very quickly with my legs bound together.

Please do not let me bite it, I prayed to the gods of fashion. They weren't used to hearing from me, but I hoped they'd show some mercy anyway. *If you just let me wiggle my way to that chair,* I prayed, *I will sacrifice my entire collection of coed naked T-shirts once and for all ... maybe even my worn-out Snoopy nightgown.* Just ten more steps.

Finally, we reached our designated nook on the south wall, and Randall pulled out my chair. I sank into it gratefully. Unfortunately, not gracefully. As I planted down, I teetered just the littlest bit, thanks to the shrink-wrapped skirt. Trying to steady myself, I knocked my hand against an already filled water glass. I watched in horror as a stream of water cascaded across the table and splashed Randall's suit jacket.

"Ah!" he cried out involuntarily, dabbing frantically.

"Oh—I am so—sorry, Randall, I'm so sorry!" I wanted to crawl under the table. Why was I such a klutz? Two minutes into the date, and I'd already gone and ruined his suit!

Putting down the napkin, Randall laid his hand on my arm and laughed. "Don't worry, Claire, it's honestly no big deal. I just get a little protective of my Turnbull and Asser."

"I'm really sorry," I repeated, still feeling miserable. Why'd I always have to go crashing around? I tried to regain my inner poise as I helped the waiter soak up the spill.

Randall reached out to take my hand. "He'll take care of that, Claire," he said gently, and the waiter nodded.

I pulled my hands onto my lap, wishing that I could hit the restart button. I'd rewind the tape to the moment when I walked into the restaurant and spotted Randall standing by the maître d', looking breathtakingly debonair...and then his face breaking into a huge grin when he saw me.

Of all the men I'd dated during the past five years in New York—the compulsive gambler; the artist who painted portraits of famous penises; the Legal Aid attorney with horrific, deal-breaking back-ne; and most recently James, the bass playing philanderer—I'd never felt more conscious of wanting to win someone over.

After work, I'd spent more time on my stupid outfit—which was all black and pretty boring, but hopefully in a more Carolyn Bessette Kennedy kind of way—than I'd spent getting dressed for the past three months. Then Bea had showed up at my apartment with her enormous makeup kit, trying desperately to locate my cheekbones, tweezing my eyebrows with a feverish glee that suggested she'd been waiting years for the chance.

I was glad we'd put in the effort. In a pin-striped suit (now a bit damp) and a French blue shirt that showed off his perfect Hamptons tan, Randall looked as though he'd sprung off the pages of a GQ spread. More to the point, he looked as though he should be dating a girl who'd just stepped out of *Vogue*. I wasn't nearly there yet, but at least I was closer than I'd been that morning.

"Cheers! To your new job!" Randall beamed across the table, his smile shining through the candlelit darkness. I held up the glass of wine that the waiter had just poured. "I'm so impressed, Claire. You really won Vivian Grant over, and she's no easy critic."

"Well, it would've never happened without you making the introduction. Thanks again for doing that," I said, briefly wondering what color eyes our kids would have—Randall's were blue, mine were light brown.

"So, how'd Jackson take the news?"

"Um, well—he took it pretty well," I answered vaguely. I didn't want to insult Randall by casting aspersions on Vivian, his connection, but Jackson's reaction was still weighing heavily on my mind.

That morning, I'd brought Jackson a fresh sticky bun (since he'd missed Friday's) and closed the door of his office gently behind me.

"I have some good news," I began, expecting that Jackson would be delighted to hear about the leap my career was about to take. He knew better than anyone—well, maybe anyone but Mara—how eager I was to take on a greater level of responsibility. And the timing was perfect, really, with each of us heading out the door at the same time—him to a relaxed retirement full of grandkids, me to a fast-paced environment where I could develop my skills as an editor. "I met with Vivian Grant on Friday, and she's offered me a job," I continued, filling Jackson in on the offer she'd made.

Jackson's face immediately dropped all color. He'd taken one enthusiastic bite of his sticky bun, but now he laid it back down on the napkin and pushed it away.

"Vivian Grant?" he repeated quietly. You'd think I'd announced that I'd met a nice boy named the sultan of Brunei who'd graciously invited me to join his harem.

"I—I know she's a little high-strung, Jackson," I stammered.

"Oh, she's much more than high-strung." Jackson laughed humorlessly, rubbing his brow. "Vivian Grant is arrogant and abusive and cares more about her own ego than publishing quality books. She'll chew you up and spit you out, Claire! The woman makes Attila the Hun seem like a giver."

My jaw dropped. Was Jackson Mayville trash-talking someone? He was the quintessential southern gentleman; I'd never heard him say a negative word about anyone. "Did you know her when she worked here?" I asked.

"I did, unfortunately. She made all of our lives a living hell. To put it bluntly, she's a lunatic. Listen, Claire, I know she's very successful, and her approach to publishing can seem very renegade and intriguing. But you really should not rush into this. She made the offer on Friday. Now it's Monday. Give it some time. I can't urge you strongly enough to reconsider."

I sank back into the couch, mind reeling. I was speechless.

"But what's the alternative?" I finally challenged him. I'd always deferred to Jackson's judgment and felt uncomfortable pushing back against it—but maybe he didn't understand how stagnated I'd been feeling lately. "It'll be years before I can get that level of responsibility—not to mention, salary—anywhere else. And with you gone—" I cut myself off quickly...but the words had slipped out. The last thing I wanted to do was guilt-trip Jackson about his retirement. My waterworks had been bad enough.

"Claire, listen," Jackson said in a solemn voice, "I know my retirement leaves you untethered here at P and P, but I *hate* the thought that it could in any way drive you into Vivian Grant's grip. Unfortunately, we both know that P and P won't be able to match the salary she's offered. But maybe I can convince them to come up a little—and your next promotion should be around the next corner. You're well respected here, Claire. You're young, but Gordon knows that you've got great potential. Think longer before you decide to jump ship to work for Vivian."

That was the thing. I didn't have much time. Maybe Jackson was wise to recommend proceeding with caution, but that morning I'd gotten a voice mail from Milton, Vivian's assistant. In grim tones, he'd informed me that Vivian's offer would be available until Monday morning at 10:00 and not a second later. If I was interested in taking the job, she needed to know immediately.

"Typical," Jackson grunted when I told him this.

Suddenly I felt a tiny kernel of rebellion pit itself in my stomach. Why was Jackson being so unsupportive? Maybe Vivian was tough, maybe she was even a little crazy, but where was the wisdom in stalling my career when I had the chance to push it ten steps forward? Besides, Jackson's days of struggling to make ends meet on a junior editor's salary were long behind him, and he'd published so many great books that he'd actually had *enough* of the experience. I was still starving for the experience! Did he appreciate just how hungry I was? He line-edited and discussed concepts with authors while I methodically filled out art logs, contract requests, and expense reports. He ate lunch at Michael's with Joni, Binky, and other big-time agents while I brown-bagged it at my desk and answered his phone. How could he tell me *not* to grab the reins and go for it?

The decision was mine to make.

"I'm going to take the job, Jackson," I announced. "Maybe it's not the perfect scenario, and I know it'll require a lot of hard work. But I figure if I can hang in for a year, it'll really accelerate my career—and I'll gain some valuable experience."

Jackson nodded weakly, unable to hide his disappointment. "Well, you know I'm always here if you need anything. I hope it works out, Claire, I really do." He forced a smile.

"Thanks. I know it's the right move for me," I lied, feeling not at all certain of anything at the moment.

I walked back to my desk, feeling shaky. "How'd it go?" Mara asked, popping her curly head over the cubicle wall.

I frowned. "He's not such a fan."

Mara nodded and plopped back down in her chair, not saying another word.

It was now 9:43. The window of opportunity was closing, and despite my display of bravado in Jackson's office, I was feeling less sure of my decision than ever.

But I had to do it. Before I could change my mind, I called Vivian's office.

"Grant Books." It sounded as though Milton had a bad cold.

"Milton? It's Claire—"

"Milton is no longer with the company. May I help you with something?"

"Oh. Yes, um, I was calling to speak to Vivian. We met last week and— Is she there?"

"One moment, please." The new assistant put me on hold. I wondered briefly what had happened to Milton, but he'd seemed pretty ready for early retirement.

"Claire. It's Vivian. What's up?"

"Hi, Vivian. I'm calling to accept your offer." There. I'd done it. No going back now.

"Good, good. What'd I offer you again?"

Uh-oh. She didn't remember? I repeated everything she'd said in our last meeting.

"Okay, well, that's simply too high," Vivian replied. "That's more than other editors here are making. I can't imagine I really offered that much. Let's carve off $10K and call it even."

I felt a surge of panic. Was she accusing me of being dishonest? What should I say? Vivian was lowering her offer *after* I'd accepted it? Had she changed her mind about hiring me? Even with $10,000 shaved off the top, it was still a much higher salary than I was making at P and P. Should I just take it? Or was she testing me—maybe she wanted to see if I was easy to push around in negotiations. Vivian Grant certainly wouldn't want an editor who was unable to stick to her guns.

"I'm sorry, Vivian," I said finally. "You made me an offer on Friday, and that's the offer I'm calling to accept. If the terms have changed, I'll need to reconsider my decision."

"Fine," she relented impatiently. "It's way too much money, especially for someone with your limited experience, but I really don't have time to argue about it. I need someone here now. So when can you start? How's Friday?"

This Friday? As in four days from now? I'd assumed I'd be able to give the standard two weeks' notice at P and P, adequate time to make sure that all of my projects—and Jackson's—were handed off properly. I told Vivian this, hoping she'd appreciate that I wasn't the kind of employee who would irresponsibly leave her employer in the lurch.

Turns out she didn't. "Two weeks? That's absolutely absurd. I need you here much sooner than that. How about next Monday?" Vivian countered.

Again, I felt another surge of apprehension. Was I pushing it? Haggling with my not-yet-new boss about my start date— after standing my ground about salary—didn't feel like getting off on the right foot. I wasn't used to these kinds of adversarial conversations...P and P was so bureaucratic that promotions and offers were handed down impersonally, without much discussion. I wanted to be able to say yes to next Monday, but it felt really wrong to rush out so abruptly on Jackson.

"I'd really feel better giving the full two weeks," I repeated. "Maybe I could start working weekends, or in the evenings, so that I can hit the ground running?"

"I'll have my assistant messenger some of the projects you'll be immediately taking over. But two weeks is way too fucking long, Claire, and I can't keep repeating myself! I need someone on the ground immediately. I can live with next Tuesday, but that's pushing it. Your loyalty needs to shift. *Now.*"

And with that, she hung up.

Thus marked the beginning of the pathology that was to take over my life: The feeling that my offer was precarious—that Vivian might rescind it as capriciously as she'd extended it—made me more certain that I couldn't let it go.

Swallowing hard, I knocked on the door of Jackson's office. "Vivian has asked that I start next Tuesday," I said quietly.

He winced. "Fine, Claire, next Tuesday is fine. Make this Friday your last day here. Take Monday off and get some rest. You'll need it. If you're sure you want to do this, you might as well get used to bending over backwards for Vivian."

Not exactly the blessing I'd hoped for, but I thanked him. "I'll come in weekends, work nights, whatever you need to get things wrapped up," I offered.

"Thanks, dear. But I think your hands will be full, and besides, Mara can help me if I really need anything. I'm not worried about me. I'm worried about *you.*"

Back at my desk, I called Vivian's office to say that Tuesday would be fine. This was the first lesson I learned from her: You can't negotiate properly unless you're willing to walk away from the deal. If you're scared of losing, you will every time.

"Well, it sounds like he was just sorry to lose you," Randall commented when I'd finished telling him the nutshell version of the afternoon's events. "Kind of selfish, if you ask me."

"Oh," I said, "I don't think Jackson was being selfish. He just doesn't quite see the opportunity the way I do."

"So, you liked the wine?" Randall changed the subject. "My father always keeps a few great bottles in the cellar here. By the way, Claire, my mother's *already* pressuring me to get you out to Southampton one of these weekends. You know, she and your mother were apparently inseparable in college, and she's dying to meet the daughter of Patricia Truman."

"I'd love that," I answered, gazing dreamily across the table. Meet his mother? Not exactly my usual second-date fare!

I'd just finished the most sumptuous meal of my life—Randall, much more disciplined about his diet, had ordered a tuna steak and spinach, while I'd gone in for a perfectly charred, unbelievably tender steak with a béarnaise sauce.

As Randall gestured for the check, I felt a warm glow of anticipation. The mood had been perfectly set for an easy "Want to come back to my place, Claire?"/moment of feigned hesitation for propriety's sake/ "Sure, just for a quick nightcap" sequence, and I couldn't wait to play it all out.

"I wish I could invite you back to my place for a drink, Claire," Randall groused, pulling out a Cross pen from his breast pocket and signing the check with a theatrical flourish, "but we're in the middle of closing one of the biggest deals in the firm's history, and I need to report back for duty."

Back for duty? I glanced at my watch. It was nearly midnight on a Monday. My stomach sank. Randall actually expected me to believe that he was heading back to pull another shift at the office? *Puh-lease.* After five years of being single in the city, I knew when I was getting the brush-off. Randall at least could have had the decency to formulate a slightly more credible lie, like an urgent need to clean out his sock drawer or walk his fish.

"No problem," I said coolly, willing my face not to reveal how upset I was. "Good luck with that, um, deal."

"Freddy can drive you home. I'm close enough to walk back to my office," said Randall, standing up from the table.

Whatever, I thought bitterly. *You think I don't know the code? "I'm close enough to walk" means: I'll wait a minute after you leave, walk a block, hop in a cab, and head to Marquee to pick up Brazilian models.*

What had gone wrong? I tried not to show my disappointment, but I felt pretty glum. Why had I allowed myself to get my hopes up? Why had I read so far into the peonies, the lavish dinners, the excessive compliments, the favor with Vivian, the invite to meet his mother...actually, now that I thought about it, there *had* been a lot of positive signs. In fact, the jerk had done everything possible—short of a serenade outside my window—to make me think he was interested!

Outside the restaurant, I crossed my arms and waited resignedly for Randall to begin the much less satisfying "I'm so glad we had a chance to catch up, we should do this again"/"Yeah, that'd be great"/"Well, take care" sequence.

But instead I felt his forearms rest on my shoulders, his fingers playing with the ends of my hair just a little. Huh?

"Claire," he said in a low voice, cupping my chin in his strong hands, "what are you doing Friday night?" His lips brushed gently against my neck.

"Um...," I gurgled, too blissed out to hold up my end of the conversation.

And then suddenly we were kissing...and then we were *still* kissing...and then he wrapped his arms around my waist and picked me off the ground just an inch in the most adorable bear hug. I couldn't believe it—our second kiss was even better than the first. I was kissing Pabst Blue Ribbon! And our third date was already in the works!

"So, Friday night?" Randall asked, his mouth curling into a smile. "Dinner at Nobu? Could you handle spending two nights in one week with me?"

"I think I probably could, yes." I laughed. *Two nights, a lifetime, whatever you'd like.*

"Good," he said, kissing me again. Then he opened the door

to his black town car and gallantly gestured for me to pile in. "Please bring Miss Truman home, Freddy, and then pick me up at the office around two-thirty," he instructed the driver.

Okay, so maybe he really did have to work. It was a little crazy, but there was also something undeniably intriguing about someone so dedicated to his job that he'd follow up a long, relaxing meal with a round trip to the office. Talk about having a passion for what you do.

On the drive down to Christopher Street, I thought of the kiss and felt a blush start at my toes and work its way up to my face. *I was dating Randall Cox.* Digging my cell phone out of my bag, I speed-dialed Bea and whispered the update behind my cupped hand...I couldn't keep it to myself for another block. Freddy could hear my friend's shrieks of joy from the driver's seat.

"I still can't believe you're abandoning me."

"I'm not abandoning you," I said, hugging Mara. "We'll still talk all the time. You know that."

"How's Jackson doing?" she asked.

Jackson and I hadn't spoken much since Monday, but that morning he'd dropped off a gift on my chair—an early edition of Sherwood Anderson's *Winesburg, Ohio*, a book we'd spent a good amount of time talking about during my interview five years earlier. I couldn't believe he remembered.

Actually, that's not true. It was completely like Jackson to remember.

The week had flown by thanks to a packed to-do list, and now it was 5:00 on Friday, my last day. The files had been meticulously organized. The final cardboard boxes had been taped shut.

Just one thing left to do: hit send on my parting e-mail to colleagues, giving my new contact information and telling them how much I'd enjoyed working with them. I'd been putting it off all day. Maybe because it meant this chapter of my life was really ending.

I hit send—in the forced way a person dives into cold water.

Ding. Ding, ding, ding, ding, ding, ding. You have new e-mail.

Before I had a chance to look, Marie-Therese, a pretty publicist with whom I'd worked on a few books, came charging over to my desk. Her face was flushed. "Please, Claire, please tell me that e-mail was a joke!" she cried out. "You're not really going to work for Vile Vivian, are you?"

I swallowed hard. "Well, yes, I—" I could hear new e-mails *ding*ing into my account behind me and glanced back at the screen.

```
Subject: Do you know what you're doing?

Subject: VG is certifiable.

Subject: Nooooo...

Subject: Say it ain't so!
```

And so on. My pulse sped as I clicked through a few messages. Not one of my colleagues had written back with the customary "Good luck, we'll miss you" message. Instead, everyone seemed horrified by my news.

When I turned back to Marie-Therese, I found a small but impassioned cluster of people around my cubicle.

"She came on to my friend in the men's room during a sales conference," whispered Henry from foreign sales. "Followed him in there. He wasn't into it, so she had him fired the next week for 'stealing office supplies.' Totally bogus, but he didn't see much point in pressing charges and getting stuck in a legal battle with a vengeful sociopath."

"Oh, she's famous for that," piped up Gail, a young editor at another imprint. "You kill yourself working for her, and then the second you leave, she's telling everyone within earshot that you've got a drug problem... or some mental illness... or sticky fingers... you *name* it."

"Vivian threatened to have this agent I know *beaten up* if he didn't let her get away with a blatant breach of contract. She wanted to put another author's name on the book!" swore mild-mannered Max from the art department. "She claimed it would help sell more copies!"

"She's deranged, Claire," insisted Marie-Therese. "I used to work at Mather-Hollinger, and the stories about the twelfth floor are unbelievable. There's something seriously wrong with that woman. She's almost inhuman."

Urban myth, I rationalized, trying desperately hard not to get spooked. "Thanks, everyone!" I said, false cheeriness in my voice. "But my mind's made up."

Nobody moved an inch. They just stared at me, concern etched across their faces.

Marie-Therese took a step forward. "Claire, maybe you should—"

"Hope we can all keep in touch!" I chirped, cutting her off. "Well, I guess I should be packing up now."

Finally, after a moment, they each said good-bye and wished me well.

"I'm sure they're exaggerating, Claire," Mara said kindly, but unconvincingly.

They had to be. How could it really be that bad? Vivian was aggressive and unconventional, that much was obvious, but I had a hard time believing—as one of the e-mails claimed—that she'd actually thrown a chair across a room at one of her editors. Or that she'd called a former marketing director a "filthy whore" during a meeting.

There was just no way the stories were true. For one thing, Mather-Hollinger HR would never allow that kind of behavior to take place on their premises or to their employees.

Besides, as Vivian herself was quoted as saying in a recent *Daily News* column, nobody would even mention her "temper" if she were a man—there was a deplorable double standard at play!

A few hours later, as I headed for the door, glancing back at editorial row, I felt confident about my decision. One year in the trenches, one huge breakthrough for my career. I knew I was doing the right thing.

Well, okay, maybe I didn't precisely *know* it. But I hoped it.

And I could put up with anything for a year. It would be worth it. I knew I could do it.

Well, okay. Hoped.

With one last nostalgic look at the copy machine, where I'd stood for hours on end more times than I could count, I took a deep breath and marched into my future.

CHAPTER FOUR

 MUCH ADO ABOUT
NOTHING

Thank *God* you're here, Claire," moaned Vivian, settling in at the head of the table.

This was it: my first day as an editor at Grant Books. I'd spent the morning in the HR orientation, learning all about Mather-Hollinger's prestigious history, and now I was back in the conference room—sitting in the same chair in which I'd had my interview just a little more than a week before.

"I'm about to fall apart," Vivian continued to gripe. "These fucking incompetents…Well, you'll see for yourself soon enough, Claire. I'm just relieved I have one capable editor on board now!"

The man next to me cleared his throat. To my enormous discomfort, two of these so-called incompetents—a man and a woman, both in their mid-thirties—were also sitting at the conference table with us, shuffling through files and making notes. They seemed completely unfazed by Vivian's harsh assessment of their abilities. In fact, they appeared not to have even heard her.

"Okay, so you're going to be working on ten books right off the bat," began the woman, addressing me in a crisp voice. "These projects have all been in limbo since the last editor left about four weeks ago, so I'm afraid you'll have explaining to do to the authors."

"I'm ... I'm Claire, by the way," I interjected awkwardly, extending my hand. The woman had a precise bob and bright, unblinking eyes that suggested a serious addiction to caffeine. She was also the most intensely Caucasian human being I'd ever laid eyes on. Her skin was white as the driven snow, despite the fact that it was now July.

"I'm really sorry, where are my manners?" she apologized, smiling. "I'm Dawn Jeffers, the managing editor." Vivian shot her a pointed look, and Dawn quickly cast her eyes down at her clipboard again. Apparently the small-talk portion of our program had ended. "Okay, you'll be taking over a cookbook we're doing with Chef Mario, this very charming guy with a famous Italian restaurant in the Bronx." Dawn paused, chewing the end of her pen. "Have you ever worked on a cookbook before, Claire?"

Beneath her all-business manner, Dawn's tone was gentle as she tried to determine how much help I'd need getting started. I appreciated that. I'd never worked on a cookbook before— and although I could always call Mara with questions, I'd also be grateful for any pointers that Dawn had to offer.

Before I could answer, though, Vivian answered for me.

"What does it *matter* if she's worked on a cookbook before? Claire's a smart woman, Dawn, she'll figure it out!" Vivian turned to me, a disgusted sneer on her face. "Why do so many *idiots* in this industry think that in order to know how to do something, you need to have done it a dozen times already? Why can't they understand that some people actually have *instincts*?"

Had Vivian just called the managing editor an idiot, right

in front of me, on my first day—make that third hour—on the job? I looked at Dawn for some sign of outrage, but her face remained completely placid.

"The second book you'll be working on," Dawn continued, her voice steady and even, "is a tell-all by—"

"You know what?" Vivian interrupted loudly. "I don't know why I'm fucking here, Dawn! I do not have time to do this right now. It's *your* job to fill Claire in on her projects—not mine! And Graham, the job of editorial director is to make sure these transitions go smoothly! It is not my fucking responsibility to do these things! I don't have *time* for this *shit*, people! I've got a multimillion-dollar media company to run and grow, can you *fuckwits* try to *grasp that?*" Vivian was now out of her seat, leaning across the table. A small vein on her left temple throbbed visibly.

I could hear my heart thumping in my throat. *It was happening. Already....*

"That's fine, Vivian," Dawn replied matter-of-factly. "We'll take over from here."

"No problem," echoed Graham, equally unflustered.

Vivian stomped away from the table in a huff. Then, after reaching the doorway of the conference room, she turned to face me with a radiant, completely incongruous smile. "I'll swing by your office later, Claire," she said sweetly, the anger now completely vanished from her voice. "Maybe we can grab lunch some day this week."

"Sounds g-good," I stuttered.

I turned back to Graham and Dawn, feeling oddly responsible for the fact that they'd both been screamed at. Both were busy with the stack of files in front of them on the table.

Was nobody else shaken by Vivian's tirade? She'd been screaming at the top of her lungs! Did these people have nerves of steel? How could they be so unflappable? Had they grown so used to the abuse that it no longer even registered?

The last thought was the most terrifying of all.

"So, your second book," Dawn proceeded, "is a tell-all by a fourteen-year-old student who's had a three-year affair with his teacher. He was eleven when it started. Twisted stuff. We're calling it *Sex Ed*, but that's just a working title. Obviously we've got the kid teamed up with a ghostwriter. Carl Howard. We use him a lot, Vivian likes his work. All his contact info is on the sheet I gave you."

"Third is a book on dieting by Alexa Hanley," continued Graham, not missing a beat.

Must not have heard that correctly, I thought. Hanley was a teen celebutante most famous for her severe thinness. The celebrity weeklies were constantly running photos of Alexa looking deathly skeletal in a string bikini at the Chateau Marmont—alongside headlines like "Dangerously Thin?" or "Is Lexie Rexie?" The idea that Alexa Hanley would write a diet book couldn't have been more ludicrous. What would she share...recipes for ice cubes and Ex-Lax soup?

"Vivian wants us to target teenage girls as the audience, obviously," Graham said, looking worrisomely serious, "so you'll need to work hand in glove with the art department to incorporate a fun, catchy design throughout."

He shoved the folder my way. Oh God. It was for real.

"Doesn't that seem a little...um, *wrong*?" I piped up. "I mean, marketing the advice of a celebrity who clearly has an eating disorder to impressionable young girls?"

Graham stared at me. He was a short, pudgy man with Coke-bottle glasses, and he looked as if he'd been sleeping in his clothes for a week. (I'd learn later that he had, in fact, been sleeping in them for days. Working on a book with a high-profile defense attorney had required Graham to pull a cot into his office so he could catch occasional pockets of sleep, and he hadn't made it home since the previous Friday.)

"*Vivian* bought Alexa's book," Graham replied brusquely, opening the next file in his stack. Case closed, apparently.

For the next hour, Dawn and Graham methodically walked me through the projects I'd be immediately responsible for, punctuating every sentence with, "Vivian wants," "Vivian demands," or "Vivian expects."

I got the point. On these first ten inherited projects, my job as an editor would be to execute Vivian's visions. And that was fine by me. *It'll be a good way to gain insight into how she works*, I figured. Besides, it wasn't as if I were dying to run with any of the projects I'd been assigned—they didn't exactly fire up my creative juices, to put it mildly. I'd take on more authority when editing the books I brought in myself.

"So, you got everything?" asked Dawn, tapping the table with her pencil.

"Think so. If I have questions, should I just—"

"Some questions Graham might be able to answer. But honestly, all the information we have is in those folders. Good luck, Claire. I know it's not easy taking on hand-me-downs." She smiled quickly and fled the room, and Graham, with a curt nod of his head, followed on her heels. I was left alone with the heavy stack of files.

It was time to roll up my sleeves and get to work.

One small problem: I had no idea where my office was. Or the ladies' room, for that matter. I sat there for a moment, not sure what to do next—

"I'm so sorry." Dawn popped her head back into the conference room. "Come with me, I'll give you a quick tour of the place."

"I'd like to welcome a new member to our editorial staff," said Dawn, and I waved to everyone around the table. It was my first editorial meeting, now my third day of working at Grant Books. "Claire comes to us from P and P. We're all glad to have you here, Claire."

I smiled gratefully at Dawn and quickly scanned the room for more friendly faces. Hmm. What I saw were a lot of tired, tuned-out expressions. A lot of faces not even bothering to look in my direction. Phil Stern, a senior editor whom I'd met during Dawn's office tour earlier in the week, was the only one who bothered to give me a genuine smile.

Editorial meetings were pretty universal across the industry. At P and P, they'd been forums for everyone at the imprint—editorial, publicity, marketing, and sub rights all together—to ask questions, air concerns, give progress reports, ask for second reads on submissions, and generally check in on what all the other moving parts of the publication assembly line were up to. I'd always enjoyed our weekly meetings, mainly because of Gordon's irreverent sense of humor.

Judging by Dawn's brief office tour, I'd already guessed that editorial meetings would be different at Grant Books. For starters, my new colleagues didn't strike me as the most social group—or maybe they just warmed up slowly to newcomers. After Dawn had knocked on each closed office door, the editor ensconced behind poked his or her head out timidly, shook my hand, and then ducked back inside as if taking cover. Unlike colleagues at P and P, who lingered in the hallway to chat, the staff at Grant Books seemed to hunker down in their offices during the long workday, emerging only for food, water, and bathroom breaks.

My own office was larger than I'd expected, with a big window facing downtown. It was a far cry from the cubicle I'd inhabited just a week before.

"We might as well start without Vivian," Dawn announced briskly, breaking the silence and bringing my attention back to the table. Dawn turned toward Karen Heffernan, our talented art director. Grant Books was famous for having inspired, inventive covers. While Vivian certainly played an instrumental role in that, Karen also deserved a good amount of the credit. So far, I'd been really impressed by her. A petite, cute twenty-something, Karen had a surprising amount of chutzpah—in a meeting yesterday, she'd unwaveringly stood up to Vivian and even managed to change her mind about something. I immediately liked her no-nonsense, straightforward style.

"She's not happy with the cover for *Whipped and Chained*," said Dawn. "Did she call you? She was trying to reach you. Really not happy."

Karen sighed deeply. "Yeah, yeah, I know. I'm working on it. When do you need it for the catalog?"

"Last Thursday," said Dawn, consulting her list.

Graham, seated at the head of the table, cleared his throat officiously. "Who's looking at the proposal that just came in about the behind-the-scenes making of adult films?"

Scanning the group, I could answer his question based on who was blushing the deepest magenta.

"I am," piped up Melissa, an editorial assistant just weeks out of college. "Vivian gave it to me an hour ago."

"Well? So? What'd you think?" Graham demanded impatiently.

Melissa stared at a notebook in front of her on the table with such intensity that I half expected to see it move. I could tell she was shy and not so thrilled about talking in front of the group in general—having to talk about porn no doubt exacerbated her nervousness. "Well, it's...um...it's extremely rough," she said after a pause. "Actually, the writing is incoherent. But I didn't really have a chance to finish it, because I had to update the submissions log like you'd asked and—"

"Well, that's helpful, *Melissa*," Graham huffed sarcastically.

"But is the concept a commercially viable one? Assistants, that's what we're asking you to evaluate. We can fix the writing. That's our job, in fact, to fix the writing—in case nobody mentioned it to you before. But *will* the book *sell*? And besides that, assistants, you should know that when Vivian gives you something to read, it takes precedence over anything else you're doing. She needs feedback immediately. Do not *waste* her *time*. Her *time* is *valuable*. She expects you to formulate an educated opinion about how the book will fare in the marketplace, and she expects that opinion pronto." A beet red dot appeared on each of Graham's cheeks as he finished his diatribe.

I noticed Phil Stern roll his eyes ever so subtly.

"I'm sorry, I—" Melissa looked a little shaken. I gave her a sympathetic smile and made a mental note to go chat with her later that afternoon.

Before the tense dialogue could continue, the door to the conference room was flung open dramatically. Vivian swept into the room. Phil immediately scuttled out of his chair and made room for her at the head of the table. A hushed silence fell upon the group.

Vivian had a dangerous, mesmerizing quality. It reminded me of watching a tornado approach too quickly on the Iowa horizon: You couldn't take your eyes off such an unbridled force of nature, even though you knew it would spell big trouble.

"People," she said, glowering. She tossed her calico hair over her shoulder so forcefully that I could actually hear the *swish*. A few editors smiled nervously, shifting in their chairs. The wall clock ticked loudly. Everyone seemed oddly paralyzed by her presence.

Finally Dawn regained her composure. "Hello, Vivian!" she called out. "We've got a lot of ground to cover this afternoon."

If you'd been watching the scene on mute and then been asked to guess what Dawn had said judging only by Vivian's facial reaction, you'd have surmised that some barbed insult had been flung down the table. Vivian didn't say a word back to Dawn, but her face contorted as if she'd smelled rotten meat.

More loaded silence. Dawn just stared at her notepad.

"As you probably have heard," Vivian finally said, chewing each word slowly and carefully before spitting it out, "the company is insisting that I give the assistants a raise. I've been on the phone with HR for an hour trying to understand why the fuck I have to pay higher salaries out of *my* editorial budget when *they* were the ones who bent over to get raped by the fucking unions last year." Her voice was growing louder in a crescendo of rage. "But apparently they are taking me down with them! As usual! This company is fucking bleeding me dry! Anyway, assistants, you just got an extra hundred bucks a month. Live it up."

Everyone at the table kept their eyes trained down, not wanting to make eye contact.

"Well?" Vivian demanded. "What do I need to know about this week? Go around the table and tell me what you've been doing."

What happened next was shocking. I watched in disbelief as a group of accomplished professionals took turns stammering through their notes, heads still lowered. It was as if the entire staff had wilted under Vivian's scrutinous gaze.

Only one woman—a stunning blonde with an aquiline nose, meticulously made up, wearing an elegantly tailored black suit remained completely poised and professional when giving her update to Vivian. She was the walking definition of "pulled together," from her simple, expensive-looking flats to her petal pink manicure. Maybe a little older than me, but not much. I hadn't met her during Dawn's tour or in the days since, but I hoped she might be a friendly ally.

"Lastly, Vivian, I was able to convince the author that the

cost of the ghostwriter, photographer, and publicist should all come from his advance, despite the fact that we'd previously agreed to pay," the woman concluded, clearly pleased with herself.

"Of *course* it should, Lulu," Vivian muttered in a distracted voice. Then she zoomed in on me.

"Claire!" she bubbled excitedly. "Has everyone met Claire?"

Heads bobbed, but eyes stayed down.

"Hi, everyone," I said brightly. "Very excited to be—"

"Oh, Vivian, I forgot to mention that Universal is showing strong interest in the film rights to *The Stripper Wears Pasties*," the woman—whose name was apparently Lulu—interrupted.

"Tell me about it later," Vivian snapped. "Didn't you notice that Claire was speaking?"

I quickly mentioned some of the projects I'd be taking on, plus two books that I immediately wanted to bid on, and Vivian beamed at me as if I'd just split the atom.

"Kudos, Claire!" she cheered. "I hope everybody at this table learns from watching your initiative. Just a few days into her job here and she's already bringing great books to the table! That's what I'm looking for, people . . . a little get up and go!"

And with that, Vivian got up and went, whipping herself out of her chair and out of the conference room in one swift, efficient motion. The meeting hadn't been concluded, and I could tell from the expression on Dawn's face that she had several things she'd needed to run down with Vivian. Still, nobody moved an inch.

When Vivian was out of sight, Lulu glared at me. "Enjoy it while it lasts, Claire," she sneered. There was real venom in her voice, and I involuntarily let out a tiny gasp.

Nobody seemed to notice the exchange. The rest of the

Grant Books staff just shuffled out of the conference room, not looking in my direction.

"How're you holding up, kid?" Phil Stern poked his head into my office. He was probably about five or six years older than me, but the bags under his eyes made him look older, and his thick mop of hair was already flecked with gray.

"I'm okay, thanks," I said hesitantly. I was still a little upset over Lulu's unexpected jab at the editorial meeting, but the last thing I wanted to do was fuel any office tension by talking about it.

"Don't worry about Lulu, okay?" said Phil, plopping down in the chair next to my desk. "She's been Vivian's pet for a while. And this used to be her office—one of Vivian's brilliant managerial techniques is to shift employees around to give us a false sense of promotion and demotion. Anyway, Lulu's nose is out of joint. But she'll get over it. She's just ridiculously competitive, is all."

I nodded, still feeling a little discouraged but grateful for Phil's outreach. "Thanks. I know sometimes it takes time to get to know one's colleagues. I probably caught her on an off day."

"Wish that were true, but you should expect her to remain difficult. Lulu's entire life is Vivian Grant, and she'll throw anyone under the bus if it'll help her stay in good standing with the boss. Other than her, though, the people here are so much nicer than they seem at first. The thing is, Grant Books has such tremendous turnover, it can sometimes seem futile to make an effort with new colleagues. A lot of the people on the staff are almost as new as you are, and those who've been around longer sometimes get tired of welcoming in a new editor every three weeks. It's a pretty fast revolving door here. Well, you'll see. Just don't take it personally. Everyone's actually really great—or everyone except Graham and Lulu—once they see that you'll be here long enough to merit an effort."

I smiled. "Thanks, Phil. I appreciate the insight."

"Yeah, and that brings me to my other advice." Phil nodded, leaning forward in his chair and bringing his voice down to a whisper. "How to deal with Vivian. I'm sure you've heard that this isn't the easiest workplace in the world. That she isn't the easiest boss. That the survival rate is pretty low."

"I've heard a few things," I admitted, "but I'm sure they've been wildly exaggerated."

Phil laughed grimly. "Well, don't be so sure. I'm not trying to scare you, Claire, but you should know going in that most of the stories you hear about Vivian—horrible as they may sound—they're actually understated. The *really* crazy Vivian stories—the ones that HR pays ex-employees never to discuss—are kept under lock and key. And court order."

"Like what?" I asked, a chill passing through me. Skulls in the supply closet? Human sacrifices at the office Christmas party? I felt like I was at summer camp, and Phil was the counselor with a flashlight pointed under his chin.

"Another time, another place," he answered cryptically.

"If it's that bad, how have you lasted four years?"

Phil's eyes bulged with intensity. "By obeying the five inviolable rules of Grant Books, Claire. They were handed down to me when I first started working here, and now I pass them on to you."

"Were you by any chance a theater major in college, Phil?"

"Why, yes…at Oberlin!" he answered, genuinely surprised.

"Just a hunch," I laughed. "Okay, sorry, what are the five inviolable rules of Grant Books?"

Phil cleared his throat and held up his index finger. "Number one: Under no circumstances should you give her or anyone in this office your home phone number. Not for any reason. You won't get a moment's peace."

"Really?" Vivian's assistant had just e-mailed me asking for it this morning, and I hadn't had time to write back. "But what if—"

Phil waved his finger to silence me. "Give her your cell, fine. Not your home number. Do I make myself clear?"

"Um, yes. I got it."

"Rule two: Don't trust Graham—nicknamed Himmler by the assistants—a whit more than you trust Lulu. In fact, trust him less. All the abuse that Vivian heaps upon him, he dumps on the poor assistants here. His tantrums are almost as legendary as hers. It's terrible to see. Oh, and same goes for the entire HR department. A bunch of goons. They'll betray you time and again if it means a moment in Vivian's favor."

"Got it," I said uneasily.

"Number three"—Phil reached into his pocket and fished out a business card, which he handed to me—"a good therapist. Start going now. This woman has been working with Grant Books employees for years, so she knows the drill. She's expensive, and our insurance policy doesn't cover it—but HR will. Grant Books has put her kids through graduate school at this point, but believe me, it's the least HR can do."

"Thanks, but I really don't think I need—"

"Yeah, I know you don't *now*," Phil interrupted, "but just wait. Rule four: Okay, I'm not saying our phones are tapped. I'm just saying that it's not a bad precaution to leave the building when making a private call."

"Honestly, Phil, you're telling me that—"

"And the final rule—the Golden Rule—is this," Phil whispered. "When Vivian's in a rage, never, ever, *ever* look her in the eye. And if the ax swings, duck."

"The ax?" I gulped.

"Listen, Claire, I know it sounds cowardly," he answered, "but when Vivian's in a lather about something, you'll only make matters worse if you try to stand up to her. Don't fight. Don't stick your neck out. Just duck."

My phone rang. Vivian's extension popped up on the caller ID. Phil and I both stared down at it.

"Speak of the devil," he muttered, letting himself out.

CHAPTER FIVE

 WOMEN WHO RUN WITH
THE WOLVES

O ffice walls! A window! An assistant! Oh my!" teased
Bea after I'd run down the list of new perks at Grant Books. She
and I were having our standing Thursday night dinner at Bilboquet, and with dramatic new developments in my two houses of
love and work, I'd had the floor since our salmon tartare.

"I know! I feel very important." I ravenously shoved a handful of fries in my mouth. Lunch had eluded me again, as it had
for the majority of the two weeks I'd been working at Grant.
Today I'd found time to throw some peanut M&M's down my
gullet around 3:30, but that was all I'd had since my morning
coffee.

"So have you gotten a glimpse of her famous tantrums
yet? Any staplers whizzing by your ears?" Bea had plenty of
experience dealing with ridiculously high-strung clients, but
she'd still been shocked to hear some of the rumors swarming
around Vivian Grant. I'd forwarded her a few of the scarier
e-mails that had been sent by my P and P colleagues.

"Not so much as a small paperweight has been flung," I reported. No need to mention the first meeting we'd had with Graham and Dawn or a few other minor skirmishes I'd witnessed. "Bea, I forgot to tell you, I already bought three books that I'd been trying to get green-lighted at P and P for *months*. All it took was a quick call to Vivian, explaining the concepts—she told me to go ahead and make a bid on each one! Do you know how refreshing it is not to jump through any hoops?"

"Amazing!" Bea cheered. "Just what you've always wanted! Now you can focus on looking for great material and editing instead of assisting—"

"Well, of course, right *now* I've got to spend most of my time getting the books I've inherited under control. Some of them are in pretty rough shape. But once they're all moving in the right direction, then yeah, I'll be able to build a good list for myself."

"Cheers, Claire!" Bea lifted her glass and clinked it against mine. "Sounds like you made the right choice. Just watch your back—there's got to be *some* truth to the crazy stuff people say about her, right?"

"I don't know," I said, feeling unexpectedly defensive. "I think she gets a pretty unfair rap. Vivian just wants people to work hard, to bring good ideas to the table. She's killing herself to make the imprint a success, and she just wants a team that meets the same standards she holds herself to."

"Okay," nodded Bea skeptically, taking a bite of her Cajun chicken. "If you say so."

Maybe it sounded as though I'd been sipping Kool-Aid all week—but the truth was, I felt a little bit sorry for Vivian. Minus a few blowups, I'd been nothing but impressed by her instincts, enthusiasm, supportiveness, and work ethic. "I'm learning from a genius," I gushed. "Her mind operates at warp speed."

"I'm really happy for you, Claire. It sounds perfect. And speaking of perfection, tell me about Randall!" She clapped her hands together like a child in front of an ice-cream sundae.

Randall. Things had been going so well between us—he'd been incredibly supportive during my first weeks on the job, calling every single evening to find out how my day had gone. He'd even sent roses to the office at the end of my first week. Last weekend, we'd shared yet another amazing meal—this time at Le Cirque—followed by an even more amazing good-night kiss. I was smitten. I'd named our kids.

Last night had been our fourth date. I'd rung the doorbell of his apartment at 8:05, and Randall—in an unbuttoned ox-ford and jeans—had opened the door and ushered me into his home. I was expecting Randall's place to be nice, of course, but by my standards that meant clean sheets, no visible signs of cockroach or rodent infestation. Nothing could've prepared me for Randall's sprawling bachelor pad with its wraparound windows looking out on the Met and Central Park and Fifth Avenue and the Upper East Side...not to mention a contemporary art collection that lived up to the view.

And to be honest, it completely spun me out.

"Bea, he had a Rothko in the bathroom," I whispered, still in shock, "and his bathroom—one of his *five* bathrooms, I should say—is larger than my entire apartment!"

"Well, Claire, your apartment's about a hundred square feet," she noted, "Your shower is in the kitchen."

"My point exactly!" I exclaimed. "My *shower* is in my *kitchen*, whereas Randall has a *Rothko* over his *toilet*! Come on, Bea, that is not normal! And...and he has a live-in personal chef. Her name is Svetlana, and she looks like a Bond girl! And Bea, he had a *vat* of caviar out before dinner, and this long, stretched-out dining room table, you know, the kind dysfunctional rich couples always have in the movies—"

"I cannot believe you!" Bea interrupted. "Will you listen to yourself, Claire? For years, I've heard you make ridiculous excuses for the *serious* flaws of every guy you've dated. And now you're dating the most fabulous guy on the planet—don't tell Harry I said that—the guy we've been worshipping from afar for a decade—and he seems to be really into you—and you're judging him for being too *rich*? Too *successful*?"

Well, it did sound pretty stupid when she put it that way. "But I'm really not judging him," I corrected, "I'm intimidated by him."

"Yeah, I know," said Bea, "but try to relax. This is *Randall Cox* we're talking about. You've got to get over it."

Bea was right. I was being totally ridiculous. If I could get over the fact that James slept in the dusty crawl space of an abandoned Brooklyn warehouse, I should be able to get over Randall's megapad and extravagant bathroom art. He'd shown himself to be nothing but sweet, supportive, and excellent at kissing...why was I being so ridiculous?

And then the memory came back to me in painfully vivid detail...I'd practically run out of there last night! After dinner, Randall had led me back to the living room, tried to put the moves on—and I'd felt so rigid and uncomfortable that I'd made up a weak excuse about an early morning meeting and abruptly left.

"I'm such a dork," I moaned. "Randall probably thinks...I can't even imagine what he thinks. What if I've completely blown my chances by being so awkward?"

"Guys love a challenge. Maybe it'll read as hard to get and work in your favor."

God, I hoped she was right. My phone vibrated in my bag. Caller unknown.

"Go for it. Maybe it's Randall," Bea cooed, an eager smile on her face.

I picked up.

"Claire. Vivian." I'd noticed that Vivian didn't like to waste much time on greetings. Instead, she'd state her name and then launch into whatever she needed to say before concluding with a brisk, "Call me back." It was certainly efficient, if not the most charming approach to a conversation. "I need to talk through a few ideas for tomorrow with you. Do you have a pen and paper?"

"Hi, Vivian." I raised my eyebrows at Bea and grabbed a notebook out of my bag. "Okay, shoot."

Twenty minutes later, Bea smiled sympathetically, tossed a few bills on the table, and left. I felt bad that I hadn't gotten to hear about what was going on with her—but I couldn't focus on it long. My every brain cell strained feverishly to take notes as Vivian rattled off book concepts at an auctioneer's pace. We'd spoken that afternoon, but since then she'd come up with about a dozen new ideas—half of which seemed to have legitimate potential. I kept scribbling for an hour, filling up half a legal pad with Vivian's genius. Fortunately, the waiters at Bilboquet didn't object to my hogging a table—a perk of being a regular, I guess. They even sent over a glass of rosé.

"Give me an update on these projects by ten tomorrow morning, so we can move forward immediately," Vivian concluded before hanging up.

By 10:00? I gulped audibly. How would I possibly manage to research all of these ideas, line up potential authors, fill in enough gaps in the rough sketch she'd given me...by 10:00 the next morning?

My stomach tightened, but I felt ready for the challenge. It was time to step up to the plate. Sure, I felt a little over my head—at work and with Randall—but maybe that just meant there was a lot of room to grow.

When I walked onto the twelfth floor at 6:15 the next morning, I expected Grant Books to be deserted. Instead I found that half of my colleagues had already started their work-days—approximately three hours earlier than the rest of our industry. *No wonder we're able to crank out one hundred titles a year with a skeleton crew of editors*, I thought. Doors were shut, but lights were on, and I could already hear the pitter-patter of keyboards typing.

By 10:00, I'd worked my way through three cups of coffee and six of Vivian's ideas—the six that seemed strongest to me. It was fun. I loved the creative challenge of building books from scratch. At P and P, most editors bought books that had been submitted to them through an agent, while at Grant con-cepts were originated and developed in-house—usually by Vivian herself, as she indisputably came up with the most and best ideas—and then the optimal author and ghostwriter were wrapped in. It was pretty exhilarating—pulling together the right concept and team, brainstorming the right approach—and the hours had flown by.

Still, I felt a bit nervous calling Vivian's office with my 10:00 a.m. update—I had, after all, been able to get through only half of what she'd rattled off last night. I'd get to the rest of it by noon if I continued to really crank, and I hoped that would satisfy her. I reasoned that it was better to give her something than to miss the deadline altogether.

"Vivian Grant's office," said Gregory, the guy who sounded like Milton with a sinus infection.

"Hey, Gregory. Is Vivian in? I was supposed to—"

"She's in L.A. I'm rolling calls at noon," he answered sullenly.

In L.A.? I hadn't realized how much time Vivian spent on the West Coast—yet another thing that made her stand out from other publishers. She was constantly drumming up media crossover deals for our books, pitching television show concepts, actively pushing the sale of movie rights. "Okay, I'll talk to her then. Thanks, Gregory."

There was a knock on the door and my new assistant, David, poked his head into my office. I'd had a great feeling about David from the first moment we met. A bright, ultra-competent, hardworking guy who'd recently graduated from Northwestern, David had been adrift at Grant Books for several weeks after the editor who'd initially hired him had abruptly quit. Since then he'd been reporting to three different editors, all of whom had been running him ragged with their urgent projects. I could sense that he was as grateful to have one boss as I was to have an assistant who knew the ropes a little bit. It was a little strange to have an assistant after being one for so many years—but David was so helpful, smart, and attentive, I knew that I'd get used to the new arrangement quickly.

"Roses, just delivered for you." David smiled, opening the door wider to reveal an enormous bouquet of three dozen long-stemmed red roses. I rushed over to read the note and felt a thrill rush through my entire body.

Claire,
To brighten up your day. The thought of you brightens up mine. The last few weeks have been wonderful. I can't wait to spend more time with you.
Randall

"An admirer?" asked David.

"I guess so." I grinned. I felt like doing cartwheels! What a relief—so Randall hadn't been thrown off by my aloof behavior the other night. Or at least he was willing to give things another chance. I couldn't wait to tell Bea.

"So what can I do for you this morning?" David asked, straightening his tie. I gave him two of Vivian's ideas to research, explaining the kind of information he should try to pull together. David nodded, scribbling down the few details I'd scribbled down the night before. "I'll have something for you in an hour," he declared with a confidence I envied. It was a relief to be able to delegate—hopefully, I could get through most of the remaining four ideas myself in the next two hours.

First, though, I called Randall's office to thank him. Deirdre picked up, of course, and asked if I'd be available for dinner on Saturday night. I eagerly said yes. She told me that Randall would call me after his meeting ended.

Exhilarated, I set back to work, stopping every few minutes to take a deep inhale of the roses and reread the note.

Around 12:30, when I still hadn't gotten a phone call from Vivian's office, I asked David to go check in with Gregory. David came back a minute later, scratching his head a little.

"Gregory's gone," he said. And then in a quieter voice: "I kind of figured this was coming. Apparently Vivian was irate yesterday after he failed to find her a private jet leaving for L.A. in less than twenty minutes. She let him have it with both barrels, and he was pretty shaken. He left about an hour ago and just called HR to tender his resignation."

Abrupt resignations in the middle of the day? The horror stories I'd heard from my old colleagues echoed in my head.

"Anyway, I spoke to Johnny—that's the new temp—and he seems to think she's going to be stuck in meetings all day," continued David, who seemed to be taking the disruption in stride. "My guess? She'll probably just be calling in tonight—like around eight our time."

"I can't believe Gregory would just quit like that—without any notice!"

David closed the door behind him. "Actually, Claire, Gregory was here a full week, which is only slightly less than average," he whispered. "The typical length of employment in that office is less than two weeks. Either she fires the person, or they pretty much run from the building. Or both, I guess. I've only been here eight weeks, and I've seen five assistants come and go."

"Are you serious?" I asked. David nodded, reaching for my ringing phone.

"I got it," I said, picking up. "Claire Truman."

"It's Vivian," she announced forcefully. My notes on the projects she'd asked me to research were strewn about my desk, and I scrambled to put them in order as Vivian continued to speak. "I have a few ideas I need you to look into for me. First, we should go after that girl who married the murderer convicted of killing her own sister. They tied the knot last night in his jail cell, did you read that? It was in *The Star*, tell your assistant to get you a subscription. Call and see if she'll do a book—offer two fifty. Get me a list of ghostwriters for that, we should have it on bookshelves in eight weeks, before she's gone from the headlines. Talk to Dawn about that deadline, and don't let her tell you it's not enough time—it's never enough time, I'm sick to death of her whining about it! Secondly, we need to get out of that book we signed with Chef Mario. I know there's a contract, but he's so fucking second-rate—has anyone even *heard* of him? It was Julie's lame idea to bring him on board, and now she's gone, so talk to Legal about how we can get out of the contract. We don't need to spend that much money publishing a poor man's Emeril."

My stomach sank. Julie was a former editor whose books I'd inherited—one of which was a cookbook by a legendary Arthur Avenue restaurateur. I'd called Chef Mario the day before to introduce myself and assure him that we were all very enthusiastic about his book.

"You sound like a nice lady," he'd concluded at the end of our conversation. "You've got to come into the restaurant soon! Bring your friends! On me, of course."

Drat. Getting out of the contract was not going to be a pleasant experience. I'd never had to break that kind of bad news to an author. Worse, I knew Chef Mario had been paying in good faith for the photographer, waiting for his first portion of the advance payment to come in. I hated the thought that we'd be leaving him in the hole...maybe I could just explain the circumstances to Vivian and make the argument for covering Mario's expenses. She probably wouldn't like it, but it was only fair. I'd figure out how much he'd already spent and bring it up with her later.

"Oh, and I'm sick of listening to that right-wing blabbermouth Samuel Sloane spouting off on Fox every night. The guy's an idiot—I know we published his books, but he's a moron. I loathe him. He's a bloated, disgusting, moronic publicity whore. Get me a list of authors for a book ripping him apart. They should be ready to deliver within four weeks at the most...."

Vivian threw five more potential projects my way before declaring that she'd arrived at "the studio" and would call me back in a few hours for an update. I realized I'd been holding my breath and took in a sharp inhale. More ideas to research? I hadn't had a chance to finish my research *or* debrief Vivian on the earlier list.

And the fun was only just beginning.

CHAPTER SIX

 THE WAY WE LIVE NOW

L ate!

I scurried to my subway station, iced coffee slopping out of the sweating plastic cup with each step. Phil had asked me to sit in on an early meeting with a prospective new author and her agent this morning, but I'd overslept—partially because I'd been at the office until 1:00 a.m. the night before. When Randall was out of town on business—Tokyo this week—I liked to take advantage by putting in extra hours at work.

My eyes hadn't opened till 7:00, a solid hour and a half later than the alarm was supposed to rouse me. Fortunately, if getting ready in the morning were an Olympic event, I'd take home the gold. If necessary, I could complete my entire program in less than five minutes. Jump in and out of shower, run a comb through hair, smear on some moisturizer, deodorant, and mascara, spritz a little perfume, and throw on my standard work uniform: all black. Today, because of the intense August heat, that meant a black skirt and short-sleeved lightweight sweater. I'd given up on color coordination a few years ago—one of the first indications that I'd officially become a

New Yorker—aiming instead at a wardrobe that could spit out an office-appropriate outfit to a blind person in less than ten seconds.

I took a thirsty slurp of my coffee, most of which had now trickled down my hand, before descending into the subway station.

Find your happy place, I coached myself after cramming into the packed local uptown train—but the ripe stench of the man next to me followed me there. Finally, we lurched to a stop at 51st Street and crowded out into the clammy, fetid subway air. As I edged my way up the stairs, I felt the familiar desperation of being one more cow in a slow, sticky stampede to work. Above me, the sidewalk traffic was barely inching along.

What was the holdup? After climbing two more steps, I saw for myself: There was an adult man, dressed in a baby bonnet and a sandwich board, handing out flyers to all the pedestrians he could get to accept one. I felt an itchy wave of hostility wash over me, my hands involuntarily balling up into fists.

"That's right, folks, Buy Buy Baby is throwing their annual clear-out sale," bellowed his voice down the stairs. "All inventory must go! That means spinning mobiles, baby clothes, diapers in bulk. Here you go, sir. You can't beat a sixty percent markdown, folks." I had almost made it to street level now. A few more steps.

"Never know when the stork might pay an unexpected visit!" the voice exclaimed. An older woman next to me was scandalized by that suggestion. The man on my other side—a conservative lawyer type in a navy blue suit—was having a full-blown debate with himself. And no wires, no handless phones stuck in his ears, either. Recently I'd noticed that more and more of my fellow New Yorkers—seemingly sane men and women— were unabashedly talking to themselves as they walked down the street. Apparently, the stigma of looking flat-out crazy had worn off during my five years living here.

I emerged into the open air—well, *open*, but still replete with toxic car fumes and the punch of a street vendor already roasting some sort of spicy meat (I never got close enough to learn the specifics).

"*Claire*...Claire?" I was startled by a man's voice calling my name. I looked around but couldn't find any familiar face in the disgruntled throng of people.

Oh God, it was the overgrown baby!

He was coming my way, parting the crowd. I worried for a moment that I had lapsed into some sort of *Ally McBeal*–esque episode, but then the baby ambled over and his face became sort of familiar. But who was he? And what would ever, *ever* possess a person to flag down an old acquaintance when dressed so idiotically? I was blushing for him.

"Claire Truman?" he asked. "It's Luke, Jackson Mayville's nephew. We met—"

"Of course, Luke!" It all came back to me. Luke was Jackson's starving artist nephew who'd refused to take a single handout from his parents, and was muddling by as a musician...or was he a playwright? Anyway, Jackson absolutely adored him. I'd heard about Luke often but met him only once. "Great to see you!" I said, keeping my eyes focused on his face so that it might seem like I'd missed his getup. "How've you been?"

"Right, well, regressing since I last saw you at Uncle Jack's seventieth," Luke said with a genuine laugh. "Suddenly, I feel pretty grateful that I put my foot down on the adult diaper idea."

I laughed with him. Ridiculous as he looked, you had to admire the guy's self-assurance. He definitely had the Mayville charm. Pretty cute, too, in a scruffy, Mark Ruffalo kind of way—if one could look past the bonnet. Which, granted, was a pretty hefty "if."

"Hey, my shift's almost done. Want to grab a coffee or something?" Luke asked, gently pulling my arm to guide me out of the traffic flow.

"Wish I could." I cited the morning meeting for which I was now almost late. And tried not to glance at the oversize rubber pacifier hanging like an albatross around his neck.

We caught up briefly on the curb. Turns out Luke was working a string of odd jobs to pay the bills while he got his MFA in creative writing at Columbia, and he was nearly done with his first novel.

"I'd love to read it when you're finished," I offered, digging for my card. "I'm an editor at Grant Books now—it's a much different place than P and P, as you might've heard, but I'm looking for great new fiction."

"Great! I'd appreciate that," he said. He gave me a hug (made awkward by the sandwich board) before we parted ways.

"Tell Jackson I send my love," I called over my shoulder. Jackson had just started his new life in Virginia. We'd spoken a few times since I'd started at Grant Books, but I'd been so busy that I hadn't had a chance to return his most recent call.

Luke said he would. And then I sprinted off down the block to the office.

"What the house *really* needs," chirped my mother as I cradled the phone between my shoulder and ear to free both hands for sifting through my in-box, "is more citron yellow, more petunia pink, more aquamarine blue, more dark amethyst, more eye-popping fuchsia, more..."

Loud sound of phone slamming down onto my desktop. I could still hear Mom listing her rainbow of colors, though, so apparently she hadn't noticed the loud crashing noise (when she gets on a roll, her usually high level of perception plummets).

Mom had home improvements on the brain. We still had several months until our annual party in my dad's honor, but Mom was already hard at work trying to spruce up the house in preparation. The party was a really big deal to her, as it was to me, and I knew she wanted every detail to be perfect.

It was a tradition we'd started five years ago. On the Saturday closest to my dad's birthday in January, we open up our house to all the friends, family, and community members who feel like dropping by, and everyone gathers to eat and drink and recite their favorite poems. Last year, we raised enough money in donations to start a university scholarship in Dad's name. What started out with a dozen or so people gathered in our living room had quickly grown into a popular campus event. This year, Mom was expecting upward of two hundred people at the house.

"So do you think the kitchen would look better in a mint green or tomato red?" she asked.

"Go with the green, Mom. And what do you need me to do? Should I deal with the caterers and the menu? Or I could call Prairie Lights and see if they'll donate books for the raffle?" Prairie Lights was an independent bookstore in the city. Every year on my birthday, my father used to take me to Prairie Lights—which had one of the best children's book sections in the country—to pick out five new books. They'd always been generous in helping us with Dad's poetry party.

"That would be great, honey, but are you sure you'll have time?" Mom fretted. "You just started your new job. Why don't you leave things to me this year?"

I hated to admit it, but she had a point. I'd been at Grant for only a month, but my to-do list was growing at an alarming clip. In the past week alone, I'd been asked to take on five new titles, all inherited from an editor who, according to Vivian, was "a looney tunes who couldn't handle the demands of the job." I wasn't sure about the accuracy of Vivian's diagnosis, but in any case, the new titles filled up my plate.

Still, I had to do my part in planning Dad's party. After all, Dad had never once let his work prevent him from helping me with my homework, watching my dance recitals and soccer games, tucking me into bed at night. I'd just have to make the time.

"Okay, dear," Mom consented reluctantly, "but you just say the word if you get too busy. Don't stretch yourself too thin."

"Deal," I agreed, rubbing my growling stomach. New e-mail popped up in my Outlook. I could tell at a glance that it was from Vivian: It was written in her trademark sixteen-point font, which had the effect of making every e-mail read like a shout. "Hey, Mom, could I call you back later, or tomorrow? I haven't eaten lunch yet, and I'm famished—"

"You haven't eaten lunch? Claire, it's nearly four in the afternoon! I know this new job of yours is stressful, honey, but please don't forget to take care of yourself."

"I know, Mom, I will."

"Bea tells me that you've lost weight!"

Argh. I hated when Bea got Mom worked up. "Mom, I'm fine...I'm just getting used to the new pace."

"And she told me that you've been working past midnight all this week."

Beatrice and Mom spoke all the time. In fact, they probably spoke to each other more than they did to me, especially since I'd started at Grant. I loved that they were so close—except when Bea leaked details about my life that made Mom lose sleep.

"It's no big deal, Mom. I'm just getting up to speed here, that's all."

"Well, okay. Just don't let this Vivian woman push you around. Bea tells me—"

"Mom, she's not pushing me around," I interrupted. "She's teaching me a ton! It's the opportunity of a lifetime! I don't know why I'm the only one who seems to appreciate—"

"Okay, I know. I'm sorry." Mom sighed a little.

"I'll call you later this week, Mom. Love you."

I felt bad for snapping, but I was so famished that I could see dots in front of my eyes. I quickly checked Vivian's e-mail—nothing that couldn't wait ten minutes—and grabbed my wallet. Burger Heaven—the aptly named diner across the street—was calling my name.

Unfortunately, the door to my office swung open before I could leave.

"*Hel-lo*, you gorgeous, sexy pants mamasita!" bellowed the one and only, larger than life Candace Masters, teetering into my office in her four-and-a-half-inch stilettos.

Candace, one of my new authors, had been an international supermodel in the 1980s, partied at every hot spot from Studio 54 to Bungalow 8, adhered to a strict "billionaires only" dating policy, battled through addictions to every substance on the planet, gone under the knife more times than she could count, married a few times, had a few kids, and pumped out a few best sellers about all of it along the way. She was still very striking, although her regular visits to Dr. 90210 were starting to give her a slightly Madame Tussaud look. And she was incredibly vibrant and vivacious—so vivacious, in fact, that one might suspect she hadn't quite kicked *every* chemical substance out of her diet.

"Hey, Candace! How's it going?" I said, wishing I'd had a heads-up on her visit. David stood outside in the hallway, his shoulders raised apologetically, but it wasn't his fault. Stopping Candace from barging into my office would've been on a par with halting a charging elephant.

"It's going, baby love, it's going," she answered, running her fingers through her spiky platinum hair. "What do you think of my new micro-mini? Gucci, baby. This is a four Gooch day for me." With a Vanna White flourish, she pointed to her shoes, her bag, her skirt. Then she reached her hand down her skirt ever so slightly and fished out the skinny leather strap of her G-string. It was a sight that a few generations of men across America would've lined up to see, but it just left me feeling awkward. "Gooch," she boasted.

"Um, very nice!" I nodded.

"I thought of the subject for my next book!" she shrieked, stooping down to give me two air kisses. "Wait, doll, before I forget, I brought you a little somethin'-somethin'." She reached into her bag and fished out a balled-up red lacy thong, which she tossed playfully in my direction.

I thanked her, not picking it up. I couldn't help wondering whether the thong was clean—or something she'd peeled off the night before and shoved in her handbag.

"Wear 'em in good health, doll!" She blew me a loud kiss, and then she was off again, flitting over to my bookshelves where she proceeded to pull out dozens of Grant books, tossing each one into an enormous Chanel shopping bag. "I like to stock up while I'm here," she explained, working her way through each shelf. Phil had warned me about Candace's compulsive book-hoarding sprees. One time she'd brought four assistants into the office to help her haul her loot. Phil was convinced she was selling them on eBay.

"Okay, so my book," she finally said, handing off the Dumpster-size shopping bag to her intimidated young assistant, who'd materialized in the doorway. "My search for Mr.

Right—and all the perverts, scoundrels, and dogs I've endured along the way. Like this one guy I dated last summer in the Hamptons. Huge textile fortune, drove a big red Hummer, major spread on Gin Lane, always VIP at Jet East—seemed like the catch of the day, you know? Until one night he peeled off his shirt with the light, and I realized that he had vaginas tattooed *all* over his body! Freak! Can you imagine? So, you know, it'd be a book about extreme red flags and the men who wave them. Sound good? You like?"

A book about bad men and gritty sex? That had Vivian's name all over it. More than one agent had confessed that they sent Vivian any proposal in which the woman was persecuted, the man to blame—knowing she'd get behind those authors 100 percent. Add in some crazy sex, and you had her favorite formula.

"It sounds good, Candace," I encouraged. "Why don't you start jotting down the specific stories you want to include—obviously, we'll want to go for the juicy stuff you haven't covered in your earlier books—and have your assistant get that list to me. Then we can go from there."

"Perfect, doll. Kendra!" The assistant popped back into the office, eager to serve. "Please collect my things. And is the driver outside?"

"Yes, Candace, on Fifty-fourth Street."

"Rock on. Okay, I'm just going to say a quick hello to my man Phil, and we'll be on our way. Thanks, Claire. I hope you stick around." With a wink, Candace gave me two more air kisses and floated off down the hallway towards Phil's office.

As I was gingerly lifting the thong off my desk and into the trash can, the phone rang.

"Any chance you could get out of the office at a reasonable hour and come to yoga?" Bea asked. "There's a class at Om that starts at eight. It's right next to your office, and I think it'd be great for you to unwind a little. And maybe we could grab a bite afterwards—you know, since you've bagged our last two Thursday dinners."

At the moment, yoga sounded torturous—I had less than no energy. But maybe after I got some food in me, it would become more appealing. I agreed to meet Bea there.

Burger Heaven. Time to make a break for it.

"Back in five," I shouted over my shoulder to David, rounding the corner to the elevator bank at the exact same time as Lulu. She pulled a sour face. Oh crap. Now we had to pretend to be friendly for twelve floors.

And it would definitely be an act on my part. Lulu had done nothing but undermine me since I'd started. During our editorial meetings, she went out of her way to argue against every point I made. If I said a submission looked interesting, she'd stifle a yawn. If I said it was the worst thing I'd ever read, she'd ever so politely ask if I'd mind giving her a copy. You know, just for a second opinion.

Well, I'll suck it up and make the first effort, I thought as we stepped into the elevator in silence. "Hey, Lulu, how's it going? That's a pretty shirt."

Lulu pressed the button for the lobby and kept her eyes fixed straight ahead. "Claire," she pronounced slowly in a low voice.

And that was it. No friendly chitchat on our way down—not even a hello! Just my name. No other sound escaped from Lulu's perfectly lipsticked lips.

Forget it. Why did I even bother? Each floor seemed to take an eternity, but we finally reached the lobby and the golden doors opened to release us. Lulu stepped off first, of course, striding through the lobby with a glassy smile on her face, wiggling her fingers at the security guard as if she weren't the biggest bitch on the planet.

Fortunately, there was no chance she was also heading to

Burger Heaven. According to Phil, Lulu only ordered salads from the organic health food place down the street. Tofu Hell, as he called it. Well, as far as I was concerned, she could burn in it.

Bea and I lay flat on our backs, waiting for class to begin. The room was crowding fast, but there was still some space next to my mat. I shut my eyes for a moment, willing myself to relax from the stresses of the day. None of the petty irritations were important. I would *let go* of Alexa Hanley's slime-ball manager calling me "sweet cheeks." *Let go* of the irate phone call I'd received from an agent hunting down an embarrassingly over-due acceptance payment. (We'd already published the book in question, but for some reason Vivian refused to accept that the work had been done. "I hate that book," she explained, as if that were a valid reason for not paying the author.) *Let go* of the image of Lulu's smug face during the elevator ride.

When I opened my eyes, a meticulously groomed blonde—right down to her perfect French pedicure—was unrolling a sticky mat with Louis Vuitton logos emblazoned all over it. It took me a second to recognize her.

Lulu. Even her name sounded unnecessarily cute.

Her mat was less than a foot away from mine. What were the odds? Should I try to be friendly again? I couldn't exactly pretend not to see her, and besides, I didn't want to stoop to her juvenile level.

"Hey, Lulu!" I whispered.

"Oh, hello," Lulu said coldly. Then she folded into a front bend, resting her forehead between her knees on the mat. For a rigid, uptight girl with a pole up her butt, she was shockingly limber.

"Please come to a comfortable seated position at the front of your mat," said the instructor.

As class stretched on, Lulu executed each pose with flawless form. I noticed a subtle sheen on her brow, but nary a drop of sweat fell to the ground.

I, on the other hand, couldn't seem to restrain myself from grunting like Maria Sharapova and turning my sticky mat into a small slip 'n slide of sweat. By minute twenty, every time I downward dogged, my hands and feet slid around as if they were on roller skates. My hair was dripping wet. My T-shirt and shorts looked as if they'd been left on a clothesline during a heavy rainstorm. When class was finally over, I mopped my brow with the square inch of my T-shirt that hadn't been saturated. Even Bea had to raise an eyebrow.

I rolled up my mat and turned to Lulu, determined once and for all to make nice. We'd just spent a good chunk of time aligning our chakras, so maybe she'd be more receptive. "You're really good, Lulu," I said, "I'm impressed. Have you been doing yoga for a long time?"

Lulu didn't say anything, and for a moment I wondered if my words would just hang in the air as they had in the elevator. She stared at me. Then she deigned to speak, flinging her words at me as if they disgusted her as much as I did. "One doesn't 'do' yoga, Claire, one 'practices' yoga. And not *everything* is a competition, you know," she snapped, pulling the strap of her bag onto her shoulder. Then she headed for the door.

So much for making nice.

∞

"Hey, babe. Just landed. Any chance you can meet me at my apartment in an hour?" Randall asked.

"Of course!" I answered quickly, figuring Bea would give me a pass on dinner. I did the math: I could run back to my apartment (fifteen minutes), shower quickly (five minutes), get dressed (fifteen, since it was to see Randall and thus would require an extra four minutes to scrounge for matching under-garments), and head straight up to his place (twenty minutes). I hadn't seen him in a few days—he'd been working on some big deal in Tokyo, and it had been difficult even to connect on the phone. Fortunately, I'd been so swamped with work that I hadn't had time to mope too much over his absence.

"Was that Randall?" Bea asked when I'd hung up the phone.

"Uh-huh." I nodded.

"And could tonight be the night?" she asked.

The thought hadn't crossed my mind, but now that she mentioned it...Randall and I had been dating over a month, seeing each other a few times a week...I'd heard him refer to me as his girlfriend on the phone with a work colleague....And I was head over heels for the guy.

"Actually, yes." I smiled. "Tonight very well could be the night."

CHAPTER SEVEN

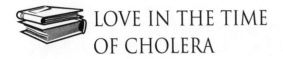 LOVE IN THE TIME
OF CHOLERA

C laire?" David knocked on my door. I'd been huddled
over a manuscript for a four-hour stretch, and my back felt
solidly fused into a curve. "Someone's in the lobby to see you.
His name's Luke?"

Luke Mayville? I told David to bring him up.

"And Bea's on line one. Again."

"Hey," I said quietly, picking up the phone. It was the third
time she'd called that morning.

"So?" Bea demanded hungrily.

"Yup, last night was the night," I answered. I didn't feel like
discussing it, analyzing it, or, frankly, even thinking about it.
Because I was busy with work and a day packed with meetings. And because, unfortunately, I'd had sneezes that lasted
longer. I wasn't worried: Randall and I just needed some
time. First times were supposed to be a little disappointing.
It was practically a rule. Still, I didn't feel like rehashing the
experience with anyone, even Beatrice.

Luke poked his head into my office. When he saw I was on the phone, he quickly backed out again.

"Can I call you back?" I asked Bea. "I've got someone waiting. . . ."

"Fine," she said, clearly let down that she wouldn't be getting a detailed version of last night's events. "By the way, Harry and I just booked our tickets to Iowa. I'll e-mail you our itinerary. I know we've still got plenty of time . . . but you know how hot Iowa is as a mid-January destination."

"Right up there with St. Barth's, I know. Mom will be so thrilled you guys are coming. I was thinking I might ask Randall, but it's still ages away—"

"You definitely should. Okay, don't forget to call me back."

I stepped out in the hallway to look for Luke. He was studying bookshelves that held at least one copy of every Grant book published for the past decade.

"You guys have some really terrific authors!" he commented somewhat incredulously, as people generally did when they realized that Grant Books' list wasn't entirely porn, pulp, and politics. "Hey, am I interrupting you at a bad time? Sorry to just drop by unannounced."

"Are you kidding? You can always stop by." With Jackson already settled into retired life in Virginia, Luke was my only hope for a Mayville fix. The family resemblance was strong, although it had little to do with looks. Luke was a few inches shorter than Jackson, who was a lanky six feet five, and his features were sharper and darker. But there was something similar about the way that both Mayville men carried themselves.

I had to admit, Luke was looking pretty cute today in a faded T-shirt and cargo pants—at least it was a definite improvement on the sandwich board and pacifier. Hmm. I'd have to brainstorm a great girl to set him up with, provided he was single.

Now that I'd found Randall, I wanted the whole world to fall in love. Maybe Mara? She'd had a rough streak lately, and it'd be great to introduce her to a guy like Luke.

"Well, thanks. I really am sorry to barge in on your day like this," he apologized. And then he held a big stack of papers over his head like a heavyweight champ. The bags under his eyes...the relieved expression....

"This must be the magnum opus!" I exclaimed. "Is it done?"

Luke laughed, plopping down in my guest chair and stretching out his long legs. "Well, sort of. I can't even tell at this point. But you'll love it if you're having trouble sleeping."

"Yeah?" I laughed. "Speaking of, when's the last time you've slept?"

"Don't be fooled." Luke rubbed his eyes a little. "I'm actually very well rested. But I do everything possible to cover that up when visiting publishers. Gotta look the part of ink-stained, chain-smoking, pallid, starving, death-warmed-over wretch if you want to be taken seriously as a writer in this town."

"Sure. Or dress up like a grown-up baby?" I was unable to control a tiny snort of laughter at the memory.

"Precisely." He nodded seriously. "Either look is pretty much guaranteed to impress."

Then, without further ado, he handed me his manuscript. It felt heavy in my hands. "It's still very rough," he explained. "It needs a lot more work. The ending's rushed, the plot's slow, and I can't think of a title to save my life. So, I mean, don't worry if you don't have time to—"

"Luke," I interrupted, and he took a deep breath, "I'd love to read it. Thank you."

I've always imagined that for a writer, this moment would be comparable to the feeling of dropping one's child off at school for the first time—proud, expectant, but also fearful that he or she will be judged, picked on, or simply ignored. Not prolonging that agony a second longer than necessary was one of my main priorities as an editor.

I could tell Luke had more than the average dose of separation anxiety, so I promised myself that I wouldn't let his manuscript gather so much as a speck of dust. No matter how much work I had ahead of me, I'd find the time to read a chapter or two right away. I was genuinely curious to read it; Jackson had always bragged about how smart his nephew was. After opening up the first page, I glanced at the first few lines—and then looked up, suddenly aware that I must have been making Luke more nervous by reading in front of him.

"So, I figure I should probably celebrate," he declared, breaking the momentary silence. "Just the fact that it's finished, I mean. Who knows if I'll be able to sell the thing, of course. Unless you're willing to make an offer based on the unadulterated brilliance of the first sentence...."

"I'll think about that. You definitely should celebrate, though. It's a major milestone."

"Any chance you feel like having dinner with me tonight? Lately I've become addicted to this great little Italian spot in the West Village called Mimi's, it's—"

"I love Mimi's!" I blurted out, shocked that anyone else would be acquainted with the hole-in-the-wall, charming mom-and-pop restaurant that had served as my own private kitchen for the past few years. Their buttery pasta with zucchini and squash was the stuff of dreams, and their gnocchi...I could honestly drool just thinking about their gnocchi.

"Great! How's eight o'clock?" Luke asked, seeming to take my previous declaration as a yes. I didn't correct him. It wasn't as if he were asking me out on a date, after all. We were friends. Or maybe not quite friends yet—but we had Jackson in common. And Luke was probably trying to butter me up before I read his novel.

Besides, now that the thought of Mimi's had been planted in my head, there was no turning back. After six weeks of being so busy that I was lucky to get down one solid meal a day, the prospect of a Mimi's feast sounded like pure heaven. And Randall would be stuck working late, anyway—so it wasn't like I was missing out on a chance to spend time with him.

My phone rang, and Vivian's extension flashed on the caller ID. "The boss," I apologized to Luke. "Eight o'clock sounds perfect."

"See you tonight, Claire," Luke said, waving and ducking out the door.

"She hasn't returned my calls in three weeks, Claire. My client has no idea what's going on! I can't get her or Graham to pick up the goddamn phone." Derek Hillman, a bottom-feeding L.A. agent who represented porn queen Mindi Murray, sounded distraught. Normally he just sounded pissed and pushy—things were starting to escalate.

The issue at hand: Mindi had turned in a proposal for her second book more than a month ago—a steamy how-to guide for women who wanted to lure the men in their lives off their porn addiction and back into bed—but for some reason, despite Vivian's expressed interest, plus a dozen messages and e-mails, I could not get my boss to commit to an offer. I'd thrown Derek every excuse in my arsenal, but I couldn't hold him at bay much longer.

"Well, Derek," I began, "we're just figuring out our P and L and what we—"

"Okay, bullshit. I've done twenty books with Vivian, sweetheart, and I know she doesn't need to see any P and L to decide how much she wants to offer. What's her problem? Is she in the office today? At this point, I'm about to sic Harold

on her. Tell her that, will you? Maybe *Harold* should negotiate this contract." Harold Kramer, a cutthroat lawyer who
could sue the sweat off a racehorse, was high on Vivian's
most-loathed list. Without question, she would *not* want him
to get involved.

"Just hold on, Derek, I'll get an answer from her by the end
of the week. She's coming back from L.A."

"Vivian's in L.A.? Why, I had no idea! Normally I can sort of
tell when she's in town...a pentagram forms in the sky, blood
weeps down walls. Listen, sweetheart, I need to know what's
happening by the end of the day, or we're going elsewhere.
Enough is enough."

"Derek, I'll do my best. I'm sorry, it's just—"

"Been unusually busy. I know. Skip the apologies, skip the
excuses. Just call me back today with an offer." He crashed the
phone down on my ear.

"How're you doing, kid?" asked Phil, materializing in my
doorway. He had about twenty files stacked in his arms. "You
coming?"

"Coming where?" I asked, feeling immediate alarm. Had I
forgotten about a meeting?

"The sales meeting, of course. Don't you have, like, a dozen
books on the spring list?"

I could hear blood pulsing in my ears. The marketing meeting—the one chance we editors had to present and promote
our titles to the entire sales team—was scheduled for *next*
week. "I think you've got the wrong date, Phil," I said, trying to
remain calm. "That meeting's not until next Wednesday."

Phil just stared at me. His face blotched up as if he'd been
playing football in subzero weather. "She wouldn't have—I
can't believe—Claire, Lulu sent out a staff e-mail on Monday saying that the meeting had been moved a week earlier.
It's taking place today, in about ten minutes! We've all been

scrambling to get our pitches squared away! Are you *sure* you didn't get that e-mail from her?"

With trembling fingers, I scrolled down in my Outlook. I hadn't received anything from Lulu in the past week. "Is it actually possible that Lulu e-mailed everyone but me?" I asked, not wanting to believe she could be that evil.

"I didn't get anything, either," piped up David from behind Phil.

Bitch.

But I didn't have time to feel enraged. Or calculate my revenge.

"Exactly how many minutes do I have?" I shouted at Phil, lurching for my filing cabinet and pulling out manila folders. Twelve books. Twelve books I needed to compellingly position and pitch to our sales team—so they could determine how to position and pitch to our major accounts. My first sales meeting at Grant Books—arguably the most important meeting on the calendar all season—and Lulu had completely sabotaged me!

The last-minute notice wasn't the only reason I felt panicked. I was petrified of speaking in public; I always got nervous and tongue-tied. My only hope had been tons of preparation— I'd planned on spending the entire weekend going over my notes—and now that was shot.

"I'll bat first and talk slowly, to buy you a few extra minutes," said Phil, still stunned. "I'd say you've got fifteen. Honestly, though, I wouldn't push it past that."

I glanced at David, my wingman, who'd rushed over to the filing cabinet to help. "You take the top six," I commanded, pointing to the list he'd pulled out, "and I'll take the bottom. Three talking points on each book. We'll keep it simple, straightforward." David nodded and went to work. We both scribbled notes and assembled materials in frenzied silence.

"Two minutes left," David said, checking his watch. "I'm done with mine."

"Me too. I'll review in the elevator. Let's go!"

We sprinted for the elevator bank and hit the button for the third floor. I ran my eyes over the notes as the elevator plummeted.

"Where's the conference room?" I panted, looking both ways at the intersection of two hallways.

"Hang a left—" David pointed toward double doors about forty feet away. I sprinted toward them, heaved them open, and—

"Claire!" Graham exclaimed, looking up from one end of an enormous conference table that was crammed with people. The entire editorial staff of Grant Books—save for Vivian, who was in L.A.—was seated along one edge. I spotted an empty seat next to Phil and glared at smug Lulu, who sat with an expression of wide-eyed innocence.

I'd kill her later. Right now, there was a job to be done.

"Everyone, please meet our newest editor, Claire Truman," said Graham. "Claire, you're just in time to tell everyone about the twelve books you have on your list for spring."

I sat down and pulled out my index cards. And that's when it hit me: I didn't feel nervous. Somehow, the panic of the last fifteen minutes, the adrenaline coursing through my veins, and the mad dash down the hallway had magically cured my usual fear of public speaking. As I launched into my first title, I felt more relaxed, confident, and articulate than I ever had before in front of a crowd. David's notes were right on target, and I was able to answer all the reps' questions.

When I'd finished, I looked at Lulu. She had her arms crossed across her skeletal body, and her face had tightened into a nasty little pout. I could tell she was fuming.

"You did good, kid," said Phil, throwing his arm around me as we all headed back up to the twelfth floor.

"Thanks to David," I said as the staff piled into the elevator. "Lulu, I didn't seem to get that e-mail about the scheduling change. Do you know why I wasn't on the list?"

"You weren't on the list?" she answered, not turning to face me. "Maybe I need to update it."

"What a beautiful, heartfelt apology, Lulu," Phil said as we stepped off on twelve. "You know, if Claire and David hadn't exhibited such grace under pressure, you could have really done some damage to a dozen books on our list. I wonder how Vivian would feel about that."

Lulu whipped her head around, fear in her eyes.

"Check your staff e-mail list," I said to her, veering off toward my office. I'd watch my back from now on, but my anger had mostly dissipated. Phil was right: I *had* done good.

"Claire!" Mimi barreled across the floor of the tiny restaurant to envelop me in a hug. "Look at you! Skin and bones, my *bella*! Why you're so thin?" Then she turned to face Luke and pinched his cheek hard. I could tell it hurt, but he smiled bravely through the pain. "My two favorite customers, in here together! Ah, Mimi is so happy!" she clucked, showing us to our table.

The decor at Mimi's was a complete cliché—red-checkered tablecloths, candles dripping over the sides of old wine bottles, soft Sinatra playing in the background—but no restaurant in New York could compete with the experience of being greeted by Mimi herself at the door. A cannoli away from two hundred pounds, Mimi instantly made you feel like part of *la famiglia*.

Luke gave me a shy smile as we sat down. He was wearing a soft-looking oxford, and his dark hair was tussled just a little.

"My boyfriend loves pasta Bolognese," I blurted out, looking at the menu. It had no basis in truth, of course—Randall would never touch something so calorie laden, nor were we completely there on the boyfriend/girlfriend label. Still, despite last night's minor fizzle, I was absolutely crazy about him—and I needed to put his existence out there. The last thing I wanted to do was lead Jackson's beloved nephew into believing this was more than just a friendly dinner.

"Consider yourself lucky." Luke smiled, glancing up from the menu. "My girlfriend's a strict vegan, which means I've got to endure more than my share of meals at Zen Palate. I've *just* managed to convince myself that the soy gluten nuggets are edible." He paused, thinking it over. "Nah, actually, not there yet."

Girlfriend? I'd just assumed he was single. The presence of a girlfriend was unexpected...and frankly, a little disappointing. Luke would've been just right for Mara. Cute, smart, from a close-knit family, and those sexy dark eyes. And Mara was an absolute sucker for men with great smiles. Oh, well. My matchmaking efforts would be thwarted, but it was probably better that Luke was dating someone, too. No danger of him getting the wrong idea. I sank back in my chair and took a relaxed sip of my wine.

"I feel like I know you through Uncle Jack," said Luke. "He's such a big fan of yours."

"I miss him so much. Have you been down to Virginia yet? Carie was just telling me that she rides every day now, and Jackson has really gotten into hiking." I suppressed a laugh at the thought: Jackson was the least rugged person I knew. I couldn't imagine him hacking through the woods. I couldn't even picture him wearing shorts.

"Uh-huh. I think hiking, for Uncle Jack, means forgoing the valet."

I smiled. "I just wonder how he's getting through each day without his red pen. Have you ever met anyone who loves to edit more than Jackson? I mean, I've seen him mark up published books with that pen."

"Oh, I know. One time, he and I were walking down a street, and he stopped to correct some graffiti scrawled on the side of a bus stop. Uncle Jack might've retired, but I guarantee the red pen is still working overtime."

I drizzled some olive oil over Mimi's freshly baked bread. "It still must be a strange transition, retirement. Not being in the office. I can't imagine not working full-time."

"Yeah? So you're born to edit, too?" Luke smiled.

"Well, that might be a slight overstatement. But I do love it. It was my father, really, who taught me to edit. He bought me my first *Chicago Manual of Style*. I can still hear his voice in my head sometimes, reminding me when to use 'which' and when to use 'that'—catching me when I accidentally split an infinitive—"

"And I thought *my* family knew how to have a good time," Luke teased. "Is your father an editor, too?"

"He was a poet, mainly, and also a professor at University of Iowa. He died a little more than five years ago."

"I'm really sorry, Claire," said Luke. He refilled our wine glasses, then looked up quickly. "Hang on. His first name wasn't Charles, was it?"

"Yeah, Charles Truman. Have you read his work?"

"Have I read—I *love* his work! I had 'Tranquility' tacked on the wall by my desk all through college! I've probably read that poem more than a hundred times! I can't believe Charles Truman is your father."

I could feel myself beaming. My father's devotion to his poetry had been second only to his devotion to Mom and me. That his work would be treasured by others filled my heart to the brim.

"May I tell you tonight's specials?" our waiter asked. He

whipped through the list, each dish sounding more mouth-wateringly delicious than the last.

"Maybe it'd take less time if we told you what we *didn't* want," Luke joked, eyes twinkling. We ordered as though we'd both been stranded on a desert island for months and this was our first meal back in civilization.

The hours flew by. Luke and I seemed to flow from one topic to the next—from our all-time favorite authors (his: Faulkner and Hemingway; mine: Salinger and Kundera) to our biggest pet peeves (his: food in teeth; mine: Americans who peppered their speech with Briticisms, such as "I knew him at university, he was completely bollocks!").

"Here you go," said the waiter with a warm smile, laying the check down between us. We both reached for it immediately—I grabbed it first, but then Luke's hand clasped mine, sending an unexpected shiver through my body.

"Please, let me!" I insisted. "I can expense it, you're a prospective author—" I completely hated the thought of letting him pick up the tab—he was the starving artist, so to speak, and I'd witnessed the jobs he took to make ends meet.

But Luke kept his grip firm. "Of course not, Claire. You were nice enough to come out and celebrate, despite how busy you are. *And* despite the fact that you very recently saw me wearing a bonnet."

He smiled, and I noticed again how much his eyes shone. Well, maybe things wouldn't work out with the vegan girl-friend—and Mara could have a shot after all.

After winning the battle of the bill, Luke insisted on walking me home, even though it was at least ten blocks out of his way. When we reached my awning, he kissed me gently on the cheek.

I found myself smiling as I walked up all seven flights of stairs to my studio (normally, my expression is more of a flush-faced grimace). Once inside, I slipped into my PJs, placed the cannoli Luke had insisted I bring home on a plate, climbed under the covers, and began to read his manuscript.

∾

The next day, exhausted but exhilarated, I knocked on Vivian's office door. I had a fresh copy of Luke's manuscript in hand. I'd asked David to run off ten copies first thing that morning so that I could get reads on it immediately. He'd been engrossed in it himself ever since.

"Come in," shouted a distant voice. I opened the heavy door, felt the blast of freezing air (Vivian kept her office at subzero), and found my boss poring over five or six magazines. As I got closer, I realized that they were all *Hustlers*.

"What do you think about this girl for the cover of *Just Do Me*?" she asked.

Just Do Me was a smutty novel based on twenty years of one woman's sexcapades, spanning from orgies at summer camp to a tryst with a fellow soccer mom. It would best be described as an antonym for "good" or "decent."

"I think the book will sell better if we revamp the cover," Vivian continued, flipping to a new centerfold and holding her up for my scrutiny.

Switching the cover of *Just Do Me* seemed like changing deck chairs on the *Titanic*. I evaded the question by nodding and pretending to cough.

"Vivian, I wanted to talk to you about a book I'm very interested in buying," I began seriously. "I've never read anything quite like it. I was up all last night and couldn't put it down. It's an up close look at—"

"Literary or commercial," Vivian asked, unscrewing the cap on a bottle that looked to be filled with algae. She took a swig. "New diet. All I can eat is kale and raw onions."

"Um, literary, but with universal chords that—"

"And flaxseed. But come on, it's not like anyone ever pigs out on flaxseed. The question is, will the book sell." Most of Vivian's questions came out as statements, orders. It was as if she didn't want to acknowledge that she was turning to someone else for the answer to anything.

"Yes, I think it definitely—"

"What's the title."

"No title yet. The author's name is Luke—actually, he's the nephew of Jackson Mayville. He just finished his MFA at Columbia and—"

"Jackson's nephew?" Vivian threw back her head and snorted like a wild horse. "God, why didn't you say so? Man, would *that* make old Jackson turn over in his retirement, knowing that I was publishing one of his relatives! I love it. Love it! Let's do it. How much do you think you need to offer to get the book immediately off the table?"

What? Could it really be that simple? As many times as I'd rehearsed this conversation in my head during my morning commute, it had never gone this way. Vivian hadn't read a word of Luke's manuscript—would she really make a decision based on an immature desire to irk Jackson?

"Earth to Claire!" Vivian snapped. "How much?"

"I have no idea, we haven't discussed money yet. I just got the manuscript yesterday."

"Does anyone else at Mather-Hollinger have it," she asked.

"No, but I think Luke said he gave it to another friend at FSG."

"And no agent?"

"No agent," I confirmed.

Vivian looked pleased. "Well, offer a hundred. It'll be worth every penny to make Jackson squirm."

I paused for a moment before thanking Vivian and leaving

her office. I didn't love her reasons, that was for sure, but I wanted the book far too bad to quibble. Hopefully, Jackson's discomfort with Vivian as the publisher would be offset by my involvement as the editor.

And fifteen minutes later, after he'd excitedly accepted our offer, I was officially Luke Mayville's editor.

CHAPTER EIGHT

 SHE'S COME UNDONE

O*w! Ow, ow, ow, ow, ow.*

I was bone-tired, almost limp with the exhaustion of an eighteen-hour day spent dealing with difficult authors, cranky agents, and unreasonable demands. There were a few things I could've used: a hot bubble bath; a deep-tissue massage by a gifted Swede named Hans; copious amounts of fudge.

And some things I truly didn't need—which would include my shin whacking against the unforgiving porcelain edge of the bathtub as I sprinted to find my ringing cordless phone at 2:00 in the morning.

Not bothering with the towel, leaving a trail of puddles across the floor, I ran toward the shrill ring. Who could it be at this hour? I tried not to panic as my mind scrolled through the possibilities. Randall was on an overnight flight to Europe, another business trip. Vivian didn't have my home phone number—on Phil's advice, I'd never given it out. Only in an emergency would Mom or Bea call me this late…the thought made my heart leap into my throat and I didn't notice the open drawer of my dresser, and—

OW, OW, OW. What is the mean-spirited cosmic force that dictates that once you've smacked your shin once, you'll re-smack the same spot on everything sharp and hard that comes within a thirty-foot radius? I dove across my unmade bed to rummage for the... There it was.

"Hello?" I panted.

"Claire. Vivian. What have you put together for the Sweet D-licious book?"

Vivian. My heart rate didn't slow down. How the hell did she get my home phone number? It was unlisted, and I'd lied to her assistant and said I used only my cell phone. I'd even asked Randall to keep it confidential. How had she found it? And why was she calling me at 2:00 in the morning?

"Claire? You there? Where are we with Sweet D? I don't have all night!"

The truth? I hadn't put together a single thing since Vivian had mentioned the concept to me a few days ago. Because she loaded me up with so many ideas to pursue on a daily basis, some slipped through the cracks. Sweet D, unfortunately, fell into the neglected category. He was one of the hottest stars in the rap firmament—his last album, *Bronx Tail*, had gone platinum, and he'd been shot at twice. Vivian wanted to publish a book of his lyrics, uncut and uncensored. I'd called his manager three times but hadn't heard back.

I knew it was the wrong answer. The right answer would've been: *Well, Vivian, when I hadn't heard back from the agent in twenty-four hours, I marched straight down to his office and camped out there until he finally agreed to see me. Then I convinced him that the next step in Sweet D's trajectory had to be getting a book out to his fans, Grant Books had to be the publisher of said book, and they had to agree to do it for a song. So to speak.*

"I'm sorry, I don't have much yet," I answered instead,

stomach clenching. I'd managed to last four months without incurring Vivian's wrath—which Phil insisted was a company record—but now I was sure my lucky streak was about to end. "I'll get more information together for you first thing tomorrow."

There was silence on the line. I imagined a lit fuse burning steadily toward a bomb.

"Okay," Vivian finally said.

Okay? I exhaled. That was really it? No tirade, no tantrum?

"So how are things with Randall?" Vivian asked. I shivered, wrapping my towel around me. "His father was crap in bed. Thought he was God's gift, but that man was hung like a pimple. It was better than nothing, though, which is what I've got at the moment. Do you know the last time I got laid?"

Actually, I was pretty sure I did know. In the middle of a staff meeting the previous week, Vivian had provided a graphic account of the afternoon tryst she'd had with a sexy bellboy at the Beverly Hills Hotel. He drove a Vespa and waxed his chest. "Usually," she'd confided to twenty of her nearest and dearest employees, "younger men don't know how to pleasure a woman. Like you, Harry, you probably wouldn't know which end was up. But Vespa guy was an exception." Harry, an assistant in the art department, had blushed purple. He'd quit the next day.

"I am so horny," Vivian continued as I sat down stiffly on my couch and tried to mentally detach from the conversation, "I just humped the arm of my chair. My son walked in while I was going at it and screamed, 'Mo-om!' That pretty much took all the romance out of it. Well, it gives him something to talk to his shrink about."

Something told me the kid wouldn't be hurting for material.

"You've never called me at home before, Vivian," I said,

looking at the clock on my nightstand through bleary eyes. "How'd you get this number? I'm barely at home, so I don't think I gave it out as a contact."

"Oh, Lulu passed it along," Vivian said nonchalantly.

Why'd I even bother to ask? Of course she did. How Lulu had found it, I could only imagine. I rested my head on my pillow, willing myself to stay awake as my boss launched into the story of how she'd lost her virginity.

I pulled out my day planner, adding "Change home phone" to my pages-long to-do list.

At the end of my fifth month of work, it happened.

I'd decided to stay late at the office on Friday so that I could get a handle on the ten books I'd inherited from my most recently departed colleague.

Over the past five months, I'd begun to feel much closer to the rest of the staff—through a shared grimace in the hallway outside of Lulu's office, a sympathetic smile during an editorial meeting, a quick "r u ok?" e-mail after a huge new drift of work had been dumped—but our good-byes were completely unceremonious. At P and P, we'd routinely organize farewell drinks for each departed colleague. If we did that at Grant Books, we'd all be alcoholics.

The only ritual at Grant was the passing of the files. In the wake of each exit, a huge stack of documents and folders would land on my desk. Against one wall of my office, I watched with increasing anxiety as the mountain of new files grew steadily by the week.

My newest authors had been especially shell-shocked by the time I reached them. Most had already been handed down through three, maybe four Grant editors. When I called to introduce myself, one woman wearily expressed her hope that I'd last longer than her last editor. I assured her that I would, and they pretended to believe me—but I could tell they'd heard the promise before.

Friday evening, after a week of mayhem, the twelfth floor was silent as a tomb. Vivian had flown to L.A. the day before, and the rest of the staff had trickled out for a well-deserved weekend off.

I was looking forward to a wintry weekend off, too. Randall and I had decided to "play hooky" and drive out to Long Island to spend the night with Bea and Harry in Montauk. I couldn't wait. It would be great to get out of the city, especially now that it looked like I'd be trapped here over the holidays. I had so many deadlines clustered around the end of the year, including a book that needed to be edited over Christmas weekend, so Mom had generously offered to spend the week with me in New York. Less than ideal, but at least we'd be together.

Hopefully she'd get to meet Randall during her visit. And I was eager for him to spend more time with Bea and Harry this weekend. The double whammy of our respective work demands left us with a few stolen moments together each week, not much more, which made it nearly impossible to plan double dates. It was strange, given that we'd now been dating for almost six months, but I'd still not met a single friend of his. Well, once we bumped into his colleague from Goldman on the street—a guy about Randall's age, who'd practically genuflected at my boyfriend's feet—but that was about it.

My boyfriend. It still felt like a dream. Randall was proving to be just as wonderful a boyfriend as I'd always imagined he would be. He was so thoughtful—planning dinners at the best restaurants the city had to offer, always asking about my day, showering me with flowers at the office. And I'd been right not to read too much into our false starts in the bedroom...it had just taken us a few weeks to get into the swing of things.

Deep in these thoughts, I jumped in my chair when I heard the phone ring in Dawn Jeffers's office, just to the left of mine. Then I heard it ring in Lulu's office, diagonally across the hall. I glanced at the clock on my computer screen: nearly 11:30. Had it gotten so late already?

The phone rang in my office. Unfortunately, I picked up.

"Where the fuck is everybody?" Vivian snarled into the phone. She sounded absolutely livid. "I leave the office and everyone decides that school's out? I've been up since five in the morning and I've got three more meetings tonight. Why am I working harder than the entire staff put together? And what have you been doing all week? I haven't heard a word from you—I don't know what you *do* in that office all day—"

I froze, shocked, my pen poised in midair over my notepad. Did Vivian realize how late it was in New York? Had she mistakenly dialed my extension? Did she think she was speaking to someone else? I'd heard her berate nearly everyone on the staff, but so far I'd been granted relative immunity. Not that she'd been lavishing me with praise for the past five months, but she hadn't ripped me limb from limb, either. I wasn't expecting my good fortune to run out when she'd reached me working late on a Friday night.

I took a sharp breath and forged ahead. "W-well, I'm getting up to speed on a few books I've taken over this week."

Vivian could smell fear through the phone lines, and she pounced. "Do *not* interrupt me when I'm speaking. And anyway, what's to 'get up to speed on'?" she mimicked me in a high, tinny voice. "You read the file, you talk to the author—it's not rocket science, and it shouldn't take up this much of your time. Oh, and I got your message about another literary novel you want to bid on. I've seen enough of those submissions, Claire. We can do a couple, *fine*, but they're just not profitable! Enough, enough, enough. Maybe Jackson Mayville went for all that highbrow literary crap that ten people buy, but not me. Grant Books is a tight ship, Claire, and you've got to climb out of your ivory tower if you want to survive here. You need to get in touch with what people want to read. Why am I the only one who *gets* that? Why am I the only person with goddamn *instincts*? All you elitist snobs, you out-of-touch Ivy-Leaguers. You're so fucking...so fucking anemic, it makes me sick."

I couldn't breathe. I felt as if I'd just taken a wrecking ball to the gut. Was Vivian actually saying these things to me? After I'd busted my ass to prove myself as a capable editor—after I'd taken on twenty-five books without a hint of a complaint, even though it barely left me with time to pursue my own projects—after I'd given up every weekend since I started...

"How old are you, twenty-six?" Vivian snapped, rage shooting through the phone receiver I was now gripping tightly, "You're a *child*. You're in way over your head. I don't know what I was thinking when I hired you. Anyway, I have to go. I have *work* to *do*, Claire, I can't waste my whole night on the phone with you."

Click.

My head dropped in my hands. I couldn't breathe. For a few minutes, the otherwise silent office was filled with the sound of me gulping for air.

The logical part of my brain had always expected that one day, like every other person Vivian had ever worked with, I would be on the receiving end of her anger. But a delusional sliver of my brain had harbored a ridiculous hope that maybe I'd be the exception, the golden protégée, the star pupil.

I gathered my things, heart heavy, and left my office with files strewn about. For a lifelong approval glutton, it came as a serious jolt to the system to have my boss essentially tell me that I *sucked*. Nobody had ever yelled at me before—at least, not in such a scathing, vitriolic way.

The honeymoon was officially over.

"Sweetie, it couldn't have been that bad," Randall clucked, swirling the ice in his Scotch. Since Bea had already driven out to Long Island, I'd called Randall as my backup choice for some sympathy and support—new ground for us. He'd agreed to meet me for a quick drink at Hudson Bar & Books before he had to head back to the office. "She probably had a tough day and was looking for a scapegoat. Happens all the time in the business world. When I was climbing the ladder at Goldman, I got torn a new one on a daily basis. If I took it personally every time one of my MDs yelled at me for something that had nothing to do with me . . . why, I wouldn't have lasted three days." He chuckled at the thought.

I knew Randall was right. I was being a baby, and I needed to toughen up. So my boss had yelled at me—happened to millions of employees, day in and day out. I should be able to handle it. I just wasn't used to it—that was all. I'd been sheltered for my entire life. Coddled. "Just do your best, and we'll be proud of you," my parents had always assured me. "A" for effort. Jackson had operated under the same principles. I knew they had the best intentions, but they'd turned me into a thin-skinned wimp.

But now I'd taken on a new level of responsibility, and part of that meant learning to roll with the punches. Randall was right.

By my second quickly downed glass of wine, I was feeling a little better than I had leaving the office. My tears had subsided, and now my mind felt heavy with a calm exhaustion. Still, there was a dark feeling lurking beneath it, a vestige of

Vivian's rage that an entire lake of chardonnay couldn't quite dissolve.

What if Vivian decided I was so inept that she fired me? I couldn't bring myself to admit this particular insecurity to my overachieving boyfriend, but people got canned all the time at Grant Books. I could be out of a job—maybe I'd have to crawl back to P and P after just a few months away. How humiliating! If I could incur her wrath by working hard on a Friday night, who knew how long it'd be before there was a stapler flying at my head and a pink slip on my desk? Vivian got rid of employees as thoughtlessly and regularly as most people emptied their trash cans.

I waved to the waitress for a refill. The hopes I'd had five months ago—proving myself as an editor at Grant, finding great books, moving my career ahead several paces—now seemed like delusions. Who was I fooling? I *was* just a kid, and though I'd been killing myself to do a good job, maybe I didn't have the experience I needed to take on so many projects. Maybe I *was* in over my head.

"I hate seeing you this upset, Claire-bear," said Randall, using his newly coined nickname for me. He rubbed my shoulder gently. "Maybe it's not worth the stress. Maybe—"

"No way," I interrupted him, shaking my head. As shaken as I felt, I knew I couldn't quit. I'd vowed to last a year, and it would take more than one beating to throw me off the track. "I'm going to prove her wrong," I muttered, more to myself than to Randall. I'd just have to try harder. I took a big gulp of wine.

"I'm sure you will, sweetie," Randall said encouragingly. "You're a star, and Vivian Grant is lucky to have you. She knows it, too—she just had a bad night, and you happened to step into her line of fire. I'm sure this will blow over, Claire-bear."

"Thanks, Randall," I said, kissing his cheek. "I'm feeling better already." He'd done a great job as Bea's stand-in.

"I'm glad." He kissed my nose. "I hate seeing you so upset. I wish I didn't have to go back to the office"—Randall frowned, checking his watch—"but if I don't get this memo done to-night, I'll have to deal with it tomorrow."

"No, I promise I'm good," I assured him. Secretly, though, my heart ached at the prospect of heading back to my apartment alone. I didn't feel like hearing my own thoughts tonight...or worse, the echo of Vivian's. I could go back to Randall's and wait for him—but who knew how long he'd be stuck at the office, and I always felt uncomfortable being alone in the apartment with Svetlana.

Randall strode over to the bar to settle our tab. I took an-other glum sip of my wine, watching the attractive female bar-tender gazing at my boyfriend as he waited. It didn't faze me, strangely enough—I knew what a solid, trustworthy guy Ran-dall was, and I'd never seen him so much as glance at another woman. Not a chip off the old block in that regard. Besides, I couldn't blame the woman. In his expertly tailored suit and Hermes tie, Randall, as always, looked beyond handsome.

Well, I cheered myself, *maybe my job has hit a huge brick wall, but at least I still have the perfect guy.*

He walked back to the table and rested a hand on my shoul-der. "Pick you up tomorrow at three? Oh, and I almost forgot. My parents are in Southampton, very unexpectedly, for the weekend—I think they're meeting with a contractor about a new guest cottage on the property. Anyway, do you think we could carve out an hour to visit with them before heading out to Montauk? If we stop by for a cocktail at six, that'll give us plenty of time to get out to Bea and Harry's for dinner."

"Your parents? Sounds great," I answered, standing up to kiss him good-bye. *The perfect guy who's dying to introduce me to his mom and dad. Yeah, life could be worse.*

CHAPTER NINE

 EAT THE RICH

O f course I want you to meet my parents. Unless you feel—"

"No, no, I'd love to meet them, it's just that—"

Randall put his finger to my lips. We'd been intermittently having the same conversation for two hours since leaving the city, neither of us capable of completing a sentence. Yes, I'd agreed the night before to having cocktails with Lucille and Randall Cox II before our dinner in Montauk with Bea and Harry. And of course I wanted to. But I was a little nervous. What if they didn't think I was a suitable girlfriend for their son? One crushing blow to the ego per weekend was about all I could handle—and thanks to Vivian, I'd already hit my quota the night before.

"You have nothing to be nervous about. My mother is absolutely euphoric that I'm dating the daughter of Patricia Truman," Randall insisted. "Believe me, it's her wildest dream come true." From the driver's seat, he reached his arm around me, then pulled my head down so that it rested awkwardly on his muscular shoulder. I stayed put for a few uncomfortable moments until he hit a pothole and my temple banged against him. I shifted back into the upright position.

"We're here!" he announced a few minutes later, squeezing my knee.

We were? I thought we'd been driving down a quiet lane, lined on either side by huge oak trees, but now I realized that it was actually the long private driveway to the Cox estate. Randall put his Porsche in park, and I climbed out of the car, taking in the full view: the enormous, shingled Stanford White home, the rolling lawns, the perfectly kept tennis courts, and the sun setting on the water just behind the house. I'd stumbled into *The Great Gatsby*. And Randall—stretching athletically, his polo shirt lifting to reveal a strip of taut stomach—was perfectly cast in the scene.

"We made great time," he said, affectionately patting the hood of his car.

As we entered the enormous marble foyer, I could hear a rich bass laugh mingle with a trilling soprano giggle. Randall took my hand and pulled me toward the sound of laughter and clinking glass.

"Darling!" Lucille Cox flew up at us the second we entered the living room, grabbing us both in a tight embrace and planting a slightly damp kiss on each of my cheeks. She was the tannest, thinnest woman I'd ever seen, impeccably dressed and topped off with a meringue of bleached hair. "Randall, my darling! And you must be Claire. We've been so looking forward to meeting you, my dear. Randall says the most glowing things about you." My heart warmed instantly. Randall had glowed about me?

Randall's father, previously unable to get a word in edgewise, inched forward and shook my hand. I could see where Randall got his looks. Now in his sixties, his father was still handsome. His jowls drooped a little, and clots of hair poked out from his nose, but his face hadn't given up its original design. "Pleasure to have you here, Claire," he declared in a stentorian voice. "Now, first things first—what I can get you to drink?"

Two shockingly stiff vodka tonics later, we'd become a quartet of laughing voices, and I gazed tenderly at everyone in the room. *This is a family I can get used to,* I thought as Randall II topped off my glass once more and Lucille offered me another Dunhill. It was refreshing to meet people who refused to outgrow their vices.

My stomach grumbled quietly—I hadn't eaten more than a bite all day, my nerves were too jangled from the combination of Vivian's tirade and the parental meeting—and on cue, a maid dressed in a crisply ironed uniform materialized with a tray of hors d'oeuvres. I gratefully took a piece of melon wrapped in prosciutto. Just in time. If I didn't get something in my stomach, I'd never make it to dinner. Randall's dad didn't mess around with his vodka.

"No, thank you, Carlotta," Lucille demurred, not so much as glancing at the tray.

"Not for me," echoed Randall.

The maid rested the silver tray between me and Mr. Cox, who happily gobbled up a few mini–crab cakes. "These are delicious," I said, snagging my second.

Mr. Cox nodded. "Try the salmon puffs," he suggested helpfully.

"How *do* you keep your lovely figure, my dear?" asked Lucille with a tight smile as I picked up a puff from the gleaming tray.

"Mother," Randall whispered in a warning tone. I dropped the puff into my cocktail napkin, suddenly feeling as though I should have a snout. No wonder this woman had a grown son who chewed every bite of food one hundred times.

"Claire, I just adored your mother in college," Lucille

purred, resting her bony fingers on my arm. Instantly the conversation split in two. Randall and his father launched into a discussion about investments, legs crossed toward each other, revealing identical cashmere socks above their matching Gucci loafers. Lucille pulled her meager body closer to mine.

"Oh, thank you," I replied. "She's said the same—"

"We were like sisters at Vassar! We shared absolutely everything—hairbrush, study notes, clothes, even *boys* on occasion!" Lucille let out a trill of laughter over the memory. "You know, I've never had such a close friend in my life, before or since. Tish-Tish was one of a kind."

Tish-Tish? I'd never heard anyone refer to Mom by *that* dreadful nickname before. How sad, that a friendship could drift as far apart as theirs had. I thought of Beatrice. Lately I'd been so preoccupied with work and my new relationship that our conversations had been reduced to two-minute "check-ins." Could *our* lives ever diverge in the polarized way that Mom's and Lucille's had? It had never occurred to me before—and it was a chilling thought. To hear Lucille tell it, she and Mom used to be inseparably close, too—but it'd been more than a decade since they'd last seen each other.

"I miss your mother more than I can tell you," Lucille continued melodramatically. Her little forehead quivered slightly—if her commitment to Botox were any less resolute, my guess was that I'd be seeing a brow knit with sadness. "It's just too bad, Claire. You know, how she's living out there. My heart goes out to her. I *so* wish we could convince her to move closer to New York."

How Mom was living? The last time I'd checked, she was living in a beautiful little farmhouse on a gorgeous piece of land. She was living among a community of friends who loved her and had known and loved my dad. Her work had never been stronger, and to her enormous delight, she'd started to sell to small galleries across the country.

"I think she's pretty happy with how she's living, actually," I corrected Lucille.

"Oh, I know she *says* she's happy, my dear, but really, how can she be? Living in the sticks? Isolated from culture, unable to travel much, and even forced to sell some of her own paintings? If only your father had been able to...well, I suppose we shouldn't blame the dead."

Blood rushed hotly to my face. I shot Randall a sharp look, but he remained absorbed in whatever his father was saying and offered no buffer. Was his mother trying to make me fly off the handle within twenty minutes of meeting her? Because if she was, making an insulting insinuation about my dad and a patronizing comment about my mom was a pretty reliable way to go.

Don't lose your temper, Claire. I took a deep breath.

"Mrs. Cox, she really is happy," I said firmly. "Iowa City isn't exactly bright lights, big city, but you'd be surprised by how rich the cultural life actually is. And Mom is thrilled that there's a growing demand for her paintings. I think that's satisfying on several levels, including a financial one."

"Uh-huh." Lucille nodded, clearly unconvinced. "Well, dear, I do hope you're right."

Mom liked this woman? They'd been friends?

"I know Vivian Grant, too, you know," Lucille continued, gesturing for Carlotta to refresh our cocktails. I noticed that Randall's father looked up ever so briefly from his conversation at the mention of Vivian's name, but Lucille didn't notice. "*Dreadful* woman, Vivian. She was always so *driven*. Oh, I respect what she's done with her career, I suppose. But what about the rest of her life? It's important to keep a balance between the demands of work and home, don't you agree?"

Lucille was right: Vivian *was* dreadful. And after the lashing she'd given me last night, I was particularly in the mood to hear criticism of her—no matter what it was. I took another sip of my vodka tonic and nodded vehemently in agreement.

Uh-oh. The room kept wobbling a little after my head stopped.

Lucille smiled warmly at me, as if I'd cleared some invisible hurdle. "It's so refreshing to meet a young woman who feels that way, Claire. Especially one with whom my son seems so smitten. Perhaps I shouldn't tell you this, but his last girlfriend, Coral"—she pulled a face that let me know exactly where she stood on Coral—"was *so* focused on her career. It was all she could talk about, really. Not that there's anything wrong with a woman wanting that, it's just—selfishly, as a mother, I'd like to see Randall with someone a little...softer in her ambitions."

What? Was I soft in my ambitions? "Actually, I work pretty hard, Mrs. Cox—"

"Of course you do, dear, I didn't mean to say that you don't take your job seriously. Forget I mentioned it at all."

Her timing, at least, was good: Having downed three whoppingly strong cocktails on an empty stomach, I might not find it hard to forget the comment.

"And then there was the whole issue of Coral's parents," Lucille rambled, still apparently fixated on Randall's ex. "How do I say this delicately...well, I can't. She was born in a trailer park, Claire. Literally, a trailer park. That may sound like an absurd and ridiculous exaggeration, but I assure you it is *not*." Lucille shook her head as if she were still having trouble digesting the fact. "Which is fine, of course, we can't hold that against the girl—she's done well for herself, Yale Law and all that—but Randall's father and I just thought that it would make it so much more *difficult*, you know, not coming from similar backgrounds. What happens when young Randall wants to become a member of the Bath and Tennis, or Shinnecock? I know, it's *terrible*, but some of the best clubs are very exacting, even when you're a Cox. And why make your life more challenging when you don't need to?"

I couldn't answer the question, because the room—exploding in peach chintz—was suddenly making me very dizzy.

"Randall," I interrupted a little too loudly, "we ought to keep an eye on the time. Bea and Harry are expecting us at eight." He just smiled, nodded, and resumed his conversation.

And Lucille kept going, too. "I know I should be a bit more coy about this, my dear," she whispered conspiratorially at a volume that the men could definitely hear, "but you're *just* the kind of girl I'd always hoped Randall would settle down with. As I said, I simply loved your mother. She was always so elegant, so refined and beautiful. She could have had any man in the world, you know. Why, it was no secret that Harrison Westville the Third—heir to the Westville toothpaste fortune—would've snapped her up in half a heartbeat." Lucille made the tiniest clucking sound.

"What are you ladies chatting about over there?" Randall finally interjected. "Mother?"

"Oh, just girl talk." Lucille giggled. "Listen, darling, can't we persuade you to stay for dinner? The cook made her famous Cornish hens, and we'd love to spend more time with you two!"

"What do you think, Claire?" he asked. "Would Bea and Harry mind if we made it brunch tomorrow instead and spent the night here?"

What?! The room finally stopped its slow spin and ground to a screeching halt. Bea and Harry had spent the afternoon gathering ingredients for tonight's menu and getting ready for our visit. We couldn't possibly cancel at the last minute! Even in my slightly blurry state, that much was clear to me.

"I really wish we could," I said to Lucille after a pause, "but I'm afraid my friends would be upset. They've been looking forward to spending more time with Randall, and this dinner has been planned for a while."

"Of course. It's a shame, but we understand," said Lucille, "Another night. I do hope we'll see you again soon, Claire. And your mother! You must tell me when she's next in town. I would be so delighted to see her." The four of us stood and kissed our good-byes. I focused on staying vertical.

As Randall helped me into the Porsche's deep bucket seat, I waved at his parents and tried to hold back my scowl. "I can't believe you did that!" I fumed as soon as he shut the car door.

"Did what?"

"Tried to bag on Bea and Harry? Put me in the position of telling your mom we couldn't have dinner with them?"

Randall kept his eyes steadily on the road ahead. We drove in heated silence for a minute, snaking down the driveway with a rising moon overhead.

"I'm sorry, babe. I wasn't thinking," he said finally, kissing my hand.

But for some reason (likely vodka), his knee-jerk capitulation only fueled the fire. "And what's the deal with your mother not liking your ex-girlfriend because she wasn't . . . to the manor born? Or because she was too focused on her career? That's really narrow-minded, Randall, and those same things could be said about me!"

"My mother really should not have said that about Coral! She shouldn't have said *anything* about Coral!" Randall sounded genuinely pissed. He took a moment to collect himself. "But of course, your background's not like that. Your mom came from a very good Boston family, and your father was a respected academic. Hardly the trailer park, Claire."

"That's not what I'm upset about, Randall!" I slurred in

outrage. Why didn't he understand that it was his mother's haughtier-than-thou attitude that I objected to? And he sounded as though he'd actually given the question of my "suitability" some thought! And what about the career stuff? "You know my job's very important to me, right?" I asked, swiveling around in the passenger seat to face him.

He glanced over at me quickly. "Claire, there's an Evian in the backseat. Why don't you drink some? I think you've been overserved."

"You know I care a *lot* about my career?" I repeated. I knew I sounded belligerent, but I couldn't seem to stop myself.

"Of course I do, Claire. My God! I honestly don't know what you're getting so riled up about. If you'll remember, I was the one who helped you *find* that job you care so much about in the first place. Drink some water. You're behaving like a child."

His words hit me like a slap. A *child*. First my boss, now my boyfriend.

"Listen," Randall said in a much calmer voice, resting a hand on my knee, "I'm sorry. I'm sorry Mother upset you. She means well, but sometimes she says things without thinking them through. She definitely shouldn't have brought up Coral or talked about that career nonsense. I think she was a little nervous about meeting you, and it made her run off. Anyway, I am *sorry*. And about suggesting that we change our plans. It's just that I don't get to see my parents all that often, given my work schedule, and I felt bad that we couldn't visit with them longer. They've been looking forward to meeting you for weeks. It's all that my mother's been talking about."

I felt all my anger deflate. What was I doing? So Lucille had rubbed me the wrong way. Did I really have to unleash that on Randall as soon as our car doors shut? So he'd goofed about the dinner situation. He was just a good son who had a hard time disappointing his parents. Why was I ruining the first full weekend we'd been able to spend together in months?

"I'm sorry, Randall, I don't know what's come over me," I said quietly, feeling ashamed of myself. He handed me the bottle of Evian, and I took a long gulp.

"Don't worry about it. Let's just relax and enjoy the rest of the evening, okay?"

I nodded, taking another gulp of water as Randall's Porsche hurtled through the starless winter evening. Then I leaned over and kissed his cheek, and he smiled. Handsome, smart, a good son...and forgiving. The perfect guy.

Bea waved excitedly from the house, framed by the warm porch light. I'd honestly never been happier to see her. After weeks of minimal QT and my conversation with Lucille, I was dying for a full, detailed catch-up session with my best friend.

"Hey, guys!" she called, as we got out of the car.

Fortunately, our forty-minute ride to Montauk and the liter of water had brought me back to reasonable sobriety. I'd convinced Randall to let me roll down the windows just a crack—he hated the effect of any wind on his perfectly gelled hair but made an exception—and the cold, clean ocean air had cleared my head.

"Beatrice, you look lovely as always," Randall said, giving her a kiss and clapping Harry on the back.

"Wow, the house is amazing!" I said when we stepped into the newly renovated kitchen. It had the coziest feeling to it—I loved the wainscoting, the huge antique farm table, the family portraits Bea had expertly arranged on one wall.

"Yeah, didn't she do a great job?" Harry asked, showing us to the living room.

"It's beautiful!" seconded Randall, looking around. "Say, Bea, would you be interested in decorating my new place in Nantucket? I think your aesthetic would be just right for the job."

"Really?" asked Bea, lighting up. "I'd love that! Absolutely."

"Great. I'll have my secretary get the details to you next week. Oh, I forgot—here you go, sir." Randall handed Harry a slightly dusty bottle of wine. "Petrus '85, a great year."

"Wow!" exclaimed Harry. "This is a phenomenal bottle! Thank you, Randall, it's too generous of you."

I felt a warm glow. It was a beautiful sight: my incredible boyfriend getting along so well with my best friends. One big happy family.

"So how'd it go with the parents?" Bea whispered when we'd settled into the couch next to each other and the guys were off dealing with the wine.

"Tell you later. Not a one-word answer."

"Hey, Claire, I forgot to pass along a little gossip last week," Harry said, coming into the living room with two wineglasses for us. "You'll never guess who I saw canoodling at a discreet little hole-in-the-wall diner near my office."

"Canoodling? You've been reading Page Six again, haven't you."

"Just guess." Harry laughed.

"Okay, give me a hint—celebrity, politician, or blast-from-our-past?"

"Politician and…I don't know, celebrity, sort of. I recognized her, at least. Holding hands and gazing into each other's eyes like total lovebirds. Give up?" Harry was clearly bursting at the seams to dish this one, so I nodded. "Vivian Grant and the deputy mayor."

"You saw—*wait*, who's the deputy mayor again?"

"Stanley Prizbecki. I think you'd know him if you saw him. Big bruiser with a perpetual five o'clock shadow and bulging biceps…the mayor's right-hand man?"

"*That* guy? You saw *that* guy and Vivian canoodling?" My understanding of the verb was fuzzy, but it sounded way too warm and cuddly for either of the involved parties. Wow, this *was* scoop.

The mayor—and Prizbecki, his deputy—had won the last election by a landslide with the unlikely slogan "New Yorkers need tough love." The mayor had lived up to his campaign promises by cracking down hard on organized crime and white-collar corruption—and Prizbecki had apparently been the muscle behind many of those crackdowns—but recently I'd read that the majority of New Yorkers thought they were taking things too far. I hadn't fully formed an opinion yet about their leadership, but one thing was clear: Stanley Prizbecki looked *mean*.

"Harry, isn't Stan married?" asked Bea.

"Yup, with four little kids."

Ah, okay. Now we were back on familiar ground. Vivian as seductive Other Woman, Vivian as home wrecker...now the world was making sense again.

"I hate men like that—his wife probably helped him build his career, and this is how he repays her," Bea huffed. "And his poor kids!"

I noticed Randall's forehead tense up. Ugh, why'd Bea have to go there? Decades ago, Randall had been one of those poor kids—he'd even caught Vivian in the hallway after the act, a memory she'd recounted with callous amusement. I shuddered. Another reason to despise her.

"Um, Bea, do you need a hand with dinner?" I asked, desperate to get off the subject of Vivian's affairs. "The smells from the kitchen are making my mouth water!"

"Actually, Harry's the cook tonight. His osso bucco."

"Osso bucco?" Randall repeated. "You're quite the Renaissance man, Harry! It smells incredible."

"And actually, it's probably ready. Why don't we head to the dining room?" Harry asked, pointing the way.

"That was a nice weekend," Randall said as we drove through the Midtown Tunnel on our way back from Long Island. "Bea and Harry are terrific, Claire."

"I'm glad you and Harry got along so well!" I beamed. They'd split off to play some indoor tennis that morning. Bea and I, on the other hand, had been far less active: We'd made a pot of coffee, stocked a plate with doughnuts, settled into the couch, and talked for hours. I felt so much better. Blue skies, fresh air, great friends...a reminder of how sweet life could be when one wasn't chained to a desk all the time.

"Oh—sweetie, you don't need to give me door-to-door service!" I suddenly realized that Randall was heading downtown. I'd just assumed he'd drive straight to his garage on 78th Street and I would take a cab home from there.

"I know I don't have to, Claire-bear." He smiled at me, grabbing my hand and kissing it. "I *want* to, though."

"Okay, well...um, you take a left up there." I watched Randall's eyes widen slightly as we drove down my street. He had never seen where I lived before—we always ended up back at his place, because it was so much nicer and his mornings started ridiculously early—and I felt weirdly nervous about what he'd think. When we got to a red light, he reflexively pressed autolock on all four doors—sealing us in.

A moment later, Randall pulled his Porsche in front of my building's dilapidated awning. A group of teenagers immediately began to circle the car as if it'd been dropped in from outer space.

"I can't let you get out of the car with all these hoodlums milling about," he declared protectively.

"Hood— Oh, these kids? They're always around. Totally harmless, I promise." I kissed his cheek and reached into the backseat for my weekend bag.

"Claire-bear, we need to find you a better place to live," Randall said bluntly as he looked around. I followed his stare—and just like that, the street that had felt like home for years was transformed into a total dump. There was garbage on the curb, shady guys hanging out a few doors down. As I looked at it through Randall's eyes, my block seemed completely run-down. "I *really* don't like the thought of you walking home here alone at night."

For a moment, I felt a little defensive—but I was also touched by Randall's genuine concern. "Maybe it is time I moved on," I agreed. Add moving to the to-do list. Of course, the odds of my actually finding time to look for a new apartment? Slimmer than Lucille.

Randall reached over and took my hand, a serious expression on his face. "There's something I've been meaning to talk to you about, Claire. I've been thinking about it for a few weeks, and my mother actually brought it up when we spoke earlier today. I think it makes sense."

"What makes sense, Randall?" I asked, the mention of his mother and her opinions making me instantly ill at ease.

"How would you feel about moving into my place? There's plenty of room, and you wouldn't have to shuttle your stuff back and forth—"

My heart stopped. Move in? Was he serious? He'd been thinking about it for weeks? *That* was Lucille's suggestion?

"I know we've been dating for only six months, but it feels right to me. We'd get to see each other more, and it would save you some money, and…" Randall paused, working up steam. "Well, Claire, I love you. I love you, and I'd like us to live together."

I couldn't believe it. The L-bomb *and* moving in together, both dropped in one curbside conversation? Randall Cox loved me? And wanted to live with me? This was the moment Beatrice and I had dreamed of all those years ago—it was finally coming true! I felt like running down my crummy street, cheering at the top of my lungs, and—

"I'll understand if you need some time to think about it," Randall said somewhat somberly.

Oops! Sometimes I forgot that men couldn't mind-read. "I love you, too, Randall!" I said, flinging my arms around his neck and kissing him. "And of course I'd love to live with you."

Really, what was there to think about? Sure, it had come out of the blue—I certainly hadn't been expecting him to ask—but I was used to commitment-phobic James, who'd resisted my leaving a stick of deodorant hidden under his bathroom sink. Of course I wanted to live with Randall. If Randall was ready to take this enormous step in our relationship, I was ready, too.

"Good! That's good." He nodded happily. "I'll have Deirdre call you tomorrow to work out the details. This will be great, Claire. There's plenty of closet space, and there's a gym on the second floor, and anything you'd like to eat Svetlana can prepare."

He went on with more details, but the only thing I could hear was a happy echo: *He loves me. Randall Cox loves me and wants me to live with him.*

"Okay, hop out before my car gets keyed," Randall finally said, half joking.

I kissed him and opened the car door. "I love you," I said, leaning back in for one more.

"I love you, too. Get inside!" He pointed at a drunk lurching down the street.

"How will I leave all this splendor behind?" I laughed and

slammed the door, then headed up the stairs with my weekend bag. Moving in together. Wow. *Major*. My head was spinning a little.

Part of me will miss this little place, I admitted, plopping down on my old couch with the Sunday paper. Small and crappy as it was, my studio was home, and it had been for five years. But Randall's apartment would feel like home after a while, too, I was sure of it.

I walked two steps to the kitchen area and pulled out some bread to make a sandwich, hitting play on the answering machine as I rummaged through the refrigerator.

"Claire. Vivian," snarled the first message, the machine picking up all the tense, angry notes in her voice. I froze, kicking myself for not getting around to changing the number. The trauma of Friday night's massacre sprang up fresh in my mind. "I don't know where the fuck you are, Claire. I've been trying you all day on your cell, but you seem to have turned it off. Making it difficult for me to reach you, which *you know* I find extremely irksome. Anyway, I had a few things to run down with you, so call me back."

No. No, no, no, no, *no*. I couldn't call Vivian back tonight. It would have to wait until tomorrow. I'd been at her beck and call for months, why couldn't she give me one measly weekend off…and let me enjoy feeling happy and in love for just a *few minutes*—

"Claire!" barked the second message. "Vivian! Call me back! I don't know who you think you are, or why you think you're entitled to just go AWOL like this, but I demand to speak with you!"

I looked down at the machine. The red light blinked the number 18 back at me—eighteen new messages in less than thirty-six hours. I leaned against the counter, rubbing my forehead hard. I knew the messages were from Vivian—at least,

most of them. Should I call her back now? Was it a true catastrophe, or was she just in the mood to verbally disembowel
someone?

Eight p.m. on a Sunday evening. I could take my lumps
now or in the morning. Either way, my night of relaxation had
been tainted. I picked up the phone and called Vivian back.

"Well, it is about fucking time!" she shrieked after answering on the first ring. "I am livid, Claire, l-i-v-i-d!" I heard a
voice in the background. "No! I said not to touch my feet, you
flaming retard! Just massage my legs, why is that so difficult to
understand?! Listen, Claire, we'll have to talk about this in the
morning, now is not a good time. You know, I'm trying to live a
life here. I can't just drop everything because it's a convenient
time for you. Call me when you get to your desk."

Click.

I threw the bread back in the fridge and poured myself a
big gulp of pinot grigio. I tried to cling to the happiness I'd felt
just a minute before — but my Vivian-induced dread put up the
better fight.

CHAPTER TEN

 THE SOUND AND THE FURY

C laire!?"

My head snapped up from my desk, bloodshot eyes squinting angrily in the fluorescent lighting. *Not again.* I'd only meant to give my pounding head a momentary rest, but judging from the drool puddle that had formed on top of the manuscript I was editing, I must have dozed off. No wonder, really, considering how little sleep I'd gotten the night before and the scintillating topic at hand: the memoir of the man with the world's biggest—

"*Claire, are you there?!*" the intercom bleated again, Vivian's voice full of hostile static.

"Here, here," I mumbled back, pressing down on the red button.

"*I need to see you in my office,*" Vivian crackled. "*Now!*"

Her office? My stomach lurched into my throat at the thought. I'd managed to avoid stepping into that pit of venom and destruction for more than a week. It had been a month of pure hell since Vivian screamed at me for the first time, and now I just tried to get through the day without face-to-face confrontation. Vivian could be abusive enough over the inter-com; inside her secluded, palatial, freezing office—buffered by soundproof walls—she *really* hit her stride.

"Be right there," I sputtered into the box, my grogginess burning off in a blaze of panic. I quickly ran my fingers through my shoulder-length hair, last washed three days ago (poor hygiene semi-justified by a crushing workload), and decided that spearing it in a bun with a pencil would be my best option.

Then, looking down, I realized that I'd unthinkingly put on the first shirt my hand had grabbed off the armchair this morning—the same black button-down I'd worn last Friday, a particularly stressful day. The shirt looked like a battered survivor; its armpits exuded a strong alkaline odor.

As I headed for the door, my eyes caught on my huge wall calendar. January, finally—month seven. The halfway mark. Christmas had come and gone with poor Mom sitting on my couch next to me, watching me work...and so had New Year's. Randall's holiday work schedule had been just as bleak, but he'd managed to break away for a quick coffee with me and Mom. It wasn't much time, but at least Mom finally had met him. She thought he seemed like a good guy. I could tell she still had concerns about my moving in, but she was trying to be supportive.

I crossed out Monday on the calendar. A hard-won X. The highlight of each day had become slashing a huge red X through it, watching the days and then weeks slowly add up. Sometimes I felt like a prisoner making scratch marks on the wall of my cell, but usually it made me feel better...because each red X brought me closer to the end of my self-imposed yearlong sentence at Grant Books.

The beginning of the new year had been particularly ghoul-ish. My list of inherited books had grown to thirty-two—we'd had more turnover than usual. Next week was our marketing conference, so I'd been trying feverishly to pull together something, *any*thing, to show for each of the books I had on Grant's list. That meant canceling my date with Randall and staying at the office last night until 3:30 a.m. This weekend, I was officially making the move into his place, thanks to Deirdre and Lucille, who'd stepped in to coordinate the details. Lucille was unusually excited about me living in sin with her son—in fact, she'd gotten in the habit of calling my office several times a day to discuss pressing move-in details (such as whether I preferred satin or silk clothing hangers in my new walk-in closet).

"Where the fuck are you, Claire!" the intercom blazed back to life. *"When I say* NOW, *what do you think that means?"*

My hands shook. My left eye twitched. *Five seconds to pull myself together.* My stomach flipped again. What had I done to ignite Vivian's wrath this morning? As usual, it sounded like my boss was loaded for bear.

I took a deep breath and made my way quickly through the labyrinth to Vivian's office, passing Lulu's corner and stealing a sideways glance in spite of myself. Vivian had recently switched our offices, sticking me in a windowless closet next to the interns and giving Lulu the view.

Behind her meticulously orderly desk (reeked of OCD), Lulu sat delicately sipping a Starbucks coffee and diligently typing away. Her hair was Jennifer Aniston perfect (the long, blond, pin-straight phase), and her sunny yellow sweater set *definitely* looked as if it had been recently laundered.

Damn her.

As a kid, I'd naively assumed that once I grew up I'd never have to deal with the class bully or teacher's pet again—but in the last seven months, I'd been faced with mounting evidence that these types grew worse with age. Vivian was the adult embodiment of a particularly virulent strain of elementary school bully—the kind who'd flush a nerd's head in the toilet while simultaneously stealing his lunch money, giving him a wedgie, and insulting his mom. And Lulu was the thirtysomething version of the class kiss-up, that impossibly perfect girl in the front row who shot her hand in the air to answer every question the teacher asked. Flawless on the outside, hypercompetitive and self-serving on the inside. Not to be trusted.

The fact that Lulu was back to being Vivian's little pet—and I'd been exiled to Château Bow Wow—didn't do much to bolster my warm and fuzzy feelings about her. That's understating it: Lulu was on the short list of people I wouldn't have objected to air-dropping into downtown Mogadishu.

"Phil!" I exclaimed, smacking right into him as I turned the corner to Vivian's office. He looked pretty bedraggled. I hadn't seen him much lately; he'd been as swamped as I'd been with a few big books.

"I'd avoid going in there, unless you absolutely have to," Phil warned. "T. Rex is hungry."

"Unfortunately, I've been summoned." I swallowed the bowling ball–size lump in my throat. Vivian in a notably worse-than-usual mood made me feel like running for shelter, but I had to soldier on. I gave Phil a sympathetic hug. "Sorry, buddy. Try not to take it personally."

"Same to you." He sighed before trudging back down the hall to his office.

I took another deep breath, heaved all my body weight against the vaultlike door of Vivian's office, and stepped inside. The climate was arctic, and I immediately felt my lips turn purple and the hairs on my arms stand at attention. Vivian was on the phone and held up a finger for me to wait. I sat stiffly on a couch.

I thought back to Jackson's cozy office at P and P, which had been filled with overstuffed leather couches, warm lighting, family photos, wraparound bookshelves, antique typewriters. Many a night I'd grab a manuscript and some takeout, sink into a chair, and read for hours while Jackson worked at his desk. Mara often did the same. It'd been like a family library. We'd been like family.

But that was then.

Now I was surrounded by Vivian's sleek black-leather-and-chrome couches, which were about as comfy as park benches. The lighting was icy, the artwork phallic—mainly skyscrapers jutting against the New York City skyline. Bookshelves had been forgone in favor of backlit display cases. The glass case closest to me housed Vivian's first edition of *The Prince,* and the case on the other side of the couch held her first edition of *The Happy Hooker.* You could tell a lot about my boss by the two books she treasured most.

"You don't know what the fuck you're talking about. *Jesus.* You get nominated for one National Book Award and suddenly you think—" Vivian lapsed into uncharacteristic silence, her long fingernails drumming hyperactively against the desk like the precise staccato of a machine-gun round.

She reminded me of an old-school gangster: the bizarre pin-striped suits with wide lapels, the bling of the honking canary diamond on her pinkie, the legions of spineless HR goons trained to turn the other way as she bludgeoned Mather-Hollinger's company policy. The possibility of waking up next to a horse's head had crossed my mind more than once.

If someone crossed her, Vivian was prepared to finish him or her in whatever way she could: Contracts were canceled on her whim, reputations were destroyed, psyches ravaged. Worse, though, was that Vivian opened fire in response to any *perceived* slight, which meant that she'd often level some poor soul who'd done nothing more than hair-trigger her acute paranoia. In Vivian's mind, everyone was out to screw her over, steal from her bottom line, undermine her power and position.

"What did you just say?" she snarled into the phone, motioning for me to keep waiting. "Let's get one thing straight, you worthless piece-of-shit hack. I'm not a bitch, I'm *the* bitch. And if I don't have a publishable manuscript in my hands by Thursday—yes, I mean *this* Thursday—I'm the bitch who's going to see every penny of your advance back. *Capice?* I don't care if your mother has three *hours* left to live—"

She slammed down the phone and then buzzed Tad, her assistant du jour (twenty-four, former male underwear model, who earlier that morning had written "auther" in a company-wide e-mail).

"Cross Hiram Peters off my call list," she barked into the intercom. "Fucking fairy."

Oh no. Poor Hiram. Phil would absolutely freak. He'd worked so hard to keep Hiram on board. Hiram's last epic novel had been nominated for a National Book Award, establishing him as a writer of tremendous repute, and beyond that, Hiram was just about the sweetest man you could hope to know. Phil had mentioned that Hiram was two weeks late in delivering his latest manuscript because his mother was very ill—a transgression that in Vivian's eyes reduced him to a "piece-of-shit hack."

Vivian turned her steely-eyed focus on me, and I felt my blood run cold. "Have you seen the covers for *White House Confidential*?" she inquired in a quiet voice. Too quiet.

My mind flashed to a recent Explorer channel show: A group of capsized swimmers had watched sharks circling them for almost an hour, but it was only when the circling stopped and the fins disappeared, diving deep below the water's surface, that they knew they were really in trouble. Sure enough, the sharks shot up from the ocean depths, jaws wide to seize their treading legs. Only one swimmer had lived to tell the tale. Quiet didn't bode well, for shark or Vivian attacks.

"Um, yes, Vivian, I've seen them. I think Karen did a great job. They've vibrant, they're compelling—" I cleared my throat and racked my brain for more positive adjectives. I'd learned early on in my career that the publishing industry was big on fancy adjectives. A manuscript wasn't good or bad, it was explosive/poignant/unique *or* it was unstructured/trite/derivative. "They're *provocative*," I concluded. Karen was an exceptionally gifted art director, but judging by the sound of muffled sobbing coming from behind her closed office door that morning, I guessed that Vivian had been tough on her recently. I was thrilled with the covers Karen had designed for *White House Confidential*, and so was everyone I'd shown them to.

"Provocative? Is that what you actually think?" Vivian's indoor voice had left the building. Now she was booming. "Frankly, Claire, you wouldn't know provocative if it introduced itself and *then* bit you in the ass. You're still living in your ivory tower. I shouldn't need to *tell* you that they're *fucking awful*. Awful! They are the most uninspired covers I've ever seen in my life. And you, as an *ed-i-tor*, should be *managing* the art director and making sure she's getting the right sense of the fucking book! You are supposed to be in *control* of the process, Claire."

I heard myself gulp. Vivian had an uncanny knack for making even my name sound like a vile insult.

"Why am I the only one here who *fucking gets it*?" she shrieked across the desk, her jade eyes flashing.

Nine times out of ten, Vivian defaulted to one of her favorite three tirades: 1) Why am I the only one here who fucking gets it; 2) I am not your fucking mother; 3) Why do I have to do everyone's fucking job for them? Or, if you were really lucky, some new and exciting combo platter.

"Sorry, Vivian," I mumbled. "I'll stop by Karen's office right now. It's my fault. I should have given her more insight on the book." Of course, Karen and I had already discussed the cover direction several times, and she'd read the entire manuscript. And I genuinely *loved* what she'd done. It was award-winning work. But fighting back would only incense Vivian more, as Phil had advised me when I started.

I just hoped Karen and I could come up with something that would satisfy her. Generally that required weaving a writhing, seminaked body into the cover concept, but this was one of the few books on our current list that wasn't purely about sex—so we would have to be a bit more inventive.

"I can't keep doing everyone's fucking jobs for them," Vivian spat before whipping around to face her computer. I guessed that meant I was dismissed, and I slowly edged out of the office backward, as if Vivian were a wild animal whose predatory instincts might be triggered by sudden movements.

"Are you ill, Claire?" Lulu asked condescendingly when I passed by her at the water cooler. "You look really washed out. Oh, *wait*... could it be the lack of sunlight in your new office?" She batted her eyelashes, feigning real concern for my health.

"I'm fine, Lulu," I said, unclenching my teeth just enough to speak.

The rest of the day went by in a flash of meetings, angry phone calls from agents, and a forest's worth of paperwork. I forgot about lunch and would probably have done the same with dinner if my hands hadn't started shaking a little at my keyboard. So I ate a half-eaten, slightly petrified Snickers bar I'd squirreled away weeks ago in the back of a desk drawer. I asked David to hold all calls but Vivian's and managed to plow through quite a bit of work. Around 10:00, I pulled the plug and left.

Outside, the air was brisk, invigorating. It felt good to feel the sting on my cheeks. Winter would soon enough make way for spring, another season passing me by while I spent fourteen hours a day in the office. I decided to walk down to the subway at Grand Central, just to stretch my legs a bit, and I wrapped my arms around my tote bag, full of manuscripts I'd need to tackle at home.

Randall had flown out that morning for an important pitch meeting in London. It was just as well, really—I wanted to savor my last nights in my studio. It felt like the end of an era.

I let out a deep breath, and it hung in the chilly air.

Suddenly I remembered something—I'd completely forgotten to call Luke Mayville back. He'd called that morning, but the entire day had flown by and I'd never gotten back to him. I fished for my cell phone, even though it was really too late to call. Luke picked up on the second ring.

"Hey, it's Claire. Sorry to call at this hour, I just didn't have a second free during the day, and I wanted to let you know that I'll be getting my edits back to you by the end of next week. Sorry it's taken me so long...it's been a little hectic lately."

"I'll fully accept both unnecessary apologies if you'll come meet me for a drink," Luke said. I could hear people in the background. "I'm on Perry Street, pretty close to where you live. Want to meet me at the Otheroom?"

"I'd love that," I answered, realizing it was exactly why I'd called. I needed a friend. And a drink.

CHAPTER ELEVEN

 BLEAK HOUSE

First thought on waking up this morning: *Thank God it was just a dream.* I flopped over to spank the snooze button on my alarm clock. It had gone off just as Vivian was flying at me, vampire fangs exposed, shrieking over my inability to edit a manuscript written entirely in Sanskrit.

Second thought: *I'm going to puke.*

Leapt to the bathroom in a single bound. *An often overlooked convenience of living in a shoebox,* I realized, holding my hair back with one hand.

This was *so* not good. I was still wearing my dirty button-down and skirt from yesterday. The shirt that I'd deemed smelly and gross the previous afternoon was now so repugnant that I stripped it off, balled it up, and threw it in the trash can. Uggggh. I'd never felt more disgusting in my entire life.

The night before was nothing but patchy static. Finding Luke at the Otheroom...the tremendous joy of my first sip of Jack and Coke...talking about his book...another round of drinks...venting about work, Vivian, Lulu...another round...confessing my mixed feelings over leaving my apartment to move in with Randall...another round...troubles with his vegan girlfriend (who apparently caught him eying a suede coat)...another round...and then Luke walking me home, his arm around my shoulder because I was shivering from the cold...kissing my cheek outside my building...

I cringed. Uh-oh. That was without question the part of the memory that had me feeling uneasy. I had tugged on Luke's sleeve, tried to convince him to come upstairs for one more drink. I hadn't wanted our conversation to end. Had he come up? *Had anything else happened after that kiss on the cheek?* I racked my brain for more details...but no, I remembered walking up the stairs by myself, a goofy grin on my face. Nothing more had happened, I was completely sure of it.

So why did I feel weirdly, vaguely...*guilty?*

Maybe I was just mistaking a raging hangover for guilt.

I showered and dressed my aching body for work. Today was clearly a cab-to-work day. Dealing with subway crowds was not an option.

"Morning, Claire," David said as I shuffled past his cubicle half an hour later. "Vivian's looking for you; she's been calling since eight-thirty or so. She seems to be..." He trailed off.

"In a black mood?" I filled in dryly. "You mean she didn't give you her usual greeting of 'What's-your-face, have that worthless, birdbrained twit call me back'?"

Gallows humor was all we had at Grant Books.

It was then that I noticed the shadow over David's humorless face. He was clearing his throat so vigorously, it sounded like a car engine revving. Oh no. *Please don't let her be...,* I prayed as I rotated around to face Vivian, a frothing pit bull ready for battle. *Behind me.*

"I'd lost hope for a return phone call before lunch," Vivian spat at me, rising on her toes to bridge some of the gap between our faces. I could tell it drove her crazy that at five feet one, she was more than half a foot shorter than me and had to crane her neck when we were speaking face-to-face. My stilettos had become a major act of defiance, and I wore them every single day—no matter how badly they pinched my feet, no matter how brutally hungover I was.

I glanced at the clock behind David's desk—9:03 a.m.—and then I cowered, ready for the full-body blows to start coming.

"We need to talk," Vivian snapped. "I've got four crash books that I need you to deal with. A three-week production schedule for each one, and the authors have three weeks from this *second* to deliver the full manuscript. Can you handle it?"

I'd have preferred the body blow. I might have even chosen a few bamboo shoots under the nails.

Four crash books, each on the same insane schedule, not a one written yet, meant that I'd be spending *at least* twenty-four hours a day at the office for a solid six-week stretch, and I'd still potentially not make the various deadlines. Unfortunately, it was a plank I'd been forced to walk before; in November, I'd once resorted to bringing in a sleeping bag to catch occasional doses of sleep. Phil had been known to do the same, and Graham stayed at the office almost as many nights as he did at home. No matter what Randall said, investment bankers had nothing on us—except an extra zero on the end of their salaries.

Four crash books, all at once. Man. I knew from past experience that this would be a sleepless *and* a thankless job, because no doubt something would go wrong with one of the books, at *least* one, so on top of all else, I'd have to endure Vivian's unmitigated rage.

What she was asking, really, was if I could handle full-scale martyrdom.

"That's, um, a lot," I mumbled. "I could try...but do they really all have to be on the same schedule? That's going to be tough, Vivian." God, I was lame. Where was my backbone? Why couldn't I stand up for myself? "I'll try, though—David, please ask Tad to get us the terms of each deal and we'll get started on the contracts this—"

Vivian snorted. "Deals? In case nobody filled you in, it's the job of the *ed-i-tor* to negotiate deals. You think I have time to go over the details? To hassle with semiretarded agents? I'll give you the offers I'm ready to extend for each book, and it's up to you to make it happen."

"Of course," I answered. I should've known that. In other words, I'd have to convince each agent to accept Vivian's offer to the letter (agents who'd all had dealings with Vivian in the past and felt understandably wary about waving their clients off to the wolves), explain the concept to the author, convince him/her that he/she could in fact write a full four-hundred-page manuscript in, oh, ten days, and if he/she couldn't, go through the entire process again to find a ghostwriter (those who'd actually agree to such an unreasonable turnaround time were generally hacks), and finally seal that deal to everyone's (read: Vivian's) satisfaction. Times four.

And then the *really* fun part—getting the inevitably quarter-baked manuscript at the end of the two weeks, rewriting entire chapters, harassing the poor, exhausted author/writer for more work, and turning the whole steaming pile of dung in to production in...two more weeks. *Times four.*

"But you know, Vivian, that's a lot," I repeated, bewildered. "Maybe another editor could take one of those off my plate. I just don't want to promise more than I can deliver, and frankly, that's more work than any one person can get through."

There, I'd said it.

Instead of the expected explosion, Vivian looked pleased. Smugly triumphant.

"You're right, Claire, you're probably *not* equipped," she

agreed. "Phil's got a full plate, but I'm sure Lulu would be more than happy to take on two of these books. She's already working on two crashes of her own—but you know Lulu, always happy to pull her weight and then some. Wish I could clone her!"

Grrrr. Saintly Lulu. I knew I was being manipulated, but I still loathed the thought of Lulu's pedestal being raised higher. Could my status in the Grant hierarchy fall even lower if I didn't step up? Would Vivian next expect me to move my office into a large cabinet and work by flashlight? I shook my head, temporarily unable to force words out of the emotions swirling and seething inside of me.

"Forget it," I said after a moment, hating myself for giving in. "I can handle all four, Vivian. Let me know what terms you'd like me to extend, and we'll go from there."

"Fine, then, come by my office," she said brusquely before stalking away.

I turned to David. "Would you please check with Tad to see when Vivian's free this morning?"

"I'll check with the temp," said David. Then, lowering his voice to a whisper, "Tad flew the coop yesterday afternoon. Apparently she konked him over the head with a lamp. He wasn't badly hurt, though, so that's good."

I nodded. He'd lasted two and a half weeks, which was more than average. No offense to Tad, but I suspected he was too slow to pick up on Vivian's more subtle psychological warfare—that probably bought him the extra week.

"Brace yourself for a very challenging few weeks." I tried to smile, but my facial muscles refused to cooperate.

"We'll get through it, Claire," David said reassuringly.

I ducked quickly into my office so he wouldn't see the tears of frustration stinging my eyes. *Be professional*, I scolded myself, wiping them away angrily. I'd vowed never to cry at work, even though I'd seen dozens of my colleagues do just that. The ladies' room on the twelfth floor regularly echoed with the sound of weeping, and Phil told me that the men's room was just as bleak.

I called Beatrice, needing a second to decompress before throwing myself headlong into the day. "I think my boss is trying to kill me," I whispered to my best friend. "Did anyone ever die from being overworked?"

"Of course. And it's a terrible way to go," Bea said. She paused, and I could imagine her biting her pinkie, trying to find the right words. "Claire, I know you're hung up on making it for a full year over there. But isn't it time you thought about looking for a new job?"

The thought had obviously crossed my mind—but it was hard to explain, this intensely stubborn streak that Vivian had awakened in me. Quitting before a year had simply ceased to be an option. I couldn't give her the satisfaction. I couldn't cry mercy. And I couldn't abandon Luke without an editor in the dark vortex of Grant Books. I'd brought him into this place, and now it was my responsibility to make sure he got out safe and sound.

"I don't even have the energy or time to think about a job search right now," I told Bea. "I've got the move this weekend, and then our trip to Iowa next week, and now four crash books on top of everything else…and I think I'm still a little drunk from last night."

"Last night?"

"Yeah, I ended up meeting Luke for drinks and talking the poor guy's ear off. Anyway, Bea, I've got to get back to—"

"Will you promise me you'll take better care of yourself, Claire? I'm worried about you."

"I'll try."

"Good. Call me tonight, will you? I'm running for a yoga

class that starts at ten. Oh, and are you coming over to watch *The Bachelor in Kiev* tonight?"

"Not unless it's on at three in the morning."

"Ugh! What a bummer, Claire. It's the final five! And Harry thinks that the Dallas cheerleader has something up her sleeve."

Her words brought great sadness to my heart, as I had absolutely no clue who the Dallas cheerleader was.

I hung up the phone and turned toward my computer, in whose icy sapphire glow I'd be basking for weeks. Bea got rose ceremonies and yoga, I got computer radiation and bending to satisfy my boss's every whim. Unfortunately, green was less flattering on me than blue.

My coffee mug was nearly empty. I headed to the kitchen for a refill.

"It's brilliant!" I heard Vivian exclaim from the conference room as I walked by. "I just knew Lucky's would be the perfect spot to throw tomorrow's book party. The strippers will serve the drinks when they're not performing onstage! Our sales reps will be offered complimentary lap dances—that'll spice things up! Edible underwear for door prizes! *Fabulous!*"

"Oh, my God," brayed Lulu. "You are an absolute genius, Vivian! How do you do it? And this party is genius! Genius! It's just too good!"

The girl sucked up more than a Hoover vacuum.

"I know, Lulu. This is why I'm head and shoulders above every other publisher in this business," Vivian boasted. "They're all, like...the undead. Zombies with lifeless ideas. No fresh perspective, not a drop of sex appeal in the whole sorry batch. Withered-up old snobs...."

I realized I was lingering in the hallway and continued on to the kitchen. My head hurt. Tomorrow night was the launch party for *Blow Job: An Illustrated History of Oral Sex*. I'd assumed that publishing the book put us safely at rock bottom of the canyon of poor taste—but now it was clear that there were still greater depths to plumb. Like throwing the book launch party at Lucky's, the city's most infamous strip club.

I dumped sugar in my coffee and returned to my desk. I had a mountain of paperwork that threatened to avalanche at any second and a call list that was close to a hundred names long. David had made concise little notations next to each name, and at about the fifty-name mark, I could read between his lines that several disgruntled repeat callers were getting mutinous. I'd have to start with them.

"Claire?" Phil stuck his head into my office. His arms were full with his office lamp, a large cardboard box, a framed print, a houseplant.

Shit, I thought, the word echoing around in my hollow, aching cranium.

"She's had my head on the block for the past year, Claire." Phil shrugged. "Not to mention other anatomy. Today she finally swung."

I couldn't believe it. Vivian had fired Phil, a senior editor? He was one of the best in the business, and certainly the very best at our imprint. How could I get through the week without him? Who would be my ally in skirmishes with Lulu? And much more important, Phil would be without a paycheck to support his growing family.... I felt as if I were going to be sick again. His wife, Linda, had just given birth to their second son three months earlier, and I knew Phil was already a bit stressed about making ends meet. He had an impressive résumé, but the job market was so tight.

The intercom buzzed. Her Vileness. *"Claire, I'd like to see you in my office. Immediately."*

Phil smiled wanly. "Hang in there, kid," he said, giving me a hug. "I'll be fine. I've got friends at other houses, and I'm sure something will open up quickly. Just don't let her get to you."

"*Claire! I said my office, NOW!*" shrieked my intercom. I involuntarily jumped out of my chair; her voice was like a blast of electroshock. Phil just shook his head and continued off down the hall.

Enraged, I stalked over to Vivian's office and, not bothering to knock, charged in to find Lulu—predictably perfect in a pale gray suit and pearls—already seated across the desk from our boss.

"You fired Phil?" I fumed. "How could you, Vivian—he's the best editor we have! That makes no sense!"

You could've heard a pin drop. It dawned on me, during the seconds of complete silence, that I had never questioned Vivian so boldly. I could see the shock flicker on her face, but she recovered quickly.

"Past his prime," she spat back at me. "Dead weight. I kept him on board as long as I could. Now, there's the question of who will take over his books. Where the fuck is Dawn?"

"I'm right here." Dawn pushed open the office door, carrying a stack of files almost as tall as she was. "Okay. I've got a list of Phil's books, along with his files, and I'm thinking it makes sense to basically divide them between the two of you." She shot me an apologetic glance.

"Oh, no *prob*lem," Lulu answered in a saccharine voice. "I'm excited to take on his projects, breathe new life into them!"

"Well, good," said Dawn, dropping the files heavily onto a side table and dealing them out with the emotionless efficiency of a blackjack dealer at the Bellagio.

Was I the only one here who felt completely rattled by the

fact that a senior editor—one with Phil's incredible record and commitment—could be fired out of the blue? Dawn and Phil had worked together for four years—four *Grant Books* years, which was like twenty years somewhere else—yet she didn't seem remotely fazed by the fact that Vivian had heartlessly chucked him.

Come to think of it, I'd never seen Dawn get the least bit ruffled, and she was usually in Vivian's direct line of fire. Part of me admired her stalwart professionalism. Part of me found it frightening.

"That should do it," she said briskly after we'd finished divvying up Phil's books.

"May I stay and talk to you about a few other matters?" Lulu asked Vivian as we packed up the files to leave, and Vivian nodded. Dawn and I walked back to our offices in silence.

"Is there anything you can't take in stride, Dawn?" I asked when we'd reached my office door. "To be honest, you don't seem the least bit upset that Phil got fired for no good reason."

Dawn paused. Then her eyes began to dart around the hallway as if she were a hunted animal. After a moment, she seemed satisfied that we were the only two people within earshot. "If you show her that you're upset, " she whispered so quietly that I could barely hear her, "she's won." Then she padded off down the hall.

I closed the door to my office behind me, feeling a sudden chill. I sort of wished I hadn't asked. Thinking of Dawn as some kind of a professional robot was easier than seeing her as a real human being trapped in a long-term dysfunctional relationship with her abusive boss.

No sooner had I shut the door to my office than something in me broke. I buried my face in my hands and let myself cry.

CHAPTER TWELVE

 THE BELL JAR

Bellini?" a blonde in a G-string and quill-shaped pasties asked me. Vivian had special-ordered them for all the girls.

"Um, no thanks. I'm good." I wouldn't be staying long enough to finish a bellini.

A heavy bass pulsed from the speakers, providing the beat for a topless brunette on the stage to gyrate around a pole. I scanned the room. Poor David sat huddled with a few acutely uncomfortable assistants, none of them sure where to cast their eyes.

Vivian had truly outdone herself. The whole floor had heard her battling with Sonny Wentworth, the company CEO, over whether Lucky's, a well-known Manhattan strip club, would be an appropriate venue for a book party. She'd won. But then, didn't she always?

"Claire," said Lulu, sidling up next to me. Dressed in a tight black leather minidress and a matching newsboy cap, she looked like an emaciated Britney Spears. "Isn't this party too genius?"

Lulu never made chitchat. I knew she was trying to bait me.

"It's *something*," I muttered. If by genius Lulu meant crass, fiercely inappropriate, and probably grounds for several lawsuits, then yes, this party was *genius*. If by genius she meant insanely ill-advised—throwing a party at which a crowd of top sales reps and media heavyweights were handed sex toys as parting gifts—then yes, this party was *genius*.

"Did you see my tat?" asked Lulu. She held out her scrawny little bicep, which was covered by a temporary tattoo that read *I ♡ The Boss*. "I picked it up on a Springsteen fansite. I've got to go show Viv." With that, she bounded off.

Why had I never noticed how cuckoo bananas this girl was? During the months that she had refused to speak to me, I'd just thought she was a bitch. Now it had come into sharper focus: Lulu was insane, Vivian was insane, and the inmates were running the asylum.

"Hi there, Claire," Sonny said quietly. He must have just walked in behind me, and he held his coat over his arm as if ready to make for the door again at any second.

I liked Sonny. I'd met him at a new-employee breakfast during my first month at the company, and despite being on opposite ends of the Mather-Hollinger food chain, we'd forged a natural connection right away. He was so down-to-earth and accessible, you'd never guess that he held the most powerful position at a major publishing conglomerate. Sonny was a small man, no taller than five feet five, with close-cropped hair and horn-rimmed glasses. His demeanor was quiet, understated.

"You look as mortified by all of this as I am," he mumbled.

I didn't know quite how to respond. If Sonny realized how ridiculous and wrong this party was, why had he condoned it? He was Vivian's boss—if anyone could keep her in check, it'd be he.

"I just can't believe it," I said. In one darkened corner, our author was leading a small group in a workshop on giving the perfect blow job. Mary from Accounts Payable was taking notes on a yellow legal pad. One of our sales reps was being coerced into getting a lap dance. It was extra-mortifying to witness the scene while standing next to the company's CEO.

Sonny shook his head sadly. "You're telling me," he said. I felt a pang of sympathy for him. Yes, he was a coward—but he knew it, which was the worst punishment.

And we were all cowards right along with him. I didn't want to lose my job, and Sonny didn't want to offend the company's biggest cash cow. After all, Grant Books accounted for nearly a third of Mather-Hollinger's bottom line. Given that it was one of twelve imprints, that contribution was significant—Vivian, financially speaking, pulled four times her weight. As a result, the company ignored all the other ways in which she was a severe liability—settling lawsuits with disgruntled ex-employees, taking her side in every dispute, throwing book parties at the least suitable venues the city had to offer.

"Sonny, baby!" Vivian called loudly, shimmying across the room toward us. "Is this party the sexiest thing you've ever seen, or what? We're shaking up publishing, baby! We're *doing* it!" She looked positively triumphant. Her strawberry blond hair had been yanked into a high ponytail, giving her face a look of perpetual surprise. And she'd forgone her usual power suit in favor of a tight red lace bodice, a feather boa, fishnets, and black patent-leather thigh-high boots. All in all, a disturbing ensemble to see on one's middle-aged boss.

"What exactly *are* we doing?" he muttered. I looked at Vivian. Her brash grin disappeared.

"What do you *mean*?" she sneered, lip curling. "This party is fabulous! A huge success! Where's Betsy? She'd love it!" Betsy, Sonny's wife, was a buttoned-up, ultra-conservative woman who largely kept to herself—or Sonny's side—at book parties. I honestly couldn't imagine anyone less in her element at a strip club.

"Actually, she's expecting me home for dinner," Sonny said. Then he bade us both a quick good-bye and shuffled off in the direction of the door.

"So pussy-whipped," Vivian laughed bitterly, *"My wifie's expecting me home for dinner!* Jesus. What kind of man leaves a strip club because his wife's making meat loaf? Not the kind of man who should be running this company, I'll tell you that much. I've got the biggest balls of anyone at Mather-Hollinger." She blinked at me, as if she'd forgotten that I was standing next to her. Then, hoisting up her boobs for added cleavage, she stormed back into the fray.

"Would you like a dance?" an Asian woman with double-D breasts asked me with finishing school politeness.

"No, I'm on my way out," I said, and headed for the coat check.

Then I saw him: Stanley Prizbecki, wearing a black leather jacket and several gold chains. He and Vivian eyed each other seductively across the room as a Barbie-doll blonde writhed all over him.

Suddenly I knew that if I didn't get some fresh air immediately, I'd be sick in the lobby's fountain of pink champagne. I grabbed my shearling coat (a Christmas gift from Randall) from the girl behind the counter and ran to the door, barely making it to the curb before losing my lunch. For the second time that week.

"I told you to take Lexington!" Vivian barked at the driver, leaning into the front seat of the Lincoln Town Car to get right up in his face. He veered quickly to follow her instruction, the sharp turn slamming Vivian and me to one side of the car.

"Motherfucker! Are you trying to kill me?" she screamed.

I saw him raise his eyebrow in the rearview mirror. The idea had probably crossed his mind.

It was 8:00 a.m. on Friday of the longest week ever. Vivian and I were heading uptown for a meeting with a hot young nutrition expert, Rachel Barnes, who'd gotten press recently for transforming many already thin women on Manhattan's Upper East Side into the fat-free twigs they longed to be. Her secret? A life-consuming, U.S. Navy SEAL–inspired exercise program, coupled with a five-hundred-calorie-a-day diet that she swore was healthy. For the low, low price of $10,000 a month, Barnes's clients learned that eating nothing and working out like an Olympic athlete would reward them with a skeletally thin look—so in this season.

"Three best sellers this month alone. Can't argue with that kind of success!" Vivian brayed into her cell phone as the driver, who'd been instructed to get us there as fast as humanly possible, wove through traffic at a death-defying speed. I stared straight ahead, trying to keep my bearings. It was all I could do to avoid getting sick yet again. Lately I couldn't trust my own stomach.

Vivian looked up sharply from her phone call. "What are you doing, Claire?"

"I'm not feeling all that well. I just need to—"

"Ew, you're sick? Stay away from me, I do *not* have time to be sick right now."

"I'm not sick, I just—"

"Well, sick or not sick, don't just sit there staring out the window. I'm not paying you to fucking enjoy the scenery! I want three new ideas from you before we reach Eightieth Street. You're on my time." She returned her focus to the phone. "I swear, I don't know what my staff does all day! If I don't crack the whip constantly, they'd all sit around mooning and twiddling their thumbs. It's an absolute *chore*. Okay, babe, I'll call you next week. Can you do lunch at the Ivy on Wednesday?...Fabulous. *Ciao.*"

So Vivian would be back in L.A. again next week—great news. I got so much more done when I didn't have to respond to her bells and whistles every ten minutes. She finished her call and tucked her phone into her Fendi bag.

"Actually, Vivian, I do have a few submissions that I'd like to talk to you about," I said, consulting my notepad and trying to suppress my growing nausea. "The first is a historical novel set in 1920s Chicago...." Vivian held both hands together and laid her cheek on them, indicating that the setting alone put her to sleep. "Okay, then, I have a great submission in about a chronic pain management program developed by two doctors at Harvard Medical School—"

"My God, Claire, I need chronic pain management to listen to your lame-ass ideas," Vivian groaned. "You're so...so *academic*. Such a snooze. Like the rest of the deadbeats in our business. You've got to come out of your ivory tower and think about books in a more commercial way, or you're never going to find best sellers. Smut sells. Whether you like it or not, that's what people want to read these days. So get it through your head. There's no room for myopic snobs on my ship."

A *myopic snob?* A *deadbeat?* Sometimes Vivian's abuse came so rapid-fire, it took a moment for it to sink in.

"Now take Lulu's latest acquisition—a sexy, super-provocative guide to getting away with adultery. Now *there's* a book seven out of ten married people will want to read. Lulu gets it. She just gets it. And I can't teach those instincts, Claire." We slowed down for a red light, and she yanked on the back of the driver's collar, jerking his head back. "I *told* you we shouldn't have taken Lexington! Learn to do your fucking job. It's not rocket science!"

I sank back in my seat. The driver turned the corner to head back over to Park Avenue.

"Now, Claire, when we meet with Rachel, I expect you to let me do all the talking," Vivian declared. "I'd like her to use me as the test subject for her book. You know, show how effective her program is by walking me through it for the next ten months. I think readers will appreciate seeing a model going through it."

Ah, of course. I should've guessed. Much like the design book in which the author renovated Vivian's house—for free—or the book on "do-it-yourself hair care" written by a famous stylist who now came to the office once a month to do Vivian's hair, Rachel's book deal would no doubt come attached to some big perks for Vivian. My boss was always embarking on one diet or another, looking for a magical eating plan that would somehow right her chemical imbalance *and* slim her hips. Maybe publishing Rachel's book would allow Vivian to sidestep that hefty retainer.

A few months ago, Phil told me Vivian had once paid an exorbitant half-million-dollar advance to a chef who, weeks after signing his contract, happened to move into her apartment and cook for her the remainder of the year. Had she paid him a salary on top of his book deal? Nobody who knew Vivian would guess that she'd doled out an extra penny.

"I'll let you do all the talking," I agreed.

My phone vibrated in my bag—Randall's office number. I hated having personal conversations in Vivian's vicinity, but I picked up anyway, eager to hear his voice. Tomorrow I was moving into Randall's apartment, but between his trip to London and my hectic week, I'd barely exchanged a word with him in days.

"Hey," I whispered, shifting as far away from Vivian as I could for privacy.

"Claire? It's Deirdre, dear. Calling to let you know that Randall had to extend his trip, so he won't be back until Tuesday. He told me to tell you he was very sorry and would call later. But it won't affect the move, Claire, I've worked out all the details for tomorrow. The movers will be at your apartment at ten a.m. on the dot. And don't worry about packing, they're going to take care of that for you."

My stomach sank. My first weekend living with Randall...and he wouldn't be there? What a drag. I thought about asking Deirdre if we could postpone the move, but she'd already put so much effort into it.

"Tomorrow at ten. Great. Thanks, Deirdre."

"Oh, and dear? Randall's mother has offered to spend the weekend with you, helping you get organized. So you don't feel lonely, I suppose."

I thanked Deirdre, my stomach lurching yet again. The car pulled up outside Rachel's office. I slid out after Vivian.

"Working out those weekend plans?" she asked, voice dripping with sarcasm. "Gee, Claire, I'm so glad you're not letting work get in the way of your social life!" She scoffed in disgust as we walked up the stairs.

I remembered something Phil had told me the first time we'd gone out for drinks after work. "Working for Vivian," he'd said, "tends to make people one of two things: homicidal or suicidal."

I'd laughed at the time. Now I realized he hadn't been kidding. I felt a little of both.

CHAPTER THIRTEEN

 THE TURN OF THE SCREW

*S*ally *Jones was just your average suburban housewife. That is, until the day she swapped her Windex, casserole dish, and PTA meetings for handcuffs, sex toys, and orgies....*

I couldn't continue. I'd reached my desk early this morning with high hopes of pulling together a few catalog pages that had been back-burnered for days, but it was too depressing. Instead I stared at my calendar. Just a few days until my weekend in Iowa. Almost there. And Randall would finally be home tonight, thank goodness. I'd spent my first three nights in his apartment with his mother and Svetlana—not exactly how I'd hoped to inaugurate this new chapter of our relationship.

You've got new mail.

I clicked open my Outlook, powerless to resist distraction, and found a message from Mara asking how the move had gone.

I really missed Mara. She'd recently acquired two fantastic cookbooks—one by a Beard Award finalist, another by a Napa Valley favorite—and she'd been hard at work, coordinating with the photographers, authors, and recipe testers to make sure every detail was perfect. She'd also, to my great relief, taken on Chef Mario's book after he'd been dumped so abruptly by Grant Books. I'd seen her only a few times since starting at Grant, but we e-mailed regularly—a poor substitute for our daily conversations, but it was better than nothing.

I had just started to write back when a second e-mail from Mara popped up on the screen.

> To: Claire Truman
> (ctruman@grantbooks.com)
>
> From: Mara Mendelson
> (mmendelson@petersandpomfret.com)
>
> Subject: uh-oh
>
> READ TODAY'S LLOYD GROVE. Then run for cover....I am scared for you.

I quickly pulled out the *Daily News* that I'd stashed in my bag on my way to work and flipped to Grove's column. In the past few weeks, the columnist had had an ax to grind when it came to my boss. Apparently, he'd been seated next to Vivian at a recent PEN literary gala—close enough to be in earshot, which was usually enough to fuel the horrified fascination. Last week, he'd written about Vivian's "unorthodox" publishing approach and about the routine exodus from the imprint—which, needless to say, made her mood more vicious than usual. Today, he'd gotten down and dirty about one of the books Lulu was working on:

YOU CAN'T ALWAYS GET WHAT YOU...
DON'T WANT?

Horace Whitney, the renowned left-wing political pundit and former Clinton adviser, says he's "never seen such dirty, underhanded, self-serving, morally corrupt behavior in [his] life—and I've worked in Washington for 30 years."

The object of Whitney's rage? None other than Vivian Grant, his hotheaded publisher, who, according to an e-mail from power-agent Tami Simons, "commissioned him to write a book in two months, which he succeeded in doing. Then we didn't hear back from [editor] Lulu Price for three months—not a word. Finally, after countless unreturned calls, I receive a 20-page letter with editorial changes from Vivian. At the end of it, she declares the manuscript 'unpublishable' and in no uncertain terms states that she is canceling the contract and refusing to pay the advance."

Whitney and Simons were outraged. Of course, it's hardly the first time Grant has backed out of a contract upon delivery of a full manuscript. The plot thickens in this case, though, as it took Simons less than 2 hours to find several interested publishers eager to take ownership of the project. And Grant, having apparently changed her mind about the manuscript she allegedly described in her e-mail to Simons as "a pile of horse s--t," is now suing Sampson and Evans for the right to publish.

Next to the column, the *Daily News* reprinted an old publicity still of Vivian—pouting, dolled up with heavy makeup, her hair in big, glamour-girl curls.

I groaned and took a gulp of my coffee for strength.

"Claire?" David buzzed over the intercom. "It's Candace, line one. Do you want to call her back?"

"I'll take it, thanks," I answered, picking up the line. "Hey, Candace. What's up? Have you made a decision about our offer?" Yesterday, I'd given Candace—the former supermodel penning a salacious memoir of all the Mr. Wrongs she'd known—our final offer on her third book, and I desperately hoped we could finally move forward with the contract. Unfortunately, "I deserve more" seemed to be Candace's three favorite words—not bad ones to have on hand, I suppose, when dealing with a perpetual user-and-abuser like Vivian, but more than a little frustrating for the editor caught in the middle.

Candace and Vivian had an unusually charged love-hate relationship, stemming from the fact that they had on occasion splashed in the same dating pool and were each magnetic, beautiful, and certifiable. Apparently, they were currently in a hate cycle.

"Tell that motherfucking see-you-next-Tuesday you work for that there is no way—no *fucking* way—I am accepting such a measly advance for my third book," shouted Candace through a scratchy cell phone reception. I held the phone away from my ear. They also spoke the same language, I'd forgotten that. "Does she think I don't know how much money she made off the first two? A hundred and seventy-five thousand dollars is a fucking joke. Does she think she's the only publisher in town? Just because I'm *loyal*—God, I've put up with more than my fair share of shit from that power-drunk bitch—doesn't mean I'm *stupid*. I'm not going to just sit here and take it. Tell her I need at least double that, plus I'm going to need a budget for hair, makeup, wardrobe…Oh, and we'll all be flying first class. Those are my terms, babe, make 'em happen." Then she hung up on me.

Yeah, I'm going to have to rephrase that, I thought. I forced my thoughts back to the catalog. I'd deal with the Candace headache later.

But before I could write another word, my office door was slammed open, and Alice—a sweet-natured temp who'd been filling in as Vivian's assistant for a week now—stepped inside, shutting it quickly behind her. Her pretty face was flushed and contorted with panic. Sweat beads had formed above her upper lip.

"You've got to help me, Claire," she choked out. "She's going to murder me. Vivian's leaving her apartment to fly to L.A. in twenty minutes. She just called and asked me to bring her two files from her office. I asked her where they might be, and she took my head off for it. But I can't find them *anywhere*...." Alice looked down at her watch, which only made her more panicked. "Please, Claire, can you help me? She called me a fucking imbecile and said she would write such a scathing report about me that the temp agency would never send me out again...."

Alice wiped her eyes with the back of her hand, and I held her shoulder to steady her. Why did Vivian have to be so cruel? Couldn't she just tell poor Alice where to look, the way any normal person would?

"Of course I'll give you a hand," I said. "Please don't let her upset you. She's like that with everyone. We'll get her the files in time, don't worry." Phil had given me similar pep talks countless times. He was usually able to calm me down—but I knew from firsthand experience how hard it was to "not take things personally" when someone was berating you so harshly.

"Please don't tell anyone about this," Alice whispered when we were in Vivian's office. "Vivian's really funny about the privacy of her files. She'd kill me if she knew I'd asked you to help."

"I won't say a word. Now what does she need?"

"The folder that has all the marketing team's notes from the most recent sales conference. And the one about the Prime Publishing Program."

I rummaged through the manila folders on Vivian's desk and found one labeled "Fall Sales." "Okay, here's the marketing one," I said, handing it to Alice, who looked so grateful that you'd think I'd just pulled her from a burning building. The Prime Publishing Program wasn't on the desk, so I moved over to the wall of file cabinets and pulled on drawer N–P. Locked.

"Hang on, I'll get the key!" Alice dashed off and returned a nanosecond later with the key.

I unlocked the drawer and yanked it open. It was stuffed to capacity. "Personnel"…"Presentations"…"Printers, Overseas and Domestic"…there we were, "Prime Publishing." It was an initiative designed to market and sell books directly to consumers, building the company's brand recognition to a degree that a reader would actually check the spine of the book when deciding what to pick up at the bookstore. An interesting, if grandiose, concept, and one that Vivian had helped to marshal at Mather-Hollinger.

I wiggled the folder out of the drawer, dislodging everything around it. Alice grabbed it like a sprinter taking a baton in a relay and was out the door with an over-the-shoulder, *"Bless you, Claire, please lock up!"*

As I shoved things back into the drawer, the folder behind the one I'd pulled caught my attention. It was labeled "Prizbecki." Did Vivian keep a file on her married boyfriend?

It's wrong to snoop, Claire, I scolded myself. *Put the file back.* But my curiosity got the better of me. I quickly pulled out the thin manila folder and took a peek. There was only one document in the file—an e-mail, sent to Vivian's work address.

```
To: Vivian Grant
(vgrant@grantbooks.com)

From: Stanley Prizbecki
(Stanley Prizbecki@nymayor.gov)

Hi, tasty cakes. Haven't been able to
stop thinking about you since Thursday.
Told A. that there was some public
transportation conference in Baltimore
this weekend, so I'm all yours. Meet
you downtown, 11 pm, Friday. I'll swipe
a pair of cuffs. S.
```

Yuuuuuuck. Served me right for being nosy.

I returned the document to the file, and then I saw it—a small Polaroid clipped to the bottom of the folder. My jaw hit the floor. The picture was of Stanley—wearing a pink lace teddy, high-heeled bedroom slippers, and screaming red lipstick. Lipstick and a stubbly face, never a winning combo—nor was Stanley's hairy chest poking through the feminine lace of his negligee.

An involuntary shudder passed through my entire body. I threw the folder back into the cabinet and locked the drawer.

That was wrong on so many levels, I thought as I slipped out of Vivian's office undetected. I shouldn't have looked—but really, seeing Stanley in that getup seemed like ample punishment for the crime.

The phone was ringing as I walked into my office. No rest for the weary. I picked up.

"Hi, beautiful," Randall purred when I picked up. My heart leapt. Only a few more hours till I got to see him...our very first night together in our shared home.

"Hi, sweetie. What a nice surprise—you don't usually call in the middle of the day."

"Well, unfortunately I'm calling with some bad news, babe. I wanted to let you know right away. You know how much I was looking forward to going to Iowa with you this weekend, but my biggest client just made a bid to acquire their largest competitor—it's all unfolding very quickly, and I'm leading the team. There's no way I can be away during such an important live deal. I really need to be in New York this weekend, working out all the details."

"You mean, you can't come?" I repeated. I was honestly stunned. Randall's job often required him to change or cancel plans at the drop of a hat, but I'd still somehow expected that our Iowa trip would be held as an exception. We'd had our tickets for two months. He knew how much the weekend meant to me.

"I know, babe, I'm really disappointed," he answered. "But work is work. I promise I'll make it up to you."

Work is work. Work is work. I rolled the words over in my head, tapping them for meaning. *Work is work.* What the hell did that mean? I bit my lip. Tears sprang painfully to my bloodshot, tired eyes. The adult in me appreciated how important Randall's career was to him. He was fiercely dedicated to making a name for himself outside the shadow cast by his powerful family. Still, I couldn't help feeling *crushed*.

"It's okay," I managed to squeeze out, my throat tight.

"I'm so sorry, Claire-bear. I feel horribly about it. At least let me fly another friend out there with you. Mara—whomever you like. Call Deirdre and she'll arrange everything, okay? Sorry, babe. I've got to run into a meeting, but call Deirdre. Please. And I'll see you tonight. I can't wait for that."

After I hung up the phone, I felt an actual, physical ache in the area of my heart.

Work, Claire, I instructed myself. You don't have time right now to sit at your desk feeling sorry for yourself. I turned back to the catalog page, but it felt more hopeless than ever.

David buzzed my intercom. "Now Luke's here. What a day. Do you have a minute?"

"Of course, David. Would you bring him up from the lobby?"

Without thinking, I rummaged in my drawer for some lip gloss—then I pulled my hair out of its ponytail and did a quick flip. Midflip, a strange but intriguing thought popped into my head: *What if I asked Luke to come to Iowa with me?*

Was that crazy? Luke and I had become fast friends during the process of working on his book. He stopped by the office pretty regularly—sometimes to talk about specific challenges he was facing in the revision process, and sometimes just to say hi. I always looked forward to seeing him. I knew Luke would love Dad's party, and Randall had told me to invite anyone I liked. But would it seem wildly inappropriate to invite another guy home with me for the weekend?

"How come you switched offices?" Luke asked, sticking his head into my tiny windowless closet.

"Oh, well, I got tired of the view. And sunlight."

He smiled and gave me a kiss hello. For no reason, I blushed.

"Have you had a chance to look through my edits?" I asked. I'd finally gotten them back to him the week before, taking a few extra days to be sure I'd covered everything.

"I'm only halfway through them, but so far they've been a huge improvement. Thanks, Claire. But I'm just stopping by to say hello. Haven't really spoken to you since last week at the Otheroom."

Oh yeah. The night I got hammered and talked your ear off for hours? My memory of that night had never lost its fuzziness, but I remembered yammering on about my job, my family, my dreams, my love life. It was probably better that I couldn't recall the details.

"So, how's cohabitation?" Luke continued. "You moved in with your boyfriend, right?"

"Yup, just last weekend. And it's, um, terrific." Domestic bliss with his intrusive mother and the smoldering Svetlana.

And then, suddenly, I decided to throw caution to the wind. Luke was my friend. And why *shouldn't* I invite my friend Luke to a weekend I knew he'd enjoy? Randall might feel a little uncomfortable about my bringing another man home for the weekend—but maybe he should've thought of that before he ditched me for work at the last minute. Maybe next time he'd rethink his priorities.

Not that I was using Luke to make a point with Randall. Of course not.

"Listen, Luke, please feel free to say no to this," I began, "I know it's last minute...maybe you already have plans, or maybe it doesn't sound like fun...or maybe you've got work to do, or something...anyway, seriously no pressure—"

Luke made a buzzing sound. "You've just exceeded the limit of disclaimers that can be placed before a single statement. What's up?"

"Okay, sorry. Well, I was just wondering"—why was my heart racing? why did I feel as though I were asking a boy to the prom?—"if you'd like to go to Iowa with me this weekend, for my dad's party—I mean, we have this party every year to celebrate my dad, and a bunch of people from the community show up and read their favorite poems and—really, I'll completely understand if you can't, I just thought it might be...fun."

"Are you serious, Claire? I'd love to come. Of course!" Luke grinned at me, and I could tell that his enthusiasm was genuine. "And it's actually good timing. My girlfriend's heading upstate for a 'save the silkworm' rally."

"Great! Oh, and don't worry about the ticket, I've got a...um, voucher," I said. "I'm so happy you can make it. You know, we can even get some work done! Why don't you bring the manuscript and we can go over the edits on the plane — "

"Or we can just relax and enjoy the weekend. Get you away from work."

"Even better." I smiled.

"Hi, Claire-bear," said Randall, cracking open the door to our now shared bedroom. *Yum.* Even though I still wasn't over his last-minute bailout, I had to admit that Randall looked deliciously handsome, as usual, his suit slightly rumpled after a long day at the office. I sat up in bed, resting the manuscript I'd been reading on the nightstand. From behind his back, Randall pulled out a Cartier bag.

"I'm really sorry about this weekend." He perched next to me and gently pushed my hair off my forehead. "I know I let you down, sweetie. But it's just one of those situations — I can't not be at the office while this deal is going down. Sometimes I hate the sacrifices I have to make for my job, Claire, but they do come with the territory."

I could tell his regret was genuine, and I couldn't stay angry. "I understand," I said, rubbing his back. "There'll be plenty of chances for you to visit Iowa and spend time with Mom. And as far as the party goes, there's always next year."

Next year. I watched his face for any visible signs of discomfort. Randall and I never talked about our future, really, and even my passing reference to next year felt like going out on a limb. But we were living together now — the future shouldn't be a taboo subject.

"Next year for sure." Randall smiled, completely relaxed. "Here, sweetie, a little something to say that I'm sorry." He handed me the Cartier bag. I opened the box inside to find a delicate, beautiful gold link bracelet. I loved it — but more than anything, I was touched that Randall had taken the time and made the effort.

I wrapped my arms around him. "Randall, thank you," I whispered in his ear. "It's beautiful. You didn't need to buy me a present, though."

"Let me help you put it on," he said, fumbling with the latch. I could feel the heat from his fingers on my wrist. I kissed his neck. "I thought you'd like it," he continued, finally getting the clasp fastened.

"I love it, Randall. And I love *you*. I'm so excited that we're finally spending our first night together!"

"I know. You've been so patient, Claire." He kissed me. "Hey, Deirdre mentioned that you'd called to arrange for a friend's ticket to Iowa. Who'd you decide to bring?" he asked.

"Um, actually, I invited one of my authors," I said quickly. "Luke Mayville, Jackson's nephew." Uh-oh. Would Randall be upset? I suddenly wished I'd given it more thought before—

"Yeah? That's nice, babe. I'm glad."

Huh? No reaction at all? I should've been relieved that Randall didn't feel threatened by my bringing Luke—but part of me, I'll admit, felt a little disappointed by his indifference.

"I'm going to get out of these duds and take a shower. I'll be quick, I promise." Flashing me a devilish grin, Randall loosened his tie, then headed for the bathroom.

Maybe he was just really secure. And why shouldn't he be? We were living together—we were a seriously committed couple living together. Why would he care if I shared my weekend with a friend? Randall trusted me. And he was right to—I was crazy about him.

Resting my head on the downy pillow, I tried to stay awake for Randall's return—but the sound of running water, the incredible softness of Randall's Pratesi sheets, and the exhaustion of the day were almost too much for me.

I'll light some candles, I thought, forcing myself to sit up in bed, *set the mood for when he comes back.* I opened the drawer of the nightstand to look for matches—no luck. Maybe he kept them in the top drawer of his desk. Stamps, a letter opener, some stationery…and a photo of Randall with a beautiful blonde at the beach. Great. The second photo of the day I immediately regretted seeing. And no matches.

Abandoning my mission and not wanting to inadvertently snoop more than I already had, I slipped back into bed. The shower was still running. Sometime later, I shifted in my sleep to find Randall next to me, freshly showered and in pajamas, reading through his papers. I looked at the clock—it was after 2:00. Didn't he ever sleep? The man was bionic.

"Hey, sweetie," I whispered, sliding up next to him in the bed. He smelled soapy and clean. I inhaled deeply. "I'm sorry I nodded off."

"It's okay, Claire-bear." He kissed the top of my head, turning a page. "You need your rest."

"Good night," I said, kissing his chest. Snuggled against him, I felt a kind of safety and comfort that I couldn't remember feeling since childhood.

"Night, Coral," he whispered back in a distracted voice, scribbling something in a margin of the document.

I sat up like a shot. "Did you just call me Coral?"

"Of course not! I said Claire. Night, *Claire.*"

Then why had I heard Coral? Was he telling the truth? I *had* been dozing in and out of sleep. Claire…Coral. I could see how the two might sound the same. And even if he had said his ex-girlfriend's name, what did that mean? An innocent slip, two names with almost the same letters.

I curled up next to him again. Randall trusted me, and I needed to trust him.

Still, I couldn't get back to sleep.

CHAPTER FOURTEEN

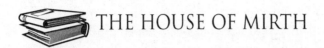 THE HOUSE OF MIRTH

My mother, of course, was waiting to pick us up—despite the fact that the airport was forty minutes from our house. The concept of taking a cab home was as foreign and "New York" to her as having dinner delivered from the restaurant on your corner.

"Mom!" I screamed through the crowded airport. Her face lit up when she saw us. Beatrice and I sprinted for her, nearly tackling her in a hug. The guys, loaded down with all the luggage, ambled up behind us.

"Honey—" Mom glanced meaningfully at Bea. "You weren't kidding, Beatrice, she's a toothpick. She was thin at New Year's, but—"

"Um, *she's* right here," I reminded them, pulling Mom into another bear hug mainly so she'd stop staring at me from every angle. "I'm so happy to see you, Mom. I've been looking forward to this weekend since you left." It was true—but at the same time, it still made me a little sad to come home and not have Dad next to Mom. It had been five years, but I never got used to it.

"Me too, sweetie. Harry!" Mom gave him a big hug. "You look great."

"So do you, Trish! And like you've been hard at work." Harry pointed to the splotches of paint on Mom's jeans.

"I woke up this morning feeling very inspired." Mom smiled. "And you must be Luke! I'm so delighted to meet you. Claire sent me your manuscript a few weeks ago, and I absolutely devoured it. You have incredible talent."

"Well, thank you," Luke said, clearly moved by the compliment. "I think it's starting to come together, thanks to all of Claire's hard work."

Mom beamed. "Claire had two great teachers in the art of editing: her father and your uncle. So I'd say you're in good hands."

"Okay, Mom." I laughed, taking my bag from Luke and leading the pack out to the parking area. When it came to me and my father, my mother found it impossible to be modest.

"You know, I've been a fan of your late husband's work for many years," Luke told Mom. "That's why—among other reasons—I was so excited when Claire invited me to join her this weekend."

Among other reasons. Bea looked at me with a curious expression.

"Thank you, Luke. It's wonderful to know just how many people Charles touched through his work," Mom said, linking her arm with his. "And please, call me Trish."

"Took her three years to throw the Trish card my way," Harry joked. "Way to get in there with the poetry."

By the time we'd all piled into Mom's beat-up Subaru to head home, it felt like Luke had been part of the group forever.

"Sorry, guys, the heater's a little temperamental," Mom apologized, glancing back at Bea, Harry, and Luke huddled together in the backseat. "There are some blankets in the back if you're freezing."

Bea immediately lunged for them, passing one to each of us. I'd forgotten just how cold Iowa could get in the winter. For a split second, I was the tiniest bit relieved that Randall hadn't made the trip. How would he have dealt with Mom's old jalopy—about as far as one could get from his Porsche—and its lack of heating? Somehow I couldn't picture Randall wrapping himself in one of Mom's handmade quilts.

"Mom, don't you think it might be time to trade Nellie in?" We'd had Nellie—the car—since my childhood. She'd more than served her time.

"Dump old Nellie? Never! You know I'd never do that."

Why'd I even bother? Mom had ridiculous loyalty to inanimate objects. Old sweaters were never too old to darn, chipped plates had "character." I could never decide if it was her *Mayflower* roots or a frugality that she'd developed over years of making money stretch. (I chose to believe that she didn't really think our Subaru had feelings.)

"Who needs heat?" asked Harry, pulling the blanket tighter around himself.

"So, it looks like the crowd this year will be even bigger than we thought!" Mom told us excitedly. "It's up to two hundred and fifty, and you know people bring friends along at the last minute . . . the tent is all ready to go. And Harriet and Suz have been in the kitchen since Wednesday, cooking up a storm."

Together for thirty years, Harriet and Suzanne had been my parents' best friends for about twenty-five. Harriet was a chef at the local inn, Suzanne was a farmer/organic soap maker, and they always handled all the catering for the party—which seemed to get more elaborate by the year.

By the time we pulled up to our house, Mom had brought us up to speed on all the preparations. Everything seemed to be under control, but she had a few chores for us before guests arrived in several hours. "Do you mind being put to work a little?" she asked Luke, who convincingly assured her that it would be his pleasure to help.

An hour later, Luke wiped his brow and braced himself to lift a heavy coffee table out of our living room. He and Harry had already moved a couch, two big chairs, and an ottoman—I would've helped, but Mom had me testing out the sound system. The sound system! I couldn't believe how much bigger Dad's party had grown since its inception—or how much effort Mom had put into it this year. Bea was busy tying ribbons onto some programs listing names of local sponsors, and Harriet and Suzanne were giving detailed instructions to the wait staff. Finally, with about forty minutes to spare, we had finished everything on Mom's list.

"Would you mind if I jumped in the shower?" Luke asked. Sweat soaked through his shirt. "I'm pretty ripe." He grinned, peeling his damp shirt away from his chest.

"Of course! I can't believe how rude we are, Luke, forcing you into manual labor within minutes of arriving. Some hosts—"

"Don't apologize, Claire. I'm happy to pitch in. All hands on deck." Luke leaned in close and kissed my cheek lightly. I froze. He had a musky, hardworking smell. Bea looked at us from across the room, her thoughts transparent in her expression.

Kiss on the cheek. Friendly gesture.

"Um, it's this way," I said, leading Luke down the hallway. I opened the bathroom closet and pulled out some fresh towels.

Luke stayed a few steps behind, running a finger along some books on the shelf. My parents had lined almost every wall in our house with shelves—their one luxury had been an extraordinary collection of books. Mom often said that being surrounded by all the books they'd read over the years made her feel as though Dad were still with her in the house. It was why she'd never move.

"Hey, did your dad write this?" Luke asked, pulling a book from the shelf.

I looked at what he held in his hands: Dad's first book of poetry. How strange that Luke happened to pull it out. A cream-colored, tiny little book, it had been published by an equally small, now defunct press when Dad was still in graduate school. Although my father went on to publish a dozen more collections of his poems, his first always remained my favorite.

"I've read every line at least a thousand times," I told Luke, feeling a familiar lump in my throat. "I've memorized the entire thing. Which is fortunate, because I somehow lost the one copy I had when I was moving out of my senior dorm at Princeton. Mom offered to give me hers as a replacement, but I felt guilty taking it after I'd been so careless. And the publisher only printed a very limited run, so I haven't been able to track another book down."

"I'm sure you'll get your hands on another copy someday," Luke said encouragingly.

"Hope so." It made me sad just to think about it. I handed Luke the towels, and he smiled, closing the bathroom door.

"Are people eating the butternut squash soup with cider cream?" Harriet fretted. "I told you it was a mistake to serve soup on a buffet, Suzanne—nobody can carry all those plates and bowls!"

"Well, sorry," clucked Suz, looking anything but. "I guess we're even, since I told *you* we'd need to prepare double the amount of asparagus-and-prosciutto crostini with fonduta!"

"Huh? What's that?" I asked, grabbing something yummy off the table and popping it in my mouth. I'd been stuffing my face since we landed—my stomach was actually relaxed enough to enjoy food again.

"What you just ate," answered Suzanne, brushing a piece of hair behind my ear. "So how you doing, kid? Your mom says you've been chained to your desk lately. But your boyfriend's real cute!"

"Luke?" I glanced over at Luke, who was chatting away with Mom at the table next to ours. "He isn't my boyfriend, Suz, he's one of my authors. Well, a friend. My boyfriend had to work, so he couldn't make it. But he sent *all* of those flowers. Isn't that sweet?" I pointed to an entire wall of white roses that Randall had sent to the house earlier that day.

"Yeah, well, I'd stick with this one," Harriet piped up. "He's handsome, funny, sweet—and look how great he's being with your mom. I haven't heard her laugh like that since..." She trailed off, circling her hand in the air.

"Luke's great, I agree. But Randall's great, too."

"I'm sure he is, Claire." Suzanne nodded. "Don't listen to Harriet. Ooh! There's your mother, taking the stage. Ssssh, everybody."

Mom tapped gently on the microphone that had been set up at the front of the tent. "Thanks for coming, everyone! I'm delighted to announce that the proceeds from this year's event will sponsor not one, but *two* students at the Writers' Workshop next year. Thanks for your incredible generosity!" Everyone in the tent burst into applause. "And now I'd like to introduce my daughter, Claire Truman, who will start us off by reading Coleridge's 'Kubla Khan.' "

I'd read the same poem five years in a row. It was one of Dad's favorites, one of a handful he used to recite when he'd tuck me in at night. I could still hear his voice when I read it; still feel him sitting next to me on the side of my twin bed.

It's good to be home, I thought, taking the stage and looking into a crowd filled with people I loved. I could feel Luke smiling, even without looking his way.

"I wish we didn't have to leave so soon," Bea lamented.

"I wish I didn't have three hundred pages to edit when we get back," I added glumly.

Harry and Luke had gone for a bundled-up nature walk, while Bea, Mom, and I stayed in our bathrobes and chatted in our newly mint green kitchen. I felt happier and more relaxed than I had in months—except for my acute case of Sunday blues.

We'd already rehashed the party and what a huge success it had been—the crowd hadn't thinned until 2:00 in the morning (the Iowa equivalent of a New York City all-nighter), and then the five of us had stayed up for a few hours after that, finishing off a few bottles of wine in front of the fireplace.

"Remind me, how many more months are you working for the dragon lady?" Bea asked.

"Five. And one week." It sounded short but seemed like an eternity. Mile twenty.

"You know, I'm not sure I like this Vivian person," Mom said slowly. Bea and I both looked up from our coffee mugs. My mother, like Jackson, lived firmly by the principle that "if you didn't have anything nice to say, you shouldn't say anything." Not sure she liked Vivian were Mom's fighting words.

"I'm *sure* I don't like her," I answered, suddenly overwhelmed by the misery of having to return to work the next day. I'd waited weeks for this trip to Iowa—and though it'd been a wonderful twenty-four hours, it had gone by in a flash. Now it was back to reality, back to New York, back to Grant Books. "I wish I could just call in sick on my entire life and stay here for a week. Maybe a year. Get under the covers and hide." I forced a laugh, but it actually sounded good.

"You know you've always got covers here, honey." Mom smiled. I could see that she had more to say but held her tongue. She cut me another slice of homemade apple pie—today's breakfast special.

"By the way," Bea whispered, leaning in toward us, "could he be any more in love with you?"

"He who? What are you talking about, Bea?"

"Captain Stubing from *The Love Boat*, Claire. Luke! Why didn't you ever mention how cute he is? You should have seen his face last night when you were reading onstage. He was, like, hanging on every word."

"It's a great poem, Bea"—I felt the blush rise to my cheeks—"and we're friends. We have a great, um, working relationship."

"Well, I think he's just wonderful," Mom declared, "and so handsome!"

"Well, Mom, Randall is wonderful, too. And probably the *most* handsome man I've ever seen. And he's—"

"He seems great, dear," Mom said gently. "I look forward to getting to know him better."

"I can't tell you how bummed Randall was when this work thing came up—did I show you what he got me, to show how sorry he was for missing this weekend?" I held out my wrist with the gold bracelet and immediately cringed. Even I could see how lame I was being—but the pro-Lukeness of my mother and best friend made me oddly defensive. I'd never expected them to see Luke as a romantic prospect—not when I had

Randall, my perfect live-in boyfriend, back at home. I was way, *way* off the market.

"That's so pretty!" Beatrice said brightly. "Very sweet of him."

Mom nodded. "It's lovely, Claire."

"I really think Randall could be, you know...the one!" I blurted out.

"Really? Well, in that case, I *really* can't wait to spend more time with him!" Mom exclaimed. "That's wonderful, Claire, that you feel that way. He must be a very special person."

"Wow," said Bea, smiling incredulously. "You know, sometimes it's still hard for me to believe that Randall our college crush is now Randall your real-life, actual boyfriend. It's just so...I don't know, so perfect!"

"I think so, too." I smiled.

Mom glanced at the clock on the wall and frowned. "We should get you girls packed—we don't have much time until we have to leave, I'm afraid."

No. I didn't want to leave. I was just remembering what it felt like to be able to breathe, relax, eat a meal, laugh with friends.

"Mom, won't you come to New York one of these weekends?" I asked. "Randall's mom won't stop hounding me about when you'll be coming for a visit."

"I'm afraid you're not the only one she's been hounding. Lucille has been calling the house four, five times a day, poor thing," Mom said. "She must be awfully lonely. I wish she had something to occupy her time. I know she serves on various charity boards, but I don't think her involvement is very challenging."

"I really can't imagine Lucille working," I mused.

"Well, she used to be a real go-getter. Of course, that was years ago."

My phone rang, and I tensed immediately. But it was Randall's office number—not my boss. "Hey, sweetie," I cooed.

"Hi, Claire-bear! Listen, I just wanted to let you know that Freddy will be there to pick you guys up from the airport. And I've asked Svetlana to make dinner for us tonight. I can get a few hours off work. I thought we could stay in, have a cozy night at home. Sound good?"

Better than good—it sounded like exactly the right remedy for my blues. "You've got a date. And Randall, the roses are so beautiful. How did you—"

"Oh, good. Deirdre was on the phone with every florist in the state of Iowa."

Harry and Luke came bounding through the kitchen door, their cheeks ruddy from the cold. "Whew! Freezing! Coffee!" Harry panted, pulling up a chair to the table. Mom immediately pulled two oversize mugs out of the cabinet and poured steaming coffee in each one.

"Perfect, thanks," said Luke, wrapping his hands around his mug and breathing in the warmth.

"Babe? You there?" asked Randall.

"Yup," I answered, suddenly self-conscious. "Okay, so...I'll see you in a few hours."

"Great. I'll see you then. I love you, Claire-bear."

I paused. "Um, you too. Bye." I hung up.

"It's so beautiful out here!" Luke exclaimed. "You just can't get this kind of nature in Central Park. This is such a better quality of life."

"Don't say that!" I snapped. "We all have to convince my mom to come to New York *more*, not less!" Bea and Mom stared at me. "And besides, we've got the Met, the opera, the best restaurants in the world—I'd say that's a pretty good quality of life."

"Of course," agreed Luke, looking surprised. "It just feels great to breathe in some fresh air."

I nodded, suddenly embarrassed by my outburst. Why was

I jumping down Luke's throat? He was just saying how much he enjoyed our home.

"I'll get to New York soon," said Mom, stroking my hair. "You know how much I love to visit you."

I wondered how Mom would feel about staying at Randall's place. Mom didn't have a judgmental bone in her body, but still I wondered if she'd be comfortable staying in his guest room with us right down the hall. And somehow I couldn't quite imagine having our traditional *Anne of Green Gables*–and–Cherry Garcia marathons in Randall's pristine media room.

"Okay, troops. It pains me to say this, but we've got to get you guys moving for the airport," Mom announced. "Here's some food for the trip home, sweetie." She handed me a huge bag filled with homemade banana bread, still warm from the oven, fresh fruit, parma-ham-and-cheese sandwiches, and juice. We'd just finished breakfast, but my mouth watered looking at the feast she'd packed.

"Thanks, Mom," I said, hugging her with all my strength, wishing I never had to let go.

CHAPTER FIFTEEN

 HEART OF DARKNESS

Carl. It's Vivian, doll. Claire Truman's on the conference call, too. She'll take notes so you can sit back and listen, babe."

"Sounds good, Viv," Carl Howard answered in his raspy, chain-smoker's voice.

Alone in my windowless office, I propped up my aching head with one hand. Was it actually possible that less than twenty-four hours ago I was sitting around the old farm table in our kitchen, sipping coffee, smelling Mom's homemade banana bread baking in the oven, listening to a distant *This American Life* on our old radio? It felt as though I'd been back in hell for a week—but it was only noon on Monday.

I pulled out a piece of Mom's banana bread from my bag and took a small bite, hoping it might bring back some of the pleasure of being home. But it didn't taste the same in the toxic air of my office. I threw it out.

"Claire, you there?" Vivian asked.

"I'm here, Vivian. Hi, Carl."

Carl was a Miami-based writer who wrote nearly half of our

books. A ghostwriter extraordinaire, Carl had a remarkable talent for getting each author's voice exactly right and telling the story in a way the author would never be able to. He could also work very quickly, which with Grant's down-and-dirty publication schedules made him our most valuable player.

I'd never met Carl, but he'd once miraculously bailed me out with an immediate rewrite on a crash book. Every editor at Grant had a few reasons to be in his debt.

Unfortunately, if you were female and remotely attractive, Carl never let you forget that debt. Rumor had it that he and Vivian had been shtupping for years, whenever the mood struck her—which made Carl's forward advances all the more awkward for her underlings.

Today, the objective of our conference call was to get Carl immediately on board to ghostwrite Morgan Rice's autobiography. And it was quite a story. Rice—the drug-addled rocker and poster girl for bad behavior—had been famously married to an iconic drug-addled rocker who'd died of an overdose at their son's fourth birthday party. She'd never publicly talked or written about her husband's death, but now she was ready to lay it all down (for a seven-figure advance). Needless to say, her book was sure to generate major buzz.

Rice had finally met with us a week ago. Her agent had set up meetings eight times before, but each time a last-minute cancellation—and a ridiculous excuse—had come our way instead. When Rice did finally make it in, her appearance was startling: hair a starchy peroxide mess, flaming red lipstick smeared haphazardly in the general area of her mouth, yellowed teeth and nails, bleary eyes, and of course, her signature track marks. Morgan Rice looked downright tragic.

And now I was her editor. We were putting together a diary of Rice's life, an appropriately chaotic collection of paraphernalia she'd collected over the years, interspersed with a running narrative. And we were doing it in four weeks. Vivian wanted to get the book out before the anniversary of Rice's husband's death—which made complete sense from a commercial standpoint but would potentially send poor Dawn to her grave. A four-color book, not a word of which was written—to be published in record time.

Dawn, of course, would figure out some superhuman way to make it happen. She always did. And then next time, Vivian would try to shave off more time in the schedule. Dawn's competence seemed to add to her burden...but then again, saying no to Vivian wasn't an option, either.

Anyway, we desperately needed Carl to put together the book. Without him on board, we had little chance of making the deadline—even Vivian recognized that. That was why she was on the call.

"So I need you to meet with Morgan, get her story out of her, pull together some art from her—apparently she's got boxes of it—and get the manuscript done in under three weeks," Vivian explained nonchalantly, as if she were asking for some cream with her coffee.

Carl whistled through his teeth. "That's a tall order, babe, even for me. Didn't she just check into rehab? Is she even coherent these days?"

"She's clear as a bell! We met with her last week. She's a doll! Anyway, I know you can handle it. The work you did on *The Crash*? Bailing us out after four other writers had failed miserably? That was absolutely amazing, Carl. You made an illiterate, half-witted moron sound insightful and intelligent. You're a phenomenal talent, Carl, and I know you can handle this. The way you use language is second to none."

Boy.

"Talk slowly, babe," Carl nearly moaned into the phone, "you're giving me a boner the size of Texas."

Oh, dear God. No, no, no. The walls were closing in. *Please don't let this conversation go the way . . .*

"Baby, you're the best in the business," Vivian purred.

"The best *what* in the business?" Carl probed. "Tell me I'm the best lay, and I'll get the manuscript to you in two and a half weeks."

"You know it, babe. Forget in the business—you're the best lay I've ever had." She made a growling noise.

Was this conversation actually happening? Had I somehow been dragged into a gross, telephonic ménage à trois with my boss and an aging lothario? It was like a horrible, horrible dream.

I cleared my throat. "Um, Carl, would you like me to over-night the contracts directly to you or to your agent?"

"What a wet blanket," Vivian snickered.

"Send 'em to me, sweetheart," Carl answered in a low voice that made my skin crawl, "and you heard what Vivian said. I'm the best in the business. You might want to keep that in mind and free up some time when I'm next in New York."

I was going to be sick.

"Actually, Claire's totally your type," Vivian answered, fill-ing in my repulsed silence. "Legs up to her neck, the whole sexy librarian thing with the glasses and the bun. You should take her out when you're in town."

My voice was caught in my throat. My boss was pimping me out? To her own on-again, off-again lover?

"Leggy, huh? Yeah, I'd love that," answered Carl. "Maybe the three of us can have a date, huh?"

"I've got to take another call," I blurted out before Vivian could answer. "I'll send you the notes and the contract, Carl."

I could hear Vivian's throaty laugh as I dropped the phone into the receiver.

I raised my fists to my temples and pressed hard, harder—

before dropping them lifelessly on the desk. What the hell was I doing? I could quit right now and be out in the free world by this afternoon.

But then my eyes landed on Luke's manuscript, resting on the corner of my desk.

Five more months until it was safely at the printer. Five more pages on the calendar. My loyalty to him was the only thing keeping me at Grant Books. If I quit now, someone else would take over—and who knew what changes Vivian might make in retribution for my leaving. I needed to remain in the ring, for Luke's sake, should there be any punches pulled before publication.

My intercom blared to life with the dreaded four digits. Not again. I'd developed a Pavlovian response to seeing Vivian's extension: My stomach clenched, and my heart began to pound like the bass from a convertible in South Central.

"*Claire?!*" she barked.

"I'm here, Vivian," I said, pressing back on the button.

"*Lulu tells me that YOU think we should pass on the teenage pimp manuscript.*"

"Yes, that's right," I said slowly. "I can't imagine paying a dime for it." It was the story of a sixteen-year-old who managed to convince a few of the girls in his high school class—some as young as thirteen—to sell their bodies for money, and it was absolutely horrible. If the book had been intended to warn parents or teens about how such an extreme situation could develop, that would have been one thing. Clearly, though, the author had no remorse for what he'd done, and his purpose was to titillate, not educate. It was smut, without any sliver of redeeming quality.

"*How fascinating. Tell me this, Claire: Are you retarded, or just very, very dumb?*" I could hear a muffled giggle in the background. Lulu's.

"Neither," I said simply, willing myself not to rise to her bait. "I just think it's pure trash."

"Well, one woman's trash is another woman's best seller. Lulu has decided that she'd like to take the project on. She and I both see enormous commercial potential, maybe a TV spin-off. That's the kind of editorial insight I'm looking for."

I knew exactly why this conversation was taking place over the intercom: Vivian wanted to maximize the number of people who could overhear it. I was surprised that she'd never thought to install a scaffold in the office to puritanically shame her employees. HR would probably let it slide—since Grant Books currently held the number one, two, and three spots on *The New York Times* Best Sellers list.

"I understand, Vivian," I said, but the intercom had gone dead.

I looked at the tiny clock in the corner of my computer screen. Not even 1:00 p.m. The hours of peace I'd felt at home in Iowa were now a distant memory.

Turning to my e-mail, I found that forty-two messages had come through in the past hour. I ordered a pizza from the deli downstairs and settled in for a long afternoon.

Before I looked up, it was nearly midnight. Without the bells and whistles of the workday every five seconds, I'd been able to catch up on the day of labor I'd missed over the weekend. I'd still have to take home a manuscript with me to edit into the wee hours, but that was fine. What else did I have to do besides sleep? Randall was still finalizing his deal, and he'd be stuck at the office all night. Curling up with my laptop on the couch was at least more civilized than sticking around at the office all night.

I threw out my empty pizza box from lunch and turned off

my computer. Then my eye caught a flash of strawberry blond hair in the hallway.

The figure stopped—and I realized it was Vivian. My body tensed. *Oh no.* I couldn't imagine anything I needed less at the moment than a Vivian attack.

"Still here, Claire?" she asked, hovering in my doorway.

"Uh-huh. Just wrapping up some odds and ends. You're here late, too," I said, hoping the conversation could end quickly.

"Yeah, well, Simon is with inseminator two tonight," she said in a bored voice. "So I wasn't in a big rush to head home to an empty penthouse." I was surprised to hear Vivian allude to feeling lonely—or to any degree of human emotion, for that matter. I looked at her. She looked especially small in her power suit, now wrinkled after a long day.

How does a human being turn into Vivian Grant? I wondered. Surely she couldn't have always been a fierce, nasty, angry tyrant. She did have two sons, after all. Sons whose anatomical endowment she liked to brag about to anyone she could force to listen—but sons nonetheless. For a moment, I saw Vivian as lonely, twisted, deeply unhappy. She almost seemed pitiable.

I thought of how I'd snapped at Mom the day before when she'd been trying to help me pack my bag. How short I'd been with Luke and Bea after they'd made the effort to come home with me. How impatient I'd been this morning when the coffee took a few minutes to perk. How completely out of touch I was with Mara. I hadn't been to the gym in months, and most of my meals cost three quarters in the vending machine. I'd spent a total of three waking hours with my boyfriend since we'd been living together.

"I've got to get back to work," Vivian said, waving a tired hand in my direction before heading off down the hall. "Somebody has to get things done around here."

I caught my reflection in my computer screen: slumped in my swivel chair, hair in a messy bun, illuminated by the blue computer screen.

And then I saw something else in the glass: All of Manhattan—bright, alive, vibrating with energy and excitement—lay outside my office window.

Five months, I promised myself, *just five more months, and then I'm getting back to life.*

CHAPTER SIXTEEN

 A TALE OF TWO CITIES

I 'll be down in one minute," I panted, not bothering to say good-bye to Randall before hurling my cell phone into my purse. I burrowed through my weekend bag...sunblock and bikinis, check. Hideously fluorescent Lily Pulitzer dress (a gift from Lucille), check. Tennis racket and whites, check. A pair of shorts, a few clean tees...okay. I was ready. Oh—except for reading material. I grabbed Luke's manuscript and headed for the door. Lately it was the only thing I could focus on.

When Randall had called earlier that afternoon to see if I could get away for the weekend, I'd been absolutely elated. Some real time together—and not just the tail end of a draining day—was exactly what we needed. Lately we'd both been so preoccupied with our jobs, we'd fallen into a pretty lackluster routine of talking for a few minutes before passing out on our pillows. So I was thrilled when he'd suggested an impromptu weekend getaway—even if it meant skipping out on some work, it'd be well worth it for some romantic one-on-one time.

Then he'd told me he wanted to visit his parents in Palm Beach.

"Hey, babe." Randall pecked me on the cheek as I climbed in beside him. "Ready for a little sun? This weather is horrible." Rain pelted the windows of his town car. The night was dreary and sludgy, ending a day that had been gray and wet.

"You bet," I said. The thought of spending more time with Lucille had significantly dampened my enthusiasm for the weekend. I'd gotten to spend a decent amount of time with her on her occasional visits to the city, but our relationship still felt strained. For starters, there was her constant monitoring of every morsel I put into my mouth—despite the fact that, thanks to daily stress, I was thinner than I'd ever been in my life. I couldn't understand why anyone would pay forty bucks for the mini-burgers at Swifty's, take off the buns, and barely take a nibble.

And then there was the shopping. I always thought I *liked* shopping. In fact, when we first moved to New York, Bea and I would hit Bloomingdale's every time a paycheck hit our bank accounts. But with Lucille, shopping felt like work—a job she took very, very seriously. Her big mission, on these jaunts to New York, was to troll Madison Avenue for clothes she "desperately needed"—suits from Chanel, gowns from Valentino, cashmere from Loro Piana, and more Manolos than the two of us could possibly carry. Lucille had charge accounts with every major designer. One Saturday afternoon back in December, she'd spent nearly the amount of money I made in a year. "Holiday parties," she'd explained breezily.

Most stressful, however, were Lucille's not-so-subtle references to my future with her son. Marriage was clearly something she had her heart set on—which should've been flattering but just felt like a ton of pressure. "Which one do you like best, darling?" she'd once asked me with wide-eyed innocence as we stood in front of a Harry Winston window full of diamond rings.

"Oh, they're all beautiful," I'd deferred, feeling very uncomfortable.

"Well, I guess it doesn't matter, seeing how Randall inherited his grandmother's four-carat diamond ring...very beautiful, and not another one like it in the world."

"Uh-huh," I'd answered, unsure of what else to say. Randall and I had never discussed the long-term future, so I certainly wasn't ready to discuss it with his mother.

"My parents have a full weekend planned for us," Randall said, patting my knee. "Lunch at the Bath and Tennis, an afternoon sail, then Mom was hoping you'd run some errands with her on Worth Avenue."

"Sounds great!" I chirped, trying hard to sound enthusiastic. Randall's family treated WASPiness like an extreme sport.

"I'm so glad that you've grown to love my parents," Randall said.

"Well, they're very devoted," I answered, trying to think of things I could say about them that were both true and complimentary. "Your mom has such boundless energy. She could run circles around me! And your dad is such a smart man."

Never mind my suspicion that Lucille's boundless energy had something to do with the little green pills she swallowed nearly every hour, or that the last time I'd seen Randall's father, he'd spent most of dinner staring at my legs. In their way, they *were* devoted to Randall. Their way was just very different from the way I'd grown up with.

"Claire, I love you," Randall said, kissing my cheek.

I looked at Randall, so handsome in his cashmere overcoat, and my heart overflowed with affection for him. He was a sweetheart—and such a model son. Sometimes it still seemed unreal, the fact that I was his girlfriend—I could still picture him in his rugby shirt, handing me that Pabst Blue Ribbon. "I love you, too," I said.

"Driver, would you mind putting on 1010 WINS?" he asked, leaning forward. "I want to hear how the market closed. By the way, Claire, we're flying Dad's new Citation 10. He's pretty stoked about it. Took him six months on the waiting list, but now he's one of the first to have it."

"Wow, his jet. Cool." I knew I should sound more excited, more impressed. But shiny new toys of that magnitude seemed to come into the Cox household as frequently as the Sunday *New York Times*.

Less than an hour later, we were aboard said jet—cashmere blankets on our laps, warm salted almonds in porcelain bowls next to us.

"It feels like a victory lap, circling over New York City in this plane," Randall mused, holding my hand as we took off from Teterboro and moved smoothly above the luminous skyline. "Oh, I nearly forgot. I have a little something for you, babe." He unzipped the leather bag he'd rested on the seat next to us and pulled out a huge white box with a black bow.

"You're spoiling me, Randall. Remember, we said no more gifts?"

Last week, on one of our rare evening walks to dinner together, he'd tried to pull me into Mikimoto to buy a set of cultured pearls—for absolutely no reason. I'd had to battle him to keep walking.

Maybe I should've just accepted Randall's extravagant gifts graciously. I could tell he got genuine pleasure out of being generous, but I hated not being able to reciprocate. At first I'd tried to, but the gifts on my budget were so much more meager in scale—an exercise book, the detoxifying tea he liked, a scarf—and I could tell Randall's excitement over them was a bit of an act. After all, how exciting can a scarf be to a man who's circling New York City in a new plane?

"Open it, darling," he prompted, placing the box in my lap and looking so excited that you'd think he were the one getting a gift.

"Oh, Randall. It's incredible!" I pulled a Chanel dress from the box—a stunning black cocktail dress with a full skirt and the most delicate lace I'd ever seen.

"Wait, there's more," he said, digging back into the bag to pull out a smaller box—which turned out to hold a gorgeous pair of Christian Louboutin stilettos.

"Randall! Wow, I don't know what to say!" The dress and the shoes deserved their own hermetically sealed closet, apart from my worn-in shoes and Banana Republic suits. I'd never seen such an exquisite outfit in my entire life.

"You like it?" Randall asked hopefully. His eyebrows lifted, and for a moment he looked like a little boy, wanting desperately to make me happy.

"I love it," I answered. "Thank you so much."

Lavish gifts from my handsome, wonderful boyfriend...I knew it was something that many women would dream of, but I still wished Randall could express his affection without breaking out his black Amex.

"Is there some formal event happening this weekend that I wasn't aware of?" I asked.

"Oh, we've got a little dinner planned for tomorrow night. Some of my parents' friends. I thought you might like to have something special, so I dispatched Deirdre at lunch today."

"Well, that was so thoughtful of you—and her," I said, moaning inwardly. Lucille's Palm Beach friends were harder to take than the last Twinkie at an Overeaters Anonymous meeting.

I'd met a handful of them during her last visit to New York. During cocktail hour (which lasted three), I'd struggled valiantly to make conversation. But really, what was there to talk about? Her friends were adamant about the purity of their leisure, outsourcing everything from the decoration of their homes to the drawing of their baths. One woman had even hired a full-time nanny to be "prepared" when her newborn grandson came to visit...with *his* full-time nanny. "He's a dear thing, but really, I can't be expected to drop everything to hold a baby for a few hours!" she'd clucked.

If these ladies were part of the weekend lineup, I'd really have to pace myself. Hopefully, I'd be able to carve out some time this weekend to sneak off and work on Luke's manuscript in peace. "I brought some work with me," I mentioned to Randall, hoping to lay the groundwork in advance. "Do you think there'll be time for me to get some editing done?"

"I hope so, babe." Randall kissed my forehead. "My little worker bee." He reached into his bag, pulled out *The Wall Street Journal*, and began to read.

"Why don't we talk a little, sweetie?" I asked gently, peeking over the corner of the newspaper. "I haven't seen you much this week."

Randall paused, then folded up his paper. "Of course, my love. What would you like to talk about? Is there something on your mind?"

"Oh, no. It's just that we never really get a chance to just relax and talk. You know? We give each other these rapid-fire updates before we go to bed—but sometimes I feel like...well, I don't know, I'd love to hear more about your life up until the point that we met. "

"Sure, Claire. What can I tell you? I think you know it all, babe. Grew up in New York, summered in Southampton, wintered in Palm Beach..."

Down the road, I'd have to break Randall of using seasons as verbs. "I know that much, yes—"

"And you know that I went to Groton, rowed crew, and got elected student body president. Then I went to Princeton, where I continued to row and started an investment club for undergraduates. And met you, of course." He smiled, tapping his finger on the end of my nose. "Then Goldman as an analyst, then Harvard for my graduate degree, and then Goldman ever since. What else are you looking for, Claire?"

I didn't exactly know what I was looking for...just more. "Um, well...what were these experiences like for you? Did you like high school? Did you go to camp as a kid? What's the most beautiful place you've ever seen?" My questions were weak, but I hoped one would spark a conversation.

Randall took a deep breath and took off his glasses. "I did enjoy high school, very much. I went to Windridge at Craftsbury Common as a child and enjoyed that very much, too. The most beautiful places I've ever been to are hmm, probably Quisisana in Capri and Eden Rock in Cap d'Antibes. I'll have to take you, sweetie, both are magnificent. Anything else?"

I wondered if Randall ever let down his guard. I didn't want to interview him, but I wanted to feel closer—I wanted to feel that I knew him inside and out. "Have you ever been madly in love, Randall?" I asked, slipping my hand into his.

Suddenly he looked very uncomfortable. "Well, I'm in love with *you*, of course."

I smiled. "I mean, before me. Alex Dixon, in college? Or maybe the ex your mom mentioned, Coral..."

"You know, Claire, I really don't see any purpose to this conversation. I'm not interrogating you about every man in your past—"

"I'm sorry, Randall, I didn't mean to—"

"I love *you*, Claire, and that's really all you need to know."

I curled up next to him. That had taken a wrong turn. It

wasn't the soul-revealing, heart-baring conversation I'd hoped for, but I did appreciate Randall's old-fashioned stance about not rehashing old flames. There was something undeniably romantic about it—as if he wanted to pretend our love lives had begun the moment we got together.

"Sweetie," he whispered, kissing my cheek, "may I resume my reading? There's a fascinating piece about emerging markets in China."

I nodded, reaching into my bag to pull out Luke's manuscript. Getting Randall to open up would take some time.

Luke's manuscript was close to perfect now, but I wanted to be sure it was all the way there. Just as I'd once read my father's early poems over and over again, I took a strange comfort in my familiarity with each line Luke had written.

I'd been working for about an hour when my eyelids started to get heavy. With the engine whirring gently and the soft cashmere blanket wrapped around me, it wasn't long before I'd nodded off.

The next thing I knew, Randall was nudging me awake. "I think we're about to land," he said, rubbing his fingers gently on my wrist. I wiggled my toes. Painful. It had been such a deep, luxurious sleep, and now there was just a quick car ride separating us from Lucille and her gaggle of girlfriends.

I threw Luke's manuscript back in my bag and slid on my shoes. "You might want to put that on, dear," advised the stewardess, pointing to the balled-up winter coat I'd stashed in the storage compartment. "It's less than thirty degrees out there, and the wind is fierce on the tarmac."

"Did you hear that?" I asked Randall, who was busy gathering his stuff. "There must be a terrible storm hitting Palm Beach."

"Mmm." He nodded.

It wasn't until I walked down the stairs that I realized we weren't in Palm Beach.

"*Bonjour, mademoiselle,*" said a young man in a spiffy blue-and-red uniform. "*Bienvenue à Paris. Puis-je prendre votre baggage?*"

"We're in Paris?" Stunned, I turned to look at Randall. He had a smirk on his face.

"Surprise! I figured that we've both been working so hard, it'd be good for us to have a romantic weekend alone. And what better city to do that in than Paris?"

"Randall! I can't believe you! What an *amazing* surprise!"

I, Claire Truman, had been whisked away for a weekend in Paris? I was stunned. Speechless, in fact. Not only had Randall tuned in to the fact that we needed to spend more time alone...he'd planned an incredibly romantic weekend to show his commitment.

"I found your passport, and Svetlana packed your bag," he explained proudly. "We're staying at the finest suite at the Ritz. Only the best, Claire. We don't have much time here, so everything will be perfect. I promise. All you have to do is sit back and enjoy."

"I can do that," I murmured, my head swimming with excitement. Paris. The city that inspired Hemingway, Gertrude Stein, Henry James. The most romantic city in the world. And I was here with Randall. It was all so perfect.

"So you enjoyed your massage? I'm glad, darling." Randall smiled, stirring his café au lait. We were having lunch at Le Deux Magots in the seventh arrondissement, a café where Sartre and George Sand used to eat croissants when they were taking a break from philosophizing. The café was a bit fussy and overpriced, but the tourist in me loved it.

"It was the best massage I've ever had," I told him, still a little dreamy from the experience. That morning, I'd been awakened gently by a chambermaid who'd led me to the downstairs spa, where I was attended to by two masseuses. It was a level of relaxation I'd never before experienced. "I can't imagine a nicer way to start the day." I reached across the table and squeezed his hand. "Well, maybe I can imagine *one* nicer way...but that's it."

Randall grinned at me. After my decadent massage, I'd pulled him off his laptop and back into bed.

"I thought after lunch we might do a bit of shopping on Faubourg St.-Honoré," he said. "It's just a short walk from the hotel and the best shopping in the world—Hermès, Christian Lacroix, Yves St. Laurent. And then I've got a very special evening planned for us. The perfect occasion to wear your new dress."

The dress! Now it made more sense. Randall had really thought of everything—even a Paris-appropriate wardrobe for me.

The day flew by. I could spend a lifetime in Paris and not get enough of it. We had a lovely, arm-in-arm stroll down St.-Honoré (it felt expensive just to walk down that street), and then we did a quick tour of the Musée Rodin before it was time to head back to the Ritz and get ready for dinner.

Back in the room, Randall and I dressed in silence. He carefully shaved and ran pomade through his hair, while I put on some makeup and tied my hair back in a loose twist. Standing in front of the mirror in a slip, I noticed for the first time just how much weight I'd lost since starting at Grant Books. Mom was right—I was downright gaunt. How had I not registered it before? My arms looked long and lanky, my stomach was flat as a drum, and my hipbones jutted out in a way I hadn't seen since I was twelve. The stomach-in-knots, too-stressed-to-eat, no-time-for-meals diet had caught up with me: I looked malnourished.

"Put on the dress, darling," Randall suggested.

I slipped it on, and Randall zipped up the back. It's hard

for a five-foot-ten-inch Iowa girl to channel dainty Audrey Hepburn, but the dress had some sort of magical properties. I didn't look like myself at all. I looked…like a girl who should be dating Randall Cox.

"You look beautiful, Claire," Randall whispered, slipping up behind me as I stood before the mirror, fixing my hair. He pulled something out of his pocket—the string of Mikimoto pearls we'd seen in the store window last week.

"Randall! I told you not to—"

"Just say thank you," he murmured into my ear. "Let's go, we've got a nine o'clock reservation at Alain Ducasse. We're on a schedule, sweetheart!"

Dinner was another over-the-top feast of the senses—the surprisingly cozy rococo salons were draped in metallic organza, the large clock on the wall had been symbolically stopped, and our table overlooked the loveliest courtyard. And the food was indescribably delicious—I ordered bisque de homard and Bresse chicken with white truffles, and for once even Randall was tempted to indulge a little.

"When in Rome…" He chuckled, scanning the menu. "I'll just run a few extra miles tomorrow."

When we'd finished our meal, Randall cleared his throat loudly. Then he cleared it again. He folded and unfolded his napkin and ran a hand through his hair.

I've never seen him fidget so much, I thought, and then it hit me—

Even before he was down on one knee, on the ground right next to me—asking me, with a plaintive, sweet, vulnerable look on his face, if I would do him the honor of being his wife—

His wife?!

Because he knew—he just *knew*—that we'd be so happy together. He'd flown out to Iowa yesterday to ask for Mom's blessing, and she'd given it. He loved me. Would I marry him?

Would I marry him?!

Half the restaurant had turned to face us now, watching the gorgeous, so-well-dressed-he-could-be-European man—with a ring in his outstretched hand that you could see from a block away—propose.

Would I marry him?!

The question hung in the air. I couldn't breathe. A proposal? I hadn't been expecting—it felt so out of the blue, and too soon—

"Claire," Randall whispered, "please say yes."

I looked into his eyes. I loved Randall. I did. I had since I was eighteen.

"Yes," I answered, and the next thing I knew there was a gigantic ring on my finger.

CHAPTER SEVENTEEN

 THIS SIDE OF PARADISE

B lack Monday," said David, stepping into my office with a copy of the *New York Post* hidden under his jacket. "Vivian's on a major warpath. She already fired an assistant and made two publicists cry, and it's not even nine yet. Did you see this?"

I gasped when he held up the front page. Stanley Prizbecki—dressed in the horrible teddy, wearing the screaming red lipstick—stared back at me from the front page. It was the photo I'd discovered in Vivian's file. "BIG DRAG FOR DEP MAYOR!" blasted the headline.

"Apparently they broke up last week," David explained. "Prizbecki's wife found out that he and Vivian were having an affair, so he ended it to save his marriage. Can you believe this picture? The papers are all saying his career is completely over. He's a laughingstock. Even the mayor can't back him up, it'd be political suicide."

Hell hath no fury, I thought. So that was why she'd kept that photo on file. Of course.

"It's going to be *such* a savage week," I noted wearily. Not to mention the worst possible week to break the news of my engagement at the office: Even during the best of times, nothing irritated Vivian more than the obvious happiness of her underlings. After an ugly break-up, my big news could unleash her very worst. I wiggled my finger out of my ring, slipping it stealthily into my top drawer while David read the article.

"Vivian is quoted as saying that she broke up with Prizbecki when she caught him wearing one of her evening dresses!"

"She's loyal to a fault."

"His poor kids, is all I can think. Anyway, how was your weekend? Good times with Randall's parents?"

"Oh, it was fine," I answered quickly. "How was yours?"

"Good, I burrowed through a lot of the submissions pile. I have a bunch of reader's reports coming your way. You were in Florida, right? You missed a huge snowstorm. The most snow we've had in late March for ten years, apparently."

I nodded. Actually, the snowstorm had played a big role in shaping our last twenty-four hours. For one thing, it had prevented us from landing until nearly 2:00 a.m. Randall had been up in arms, pacing around the plane, agitated at not getting a better night's sleep at the start of a hectic workweek. We'd decided to come back early from Paris to avoid the risk of getting stuck outside New York. Randall had the CEO and board of one of his major clients coming in early this morning. A few extra hours in Paris, he'd explained, just wasn't worth the possibility of not making it to that meeting.

I understood his anxiety, really. It wasn't as though a person got engaged and stopped caring about the rest of his or her life. Work still mattered, responsibilities still existed. I couldn't expect everything to be perfect and glossy and romantic *all* the time. Besides, I had a full workweek, too, and getting back and at it was the sensible course of action.

Still, I'll admit it: Part of me wished that the afterglow of getting engaged could've lasted longer than a few hours.

But it really had been euphoric at first. At the restaurant, we'd immediately called everyone we knew from Randall's phone, laughing with each other over the table as our friends and family screamed their congratulations. Randall had ordered a second bottle of champagne. One of the waiters brought me roses. I'd felt as though I were hovering at thirty thousand feet: Had I really just gotten engaged to Randall Cox? "It's like a dream come true!" Bea squealed into the phone, and I couldn't have agreed more. Finally, at 3:00 in the morning, we collapsed in a drunken heap on our enormous bed at the Ritz.

"Let me help you take off your dress," Randall slurred, popping up.

"Randall!" I laughed as he fumbled with the zipper. I'd never seen him drunk before, nor had he ever been so uninhibited. He slipped the dress off me, gently but purposefully, working it slowly over my now slender hips and down the length of my legs. He pulled it carefully over my feet. I lay back on the bed and closed my eyes—waiting to feel his body on mine, his lips…

But Randall seemed to be moving away from the bed. I sat up and watched as he carried my dress gingerly to the closet. He held it in his arms as if it were his bride. "There we go," he said to the dress, finding a satin hanger.

I lay down again in a pose I hoped was seductive.…

"I think I drank too much champagne," Randall groaned, flopping down lifelessly on top of me. I stayed pinned, motionless. In less than five seconds, he was snoring—and I rolled him gently off of me.

When I woke up the next morning, he was gone. The covers on his side were tucked in neatly. A maid was silently packing my things into my suitcase.

"Ze gym," she told me, pointing to the empty half of the bed. I'd expected that a champagne hangover—not to mention a fresh engagement—might've kept Randall in bed, but I was mistaken: Nothing got between him and the treadmill. "Monsieur Cox asked me to pack for you, since you will be leaving shortly," the maid explained. I nodded, bewildered.

Then I rolled over and ordered room service, staring at the enormous rock on my left hand as I dialed.

It was the strangest thing. Having never been engaged before, I couldn't say for sure how it was *supposed* to feel—but for Randall and me, it was like throwing a stone in a glassy pond: There was the initial plop, a few ripples...but then the water got smooth and flat again, very quickly. When Randall charged in from the gym—kissing me lightly on the top of my head, frowning at the eggs and sausage I'd been happily inhaling—it was as if nothing had really happened the night before. Two hours later, we were back on the plane, back to real life, back to *The Wall Street Journal* and work and barely exchanging words.

Really, if it wasn't for the diamond, I might've thought I'd dreamed the whole thing. And maybe that was why I didn't actually mind not sharing the news at work. I still needed to absorb it myself.

"David, do you have time this morning to go over the art log for the 1950s pinup book?" I asked, snapping out of my engagement analysis. "I'd like to get that transmitted by Wednesday at the latest."

"Sure. Can I show it to you in an hour? I'll finish it up now."

"That'd be perfect, thanks." Lately, I'd been delegating more and more to David. I knew he could handle it, and frankly it was the only way to stay afloat.

"Okay, I'll be at the copy machine if you need me. Do you want me to find someone to handle your phone?"

I told David I'd screen my calls myself. Then I sat back in my chair and took a sip of my coffee, which was piping hot and scalded the roof of my mouth.

It'll just take a few days to sink in. By the weekend, I'll be giddy over Martha Stewart's Weddings. *I'll be flashing my ring to anyone who comes within a ten-block radius. I'll have to hold myself back from telling every person I meet that I've found the One, and wasn't it romantic, and okay, fine, I'll tell the Paris story one more time if you insist on hearing it from the top.*

Plenty of time for flying off the handle with excitement once the news sank in a little more.

I plopped Luke's manuscript on the desk. I'd gotten through almost the entire thing on our plane ride back to New York and decided I'd ease into the day by finishing it up.

"Claire, my office," the dreadful intercom screeched before I could read the first word. *"NOW."* So I wouldn't be easing into the day. The always present anger in Vivian's voice had been ratcheted up a few notches.

I trudged down the hallway, too jet-lagged to be scared of the massacre that lay in store. "Hi, Vivian," I said quietly, stepping into her office. "What's going on?"

"What's going on?" she screamed back, already at full tilt. "Why don't *you* fucking tell *me* what's going on? Do I fucking report to you now?"

Oh boy. This was not going to be pretty. Had I really screwed up, or were the wheels just coming off the wagon? I sat down and waited to find out, feeling an odd inner calm that reminded me of that first meeting with Dawn and Graham. Maybe, after enduring enough rage, one's nervous system hit a satiation point—and Vivian no longer registered.

"Where are we on the proposal I asked you to look at on Friday?" she demanded.

"Well, I read about a hundred pages, and it's looking good — the agent said we could have it exclusively through the week, so — "

"Oh?! Oh?! Is that what he said?" Vivian scoffed, her lip curling in disgust. "My God, Claire, do yourself a favor and grow the fuck up! Do you think the nice agent man might have been *lying*? That he might be, as we speak, shopping it around to other publishers to see who else is interested? Men *lie*, Claire. They'll tell you anything they think you want to hear, if it'll get them what they want. Give me an answer on the proposal by noon. We're not playing that motherfucker's game. We're not letting him court a bunch of other publishers — "

The door cracked open, and Lulu slithered inside. "Sorry to interrupt," she lied, "I just wanted to drop off the mock-ups of *Around the Pole: A Stripper's Story*." She flopped down covers on Vivian's desk and then paused, clearly hoping to watch me get taken down.

"You're not interrupting, Lulu," Vivian said, her voice full of manufactured sweetness. "I'm glad you're here. Claire, unlike you, *Lulu* gets back to me immediately when I ask her to do something. She's a team player. Watch her! You could learn a lot!"

Learn how to be a groveling, backbiting, gutless lose-bag? No thanks.

"She's got more on her plate than I could ever expect you to handle," Vivian continued, looking me up and down with stark derision in her eyes. "All you do is dillydally over Luke Mayville's stupid manuscript like some love-drunk schoolgirl!" This thought seemed to light her fuse again, and her eyes bulged with renewed fury. "You know, I should drop that book, just to teach you a fucking lesson! Spending so much time on something that what, five people will ever read? It's *absurd*! Even *I* can't be bothered to read that boring thing, and I'm the goddamn publisher!"

I gulped, feeling truly panicked. This had been my greatest fear for months: Vivian would blow her stack with me and take retribution on Luke's book. I couldn't let it happen. "Please, Vivian," I begged, "I'll work 24/7 to stay on top of my other projects. I'm sorry, I—I'll do whatever you need me to do." I didn't care if I sounded shameless—preserving my dignity wasn't worth screwing up Luke's publication.

Vivian sat back. "You know, I could basically pull the plug on his little—"

"I know." I nodded, feeling the lump in my throat. "Just tell me what you want and I'll do it."

"Oh, I will," said Vivian, smiling like the Cheshire cat. "Don't worry, I will."

"So? So?" Bea screamed into my ear when I finally returned her fifth phone call. "I'm dying here, Claire! Give me every detail! I can't believe he flew you to Paris! How romantic!" She was practically jumping through the phone. "I mean, can you believe you're actually going to *marry* Randall Cox? Think of how many nights we lay on my old futon, daydreaming about this!"

As soon as she said it, the memory came back vividly—despite the fact that nearly a decade had passed. Bea and I used to lie flat on our backs for hours, staring at the water stains on her ceiling, dreaming about every minute detail of my imaginary life with Randall. Starting with our intimate wedding on my parents' farm—right underneath my parents' favorite apple tree, planted the first day they moved into the house. Randall and I would write our own vows, heartachingly beautiful vows, leaving not a dry eye in the crowd. I'd carry a bouquet of lilies of the valley from my mother's garden.

I tried to picture Randall and me reciting our own vows. It seemed like it would be...well, kind of awkward. Randall was a more traditional kind of guy.

"So when can I see you?" Bea asked. "Like, now?"

I glanced warily at my overflowing in-box. Files stacked on top of files—it was scary how much I had to get through in the next week, and Vivian's threat about Luke's book made everything all the more urgent. But I was desperate to see Bea. And Mara, who'd been so adorable when we'd called from Paris. She and I were having lunch the next day. I hoped that seeing them might make the engagement feel more real.

"How's tonight? Could I stop by after work?"

"Of course! And can Randall come, too?"

Randall had hit the ground running this morning, and I knew he'd be pulling an all-nighter. "Work," I summarized. "He won't be able to get out. You just get me, I'm afraid."

"You're all we need. I'll tell Harry to pick up Chinese on his way home."

There was a knock at my door. I told Bea I'd see her around 9:00.

"Claire Truman?" A heavyset woman in a pastel pink Chanel suit poked her head into my office. Her wheat-colored hair, blown into thick sheets, framed a frying-pan face. In her arms she held four enormous pink binders, each one crammed to capacity.

"Yes, I'm Claire," I answered.

The woman's face lit up. "Claire! Oh, well, you're adorable! This is going to be so much fun!"

"I'm sorry, have we met?" Was this woman a prospective author? Had I forgotten about a meeting?

"Oh, I'm sorry. Mrs. Lucille Cox asked that I call you? My

name is Mandy Turner? I'm a wedding planner based in Palm Beach and Manhattan?" Mandy spoke expectantly, as if waiting for something she said to clue me in.

I ushered her quickly into my office before anyone could overhear her. A wedding planner, already? Leave it to Lucille. We'd been back in New York less than twelve hours, and already she'd sprung into planning mode.

"Mandy, I appreciate you stopping by, but I don't think Randall and I will need a planner. We'll be having a very small wedding in my hometown...once I have a free second to start thinking about it." I smiled, glancing at the menacing piles on my desk.

"Oh?" Mandy asked, clearly taken aback. "And where's that? Your hometown?"

"Iowa City, more or less."

"Uh-huh. Uh-huh. Okay. Well, why don't I just leave my portfolios, just in case you change your mind?"

"That's nice of you, Mandy, but I don't think that it's necessary."

Mandy and I argued politely until I finally agreed to keep the binders. I couldn't spend more time discussing it, and more important, I didn't want any of my colleagues to overhear the argument.

"Oh, dear, where's your ring?" Mandy asked as I pushed her off to the elevator bank.

"It's, um, being resized," I whispered.

I'd just watched the elevator doors close on Mandy Turner and walked back to my desk when my phone rang. This time it was Lucille herself.

"Claire, darling," she began. Her voice had a steely edge. "I hear you've sent Mandy on her way, dear! She just phoned! Whyever would you do that? And let's talk for a moment about the location of your wedding. I had some thoughts. And the timing of it…why have a long engagement, really? The St. Regis has an opening at the end of June! Isn't that fabulous? Wouldn't that be just too perfect, dear?"

"That's three months away! And honestly, Mrs. Cox—"

"Lucille, my love. Call me Lucille!"

"Lucille—I need some time before I start planning anything. You know, just to enjoy being engaged, and—"

"Darling, *bingo*. That's *all* Mandy and I want. For you and Randall to enjoy being engaged—leave the boring, mundane, silly work to us."

"What do you mean, the boring, mundane—I couldn't ask you to plan—"

"You're not asking, precious, we're *offering*. To deal with planning, to cover the costs, to take the headache off your hands! Doesn't that sound lovely? Aren't you busy enough, dear? Really, why trouble yourself?"

Funny, I'd never thought of my wedding as something that'd be a trouble to plan. Although I was getting a brutal headache discussing it with Lucille.

My other line beeped. Vivian's extension. There was nothing that incensed her more than going through to voice mail, so I asked Lucille if I could call her back.

"Of course, dear. But just think about what I've said. Imagine not having to lift a finger!"

I clicked over.

"*Claire!* Why haven't we finalized our contract with Candace yet?"

"Because she's not satisfied with our offer." I'd told Vivian this three times already. "Should she take it or leave it, or are you willing to offer more?"

"Offer fifteen more, and tell her to take or leave that. And by the way, I'm going to need you to cover five or six meetings for me next week—I'll be in L.A., but I don't want to cancel them. And—you know what, just come to my office. I have a few books I need you to pursue. Not tomorrow, not this week—*right now.*"

I glanced at my in-box, which was about to double in size. Then I thought about Lucille's offer. Maybe it wasn't such a bad idea.

So what if my old fantasy of a small wedding in the apple orchard wouldn't come true. I'd be marrying the man I'd dreamed about all those years ago. I'd be marrying the perfect man.

CHAPTER EIGHTEEN

 THE CONSCIOUS BRIDE

"Tish-Tish!"

Barreling out of the side sitting room, Lucille blindsided my poor, bewildered mother, who'd just walked into the foyer of their Upper East Side town house with me. Lucille clung to Mom with such a fierce, octopuslike grip that I had to pry her off—with the help of Carlotta.

"I can't believe how *long* it's been, Tish-Tish! I can't believe you're finally in New York! I've been trying to get you here since the kids' first date!"

"I know!" Mom said, still a bit shell-shocked from Lucille's tackle. "It's great to see you, Luce. You look terrific. You haven't changed a bit."

"The miracle of Botox, Tish! If you want, I could probably swing you a weekend appointment with the best doctor in town—he'll do occasional house calls, but only for me!"

"Oh, that's okay," Mom demurred, "I think we'll have our hands full with the dress appointments you've lined up. Thanks for helping with all the planning, Lucille. You've been so generous."

Our lavish wedding at the St. Regis Hotel was now a mere six weeks away, an astonishing and alarming fact, and the only thing that was left to do was a pretty big one: find the perfect wedding gown.

"I've loved every second, Tish. And it's true, we do have a full day. Can you believe this daughter of yours?" Lucille exclaimed. "Managing to miss every single appointment I set up for her?"

"Well, I know work has been demanding Claire's every waking—"

"Oh—work, work, work," Lucille interrupted Mom, clearly not having any of it. "Well, at least it finally got *you* into town."

I could understand Lucille's frustration: The dress had become my one and only wedding-related responsibility, and I'd dropped the ball. In my semi-defense, my workload had reached a critical mass. Ever since Vivian had caught wind of my engagement, I'd needed to be at the office constantly—the fate of Luke's book, still two months away from being published, dangled precariously in the balance.

Fortunately, I'd managed to get back in Lucille's good graces when I told her that Mom would be flying in to help. Mom was a godsend, especially considering that Bea was stuck in L.A. for work. Dress shopping with Lucille was stressful enough; dress shopping *alone* with Lucille would leave permanent scars.

"Okay, let's hit it," I said, grabbing my purse and the itinerary of appointments that Lucille had printed on pink paper. I had a six-hour reprieve from the office, and the meter was already running.

"Isn't this just a dream come true, Tish-Tish?" Lucille gushed, clutching Mom's arm as we walked down Madison on our way to the first appointment. "My son, your daughter— why, just think, we'll have the same grandchildren, Tishie!"

"It's wonderful, Lucille." Mom smiled. "I couldn't be happier for them."

"Say you'll stay longer than just the weekend. We've got so much room, and Randall's gone all next week on business—so it'd be just like old times. Roommates again! We've got so much to catch up on!"

"I wish I could, Luce, and that's sweet of you to offer," Mom answered, "but I've got to finish a painting—there's a gallery in Pittsburgh expecting it next week, so I'm down to the wire."

"Pittsburgh?" Lucille wrinkled her nose. "I've got an idea—why don't I just buy the painting from you instead? Then you can finish it whenever you have time and stay an extra week! Deal?"

"I'm sorry, Luce, I've already committed to the gallery," Mom said. "But I'll show you some of my other work, and you can have anything you like. My gift, for an old friend."

Lucille beamed—I'd never seen her look happier. "And future in-law!" she trilled.

"I just want something simple," I insisted for the sixth time, a note of desperation creeping into my voice. "Like this." I unfolded a photo of a slim sheath dress with a delicate smattering of beads at the neckline. I'd torn it out of the ever-growing pile of wedding porn that Lucille had delivered to the apartment each week.

It was 3:00 p.m., and we'd already whipped at breakneck speed through Angel Sanchez, Carolina Herrera, Bergdorf, Saks, and Reem Acra. I was exhausted, starving, and about to wring Lucille's neck. She'd found a new body part to criticize in each gown I tried.

"We heard you, Claire, *simple*," said Lucille, rolling her eyes at a now stone-faced Mom, "but come on, you're not fooling anyone! What kind of woman doesn't want to look her most fabulous on her wedding day? This is the *most* important dress of your *life*, Claire! A little focus is all I ask! That sheath is fine, I suppose, but it's just so *plain*."

"Hang on, Lucille," Mom countered in her most diplomatic, let's-everyone-stay-calm tone. "Claire *will* look fabulous, but her style is much more low-key—"

"It's her wedding day, Tish-Tish!" Lucille whined like a five-year-old. "The most important day of her life! My God, must I do everything here? From pushing Randall in the...right direction, to booking the Ritz in Paris on absolutely *no* notice, to planning every single detail of the wedding, to getting the world's most coveted designers to agree to rush production on whichever gown we choose so that we can have it in less than two months—which is unheard of, I'll tell you, they would *only* do such a thing for me—so that Randall and Claire can have their special day at the St. Regis in June?"

I felt as though I'd been punched in the gut. *Lucille* had orchestrated our weekend in Paris, and she'd pushed Randall to propose? "I thought Randall had planned that trip," I said quietly, trying to hide the fact that she'd just knocked the wind out of me.

"Claire, darling, he's a man!" Lucille laughed, amused by my naïveté. "They can't really be counted on to *plan* anything, can they? His secretary is helpful with gifts, of course, but one needs clout to get the Ritz's finest suite and reservations at Alain Ducasse on a few hours' notice." She smiled proudly at her handiwork.

Mom just shook her head. From the expression on her face, I could tell that the girl she'd known in college bore little resemblance to the tiny, bossy, wired woman barking commands at us today—but she was making the best of things for my sake.

"Next stop, Vera Wang!" declared Lucille. "Let's go, ladies!"

"I really liked that first dress we saw," I said, grabbing Lucille's birdlike arm to slow her down for a moment. "At Angel Sanchez...it had such a soft, ethereal quality to it. You liked it—right, Lucille? That's the dress I want."

Mom nodded. "It looked gorgeous on you, Claire."

Lucille looked at both of us with icy condescension. "It was a beautiful dress, I agree—well, except for the way it accentuated your hips, darling—but we must see what else is out there! My dear, would you get engaged to the first man you went on a date with?"

I really didn't see the parallel but still found myself traipsing along behind her. I was too tired to defect now. We *had* to be almost done—I'd tried on at least fifty dresses. Mom flashed me a look—silently asking if I'd like her to pull the ripcord on our shopping expedition. "It's okay," I whispered to her as Lucille sped on in front of us. "I need a dress, and she means well—"

"Ladies! Stop stalling and *move*! We don't have much time!"

I prayed that Vera Wang would save the day.

Inside the Vera Wang salon, I stealthily slipped the sales attendant my magazine photo when Lucille got distracted by some tiaras. "Could you bring me something like this?" I asked.

"Certainly." She nodded and scurried off as I settled into the dressing room with Mom.

"How're you holding up?" Mom asked.

"Hanging on by a couture thread. Actually, it's nice being able to relax back here for a moment—"

"Mother! I *know* it costs ten thousand dollars, but this is the most important day of my *entire life*!" wailed a girl in the dressing room next to ours. "Do you want me to look like *crap* on my wedding day, Mother? Is that what you want?"

"Of course not, sweetie," the girl's mother answered wearily.

"This is the dress I want, then!"

"All right, dear."

"*And* the Jimmy Choos with the embedded crystals in the heel!"

There was a pause. "All right, dear."

Ugh. What had that poor woman done to deserve such a hideous brat for a daughter? Mom rolled her eyes, echoing my sentiment.

"Miss Truman? I have a few things you might like." The attendant pulled back the taffeta curtain with several gowns, each elaborate and embroidered. Lucille slipped in the dressing room behind her, rubbing her little hands together in anticipation.

And there it was. The first dress. It was a pale champagne sheath with an overlay of crystal, tulle, and delicately sequined flowers. It had a long, incredibly romantic train in the back. It wasn't frou-frou or princessy, but it was still undeniably over-the-top—which I hoped would satisfy Lucille.

"Try it," Lucille panted. Even Mom looked excited. I slipped on the dress, and she buttoned me up in the back.

I looked in the mirror. It was exquisite. Everything I could ask for in a wedding gown. This was it: the moment when I was supposed to feel transformed into the Bride. I was supposed to feel like this was the dress I'd been waiting for. The dress I wanted my groom to see when the church doors opened. The dress that made me feel like standing up in front of hundreds of people and saying I do, I do, I do.

"Yes!" shouted Lucille. "Yes!"

"You look beautiful," Mom said, watching me closely, "What do you think, Claire?"

I loved the dress.

But I wasn't having the moment. I was some kind of mutant bride. I still didn't feel the bubbling excitement I'd been waiting to feel since returning home from Paris. I hadn't felt it while leafing through the wedding magazines. I hadn't felt it when telling friends about how Randall proposed. I didn't feel it now, wearing the most stunning dress I'd ever seen. There was something seriously wrong with me.

"What's not to love?" Lucille interjected. "The dress is absolutely stunning on you, Claire."

"I love the dress." I nodded, heart heavy with confusion. Why wasn't I more excited? I actually felt envious of the brat in the next dressing room—at least she knew exactly what she wanted.

Before I knew what was happening, Lucille had called in the seamstress and was giving her commands: more hand beading on the train...House of Lesage...spare no expense...a personal friend of Vera's...I tuned out, staring at myself in the mirror and finishing off two more flutes of champagne.

"Are you sure, Claire?" Mom asked, looking a little worried. "You don't seem very enthusiastic about the dress. If you don't like it, dear—"

"Oh, I'm sorry. I do really love it, honestly, I'm just exhausted...it's been such a long week."

Mom didn't look completely satisfied, but she let it go.

"Now, veils," Lucille continued after the seamstress had been dismissed. "I was thinking a cathedral veil with a richly beaded border....Vera's got a beautiful selection."

I glanced at my watch. I'd have at least five irate voice mails from Vivian to deal with back at the office—now that Stanley was out of the picture, there was seemingly nothing to distract her from thinking about work every waking moment. Weekends were no exception.

"I'm sorry, Lucille, but I need to get back to the office."

"You work too hard," she mumbled, helping me out of the dress. "Well, I'm going to buy a veil, just so we have it."

Just so we have it? Veils at Vera Wang were, like, a $3,000 purchase—not exactly an impulse buy. I told Lucille firmly that I'd prefer to wait—uncharacteristically, she relented. As we headed out of the store, however, she suddenly "remembered" another word of advice she had for the seamstress and ducked back inside, claiming she'd catch up with us.

"You know she's buying that veil," Mom muttered as we watched Lucille's hasty retreat. "It's incredibly generous of her, but she's gotten so pushy—"

"Claire? Trish?" said a familiar voice from behind us. *Luke.* My stomach dropped to my toes. He'd walked past us and then stopped in his tracks. For a moment, I stood frozen—not sure what to say, not sure how to broach the subject that I was so overdue in broaching....

"Luke!" Mom said, kissing him hello. "So good to see you! I was hoping I'd get to this weekend—"

"What a nice surprise! What brings you to town? Just a visit?"

"Well, um, yes," said Mom, glancing down. She and Bea had been on me for weeks to tell Luke that I was engaged—they seemed to think the fact that I hadn't proved some mysterious point. I couldn't explain why I hadn't told him yet. True, I'd been talking to him nearly every day as his book approached publication...but I hadn't mentioned my engagement the first few times we'd spoken, and then it seemed awkward that I *hadn't*—so then I *didn't*, and—well, there really wasn't a decent explanation.

"I gooooot it!" The shrill sound of Lucille's voice made my stomach drop again. Oh no. She was swinging a Vera Wang bag that was almost as big as she was. "Your veil! I know you said you wanted to wait, Claire, but I just couldn't resist! Forgive me, darling! You can try it on at home and then return it to the boutique so they can send it to Paris for additional hand beading. They promised to have it done in time for the wedding."

Mom turned toward Lucille sharply. "I need to look for shoes. Will you come with me, please?" she asked forcefully, taking Lucille's arm. Lucille, pleasantly surprised that Mom was taking an interest in fashion, handed off the Vera Wang bag to me.

"It was great to see you, Luke," Mom called out over her shoulder, "hope to catch up soon!" With that, they left Luke and me standing alone on the sidewalk.

"Your *veil?*" he asked, scratching his head.

"God, I am such an idiot!" I groaned, slapping my forehead. "I guess in all the chaos of work and getting your book off to the printer, I completely forgot to tell you the, um…really exciting news! Randall and I are getting married."

I watched my words register on his face, wishing I'd told him over the phone when I had the chance.

"You're getting— Wait, is that why Uncle Jack and Aunt Carie are coming up in June? They mentioned they'd be here for almost a week and mentioned something about you having a big day, but it was such a flyby conversation, and there were multiple grandkids screaming in the background, so I didn't drill down on what they meant. I can't believe—you're getting *married?*"

I hated myself. Not only had I neglected to share the big news with Luke, but I'd forgotten that Mandy had sent an invitation to Jackson and Carie. What was I thinking? I'd invited Luke to an intimate family occasion in Iowa, but not to our seven-hundred-person wedding in Manhattan?

Mom and Bea had been right. The truth was, for some reason—some reason that I was painfully uncomfortable examining—I hadn't *wanted* to tell Luke about the wedding.

"I don't know what I was thinking," I said. "Please say you can come to the wedding, Luke. And the rehearsal dinner, Friday night, at the University Club. We'd love to have you there. Please—can you make it? And your girlfriend, too, of course."

"We broke up," he said, not responding to the rest of what I'd said.

"Oh!" I took a step back. "I'm so sorry to hear that, Luke. Well, of course, you can come by yourself, and—"

"I'm not sure that's such a good idea."

"What? Not a good— Luke, I am *so* sorry. I should've told you sooner. Please don't be—"

"See, here's the thing," Luke began, furrowing his brow. Taking my arm, he pulled me off the sidewalk and into the quiet doorway of a needlepoint store. I put down the bag and rubbed my arms a little. It was a warm May afternoon, but suddenly I had goose bumps on every square inch of my body. *What was the thing?* And why was Luke looking more serious than I'd ever seen him look before? "On the one hand, I'd love to celebrate any happy occasion in your life. I mean that, Claire. But on the other hand..." He paused, studying the lines of the palm of his hand before looking up. "I have feelings for you. Strong feelings. I've always wanted to tell you that—ever since that first time we bumped into each other, I've felt something toward you—but there never seemed to be a right time. Anyway, now is obviously not the right time, either, but I—I think I'm falling in love with you, Claire."

We stared at each other, both terrified of what he'd just said. There it was. Out there.

"God, this is awkward," he said, forcing a laugh. "I'm sorry. Maybe that's something I should've kept to myself. I see you with a veil, you tell me you're marrying someone else, and I go and blurt out—"

"No. I'm glad you told me, Luke. I just—I'm just not sure what to say."

He chewed his lip. "Did you really *forget* to tell me about the wedding, or—"

"I, um…I'm not sure, I—"

For an editor and a writer, we had some way with words.

"You can't tell me you don't feel anything," Luke said quietly, his gaze holding me in one place. He took my hand. I felt the same electric shiver I had that night he'd kissed my cheek under the awning.

"I've got to go," I suddenly spat out, pulling my hand away. Then I felt my body move, walking away from the awning and Luke and down Madison, weaving through people, the shops passing by in a blur, the warmth of the day settling in around us.

I needed time to think. Like, five years on a desert island. Everything felt so tangled and confused and—

"Claire!" It was Luke—he'd run after me.

"Listen, I can't do this right now"—I was jabbering a mile a minute—"I'm getting married, Luke, and even if for whatever reason I didn't want to share that news with you—which was wrong of me—the fact remains, I am getting married. In six weeks. Less than two months. To a great guy"—I felt the tears start streaming—"a really great guy"—dripping off my jaw, my chin—"and I can't just—you know—"

"You left your veil," Luke said, handing the bag to me.

"Oh," I said, feeling pretty humiliated as the tears continued to drip off my face. A woman with several shopping bags in tow paused on the street, staring at me with pity in her eyes. "Thank you."

"I just want you to be happy." Luke's face was close to mine. I tried not to look at his lips, the line of his nose, his shining dark eyes. I trained my eyes to the ground. "You should be as happy as you possibly can be. And if Randall's the guy who really does that for you—makes you as happy as you *possibly can be*—then you should be with him."

"Thank you," I repeated—not knowing what else to say, my head spinning.

And then Luke kissed me. Just once, just perfectly. For one brief moment, everything felt like it made sense again—even though nothing really did. If Luke hadn't pulled away, I wouldn't have been able to myself.

I lived the next few weeks in a fog. Everything seemed to wash over me—wedding details, Vivian's tirades, Bea's concern, Randall's increasing absence. Mara and I met up for drinks one night, and she asked if I'd been taking sedatives. Life just seemed muted. I hadn't spoken to Luke since our kiss—deep in my mind, thoughts of him ran perpetually, but I hadn't gotten any closer to understanding what my feelings really meant, or what I should do about them. In a way, I was grateful for my zombielike state—I just couldn't handle looking at my life with any degree of focus.

One evening in early June, I decided I'd walk home to finish my day's work. I meandered down Madison, which was packed with New Yorkers reveling in the early days of warm weather. I stopped into a deli to grab a fresh pack of cigarettes, not bothering to feel bad about the purchase. I was just lighting up in front of La Goulue when I saw her.

The blonde from the picture in Randall's desk drawer.

Across the street from me, in a light sweater and a pretty summer skirt that showed off her well-toned legs. She was phenomenally beautiful. When a cabdriver slowed down to let her walk, she waved to him with genuine appreciation. There was something about her that I involuntarily liked.

She crossed the street toward me, and began walking toward La Goulue. I walked behind her—I was headed in that direction anyway, I justified. I watched her swing open the door of the restaurant.

And then I saw Randall through the windows, opened for the summer weather. I saw him stand up at his table when she came through the doors. He looked at her in a way that I'd never seen him look at any woman before. He kissed her on the cheek, and they sat down.

That's Coral, a strangely calm voice in my head told me, and I kept walking down the street. Another woman would have charged into the restaurant and demanded to know exactly what was going on. Another woman would've waited in painful suspense for her fiancé to get home—waited for an explanation or to let him have it.

But then, another woman wouldn't have been kissing another man a few weeks before. Another woman wouldn't have been replaying that one stupid kiss in her head ever since it happened.

More for me to not think about. More to push aside, as if it hadn't really happened. I walked home the remaining blocks, catching my reflection in store windows and barely recognizing the exhausted woman staring back at me.

Hours later, in bed, I quietly asked Randall about his dinner. And yes, he admitted immediately, he'd been at La Goulue with Coral. He was sorry he didn't tell me. He'd only wanted to tell her about our engagement in person—he felt he owed her that—but there was nothing between them. He hadn't wanted to bother me with it, since it meant nothing and I'd seemed a little tense lately.

I told him I believed him. I had to believe him. I didn't have the energy to question and probe and discuss and get to the bottom of it. Almost eleven months into my career at Grant Books, six weeks to go till my wedding, I had reached a level of emotional and physical exhaustion that left me incapable of resistance. The only option was to accept Randall's explanation and push thoughts of Luke out of my head. I rested my head on the pillow, feeling hollow.

CHAPTER NINETEEN

 ENORMOUS CHANGES AT
THE LAST MINUTE

O kay, enough. I've got to leave for the church this minute or I'm going to miss my own wedding," I told Vivian firmly, capping my pen.

She looked up wide-eyed, as if startled by the news that I was getting married today. Maybe she *was* startled by the news. Given her general level of interest in the lives of people around her, it seemed entirely possible that Vivian was only now clueing in to the fact that I was wearing a white gown and heavily beaded cathedral veil.

She'd been planted in the bridal suite for nearly forty-five minutes, instead of the agreed-upon five, and Mandy and Lucille were starting to circle us like wild dogs ready to pounce. Mom was sketching in a notebook in the corner, something she did to calm her nerves. Bea, who'd passed the time by drinking flute after flute of Veuve Clicquot, was now well on her way to being hosed. I was jealous.

"Fine," Vivian relented uncharacteristically, dismissing me with a queenly roll of her hand.

"Finally! Thank you!" Lucille shouted, chucking Vivian's coat at her and pushing the entire group toward the door. "Good God! Whoever heard of such a thing?" Mandy shook her head emphatically.

"So you'll be in on Monday morning, correct?" Vivian asked as we stepped onto the elevator.

"Yes," I answered. I paused, then added, "You know, Vivian, you were invited to the wedding." Lucille had sent the invitation without asking me, wanting to stoke the crowd with as many high-profile New Yorkers as possible.

"Yeah, I saw the invite," Vivian answered distractedly, offering no explanation for why she'd chosen not to attend or even RSVP. "Monday morning, Claire, I expect you to call me first thing. We have a lot to go over. Here I am, chasing you all over the city—my life doesn't revolve around yours, you know!"

"You're both crazy," Lucille hissed, pressing the "door close" button in the elevator, and for once I was inclined to agree with her.

We rode the rest of the floors in funereal silence. The tension reminded me of my elevator ride with Lulu all those months ago. I wondered what she was doing this weekend, whether she was trapped in the office. I knew I shouldn't care—Lulu had been nothing but a headache since the day I started at Grant—but I felt sorry for her. Well, a little.

When we got outside the hotel, Vivian marched straight toward a chauffeured Lincoln Town Car and jumped in without saying good-bye. "Lulu, I don't know where the fuck you are," I could hear her barking into her cell phone through the open car window, "but I need to talk through some things with you immediately. Call me back the *second* you get this message." I watched as Vivian quickly punched another number into her cell phone.

"Drive!" she bellowed, and the driver screeched away from the curb.

Bea and Mom helped me climb into one of the white Bentleys parked out front—Lucille and Mandy would be traveling together in the second one, so they could discuss last-minute details before battle. Hands reached in to arrange my dress so that it wouldn't be wrinkled.

"You are zo pale!" clucked Jacques, ducking through the open door of the car to stab at my cheeks with a blush brush. "There, ees better." He blew us air kisses and stepped away from the car.

All brides get cold feet, I told myself as Bea poured three more glasses of champagne for the ride to the church. My mother, who barely ever drinks, downed hers in record time.

Marriage is a huge commitment. I'd be scared no matter who was standing down there by the altar.

The car pulled away and headed for the church. Twenty blocks. I prayed for red lights. I just needed some more time to think. Just a few extra minutes and I might be able to make sense of all of this. Everything had happened too fast. It was natural to feel panicked. After all, in the span of just one year, my life had changed past recognition.

One year ago, would I have ever guessed that I'd be marrying Randall Cox—the most successful and handsome man I knew, the man of my dreams since college?

Come to think of it, would I have dreamed it possible that I'd already be working as an editor on such high-profile titles? Sure, I'd edited a lot of schlock and dealt with plenty of insanity at Grant Books, but I'd also had a hand in four *New York Times* best sellers and had edited one pretty amazing piece of literature. *Luke* ... I quickly pushed my thoughts away from him, as I'd been doing for the past six weeks ... more, really.

What was wrong with me? Really, life had turned out better than I could've ever imagined a year ago. So why'd I feel like if I let myself start crying, I might never stop?

Nerves, just nerves. Twelve blocks. Eleven. I was nearly out of time. *Just get through this wedding, Claire, and you'll be fine.* All brides got cold feet.

A cab stopped to let out a passenger, and I felt grateful when our car got caught behind it.

"I'm...I'm..." I stammered, not sure what to say next. Bea and Mom leaned forward expectantly, hopefully. I gulped some champagne.

"What is it, Claire?" Mom asked gently. "Is everything okay? Because, dear, if everything *isn't* okay, now would be a very good time to tell us. You can tell us anything, Claire, and we'll support you one hundred percent."

"Yeah," piped up Bea, slurring her words a little. "Whereas two hours from now? Not so good a time to tell us."

Eight blocks. I thought about my dad. I thought about how as a little girl I'd climb up on his lap and ask him to tell me the story of how he and Mom met. And when he finished, I'd ask to hear it again. Because you never get tired of listening to a real love story. Because as his daughter, I loved the way his face lit up when he'd say, "And then your mother walked into the room."

"Here, Claire," my mother said, handing me a handkerchief. Jacques would have a conniption if he saw how wet my cheeks were. "Why are you crying, dear?"

"Just nerves," I managed to squeeze out of my tightening throat. It was too late to answer any other way. I'd let things go too far. Life had become a runaway train, and I had only myself to blame for that.

The car stopped. We'd arrived at the stony back of the church. In a fog, I allowed Mom and Bea to help me out of the car and up the short, pebbly path. I was vaguely aware of the second Bentley pulling up, Lucille and Mandy clamoring out behind us. The four of us walked into the back of the church. Mom squeezed my hand. And then—

A glass-shattering shriek pierced the air.

Lucille.

Ten steps ahead of me, sitting on a small chair in the back vestibule, was my groom.

"Bad luck!" his mother wailed like a banshee, a look of absolute horror on her face. *"Bad luck! He...can't...see...you...before...the...wedding!"* Her tiny chest began to wheeze violently, gasping for oxygen.

"Luce, you're hyperventilating," Mom said calmly, putting her arm around Lucille and guiding her into a small room. "Try to relax, sweetie. It'll be okay."

"But...it's...bad...luck! They're...not...*supposed*...to—"

"I know, Luce, but try to calm down," Mom murmured. Beatrice quickly dumped out a paper bag filled with rose petals right on the floor and headed after Mom and Lucille. She yanked Mandy along with her, shutting the door behind them.

So now Randall and I were the only two people in the back area of the church.

For a moment, we just stared at each other, not saying a word. Randall looked Cary Grant handsome in his debonair tuxedo.

"You look beautiful," he said softly.

"Thank you," I answered. "You, too...I mean, um, handsome."

We were the picture-perfect couple, about to share the picture-perfect wedding and embark on the picture-perfect life. We stared at each other again, still from opposite sides of the small vestibule.

"I guess we really upset my mother. *That's* bad luck." Randall laughed lightly, but there was no mistaking a note of sadness in his voice.

"My mom will take care of her," I said.

More heavy silence.

"Well, I guess I should be taking my post." He smiled. I nodded.

So this was it. Our last moment to—

"It isn't enough," blurted out a voice that sounded shockingly like mine.

"What?" he asked.

"It isn't enough," the voice repeated.

"What do you mean, Claire?" Randall demanded, concern now etched all over his face. "What do you mean, *it isn't enough?*"

Oh God. My words—and my voice, saying things without my permission…like some kind of out-of-body experience…my voice suddenly saying the thing I'd been thinking for weeks, months even.

"What isn't enough, Claire?" Randall repeated, now close to me, now gripping my arms tightly.

He looked terrified. His knuckles were white.

Say it, Claire, I thought. *Say it now before it's too late.*

But I had to believe that on some level, Randall wanted me to do this. I'd seen the way his face had lit up when Coral walked into La Goulue. It reminded me of my father's face whenever he saw my mother. It reminded me of Luke's face, each and every time I saw him.

I could stop the runaway train for both of us.

"Randall, you know that I love you. I think the world of you. You're an amazing person, a great man. But what we have—it isn't enough, and I think you feel that as much as I do—"

"What? What are you talking about, Claire? We're about to get married, for chrissakes—you've just got the jitters! We love each other, Claire, and what's more, we *respect* each other. Those sound like two good reasons to get married, at least to me."

And he was absolutely right. Love and respect were two excellent reasons to get married. I looked at Randall closely, seeing for the first time what a marriage to him would really be like. We would always care for each other. He'd always give me anything I needed or wanted. He'd respect me. He would be committed to our marriage.

But he'd never be truly, deeply passionate about it. Neither would I. And that wasn't enough for me.

"Randall," I asked quietly, "why did you end things with Coral?"

"*What?!* What does Coral have to do with this? That's ancient history, Claire, I really don't think—"

"When she walked into the restaurant, Randall, I saw your face. I was just curious about why you'd decided to break up with her."

Randall flushed bright red. "Claire, I told you, nothing happened between us! It was no big deal! I just wanted to tell her about the wedding in person. Please believe me, Claire, it was nothing more than that—"

"I trust you, Randall. I was just wondering why, in your mind, you'd ended things with Coral."

"Well, she didn't—she didn't fit— I don't know why, it just didn't work!"

"But you were in love with her, weren't you? So *why* didn't it work?"

"Claire, honestly, why are we talking about this? It's over between me and Coral, there's nothing to—"

"Just tell me honestly why it didn't work, and I'll never mention it again."

Randall put his head in his hands. "It didn't work because…well, my mother didn't approve of Coral…Coral's background, I guess. Didn't think she was the right woman for me. And I trust my mother. She wants what's best for me, always has."

"And you trusted her when she said that *I* was best for you."

"I— Listen, Claire, it's not like I just do her bidding. I can think for myself, of course, and I love you. You make me very happy—"

"Randall, think about how Coral makes you feel."

He shook his head in desperate frustration. "It's *over*, Claire, how many times—"

"Just think about how she made you *feel*, Randall."

He stopped shaking his head. Neither of us said a word for a moment, but the look that passed between us said everything. "It was just different," he admitted quietly. "I don't know why. But I do love you, Claire."

"Randall, we have something, and the past year has been wonderful—but it isn't enough. And it's not your fault—it's not just you and Coral. I've developed feelings for someone else, too. I didn't intend to, it just happened." We sat next to each other on the stairs. "If we got married, we'd be cheating ourselves. I don't want that for you, and I don't want that for myself."

I paused, taking a deep breath before forging ahead. "We can't get married, Randall. I'm sorry—especially for only figuring this out a few minutes before our wedding. But I know it's the right decision."

And I did know it. Finally—after a year of confusion and second-guessing and mounting doubts—I knew myself again, and I knew what I had to do. Randall nodded slowly. He leaned down to kiss my cheek, now wet again with tears—when the door slammed open and Lucille charged out.

"*What* is the right decision?" she demanded, crumpled paper bag still in hand. "Why are you crying, Claire? What's going on?"

I looked at Randall to see if he wanted me to be the bearer

of bad news. He put his hand on my arm. "Mother, Claire and I have decided to call off our wedding."

Lucille's jaw dropped. "What!? *What!?* Of course you're getting married! I can hear the organist warming up as we speak! This is some ridiculous—"

"I'm sorry, Mother, I know how much work you put into planning this—but Claire and I both know this marriage isn't right. We're not going through with it."

Lucille, stunned, fell back on her heels—before promptly collapsing into Mom's arms.

I slipped the ring off my finger and handed it to Randall. As beautiful as it was, I was glad to be free of it. I'd miss him, but I felt an enormous relief.

"Unbelievable," whispered Mandy, stalking off to give the news to the priest.

"Thank you," Randall said, kissing me gently on the cheek.

CHAPTER TWENTY

 THE AWAKENING

Luke! I hear you and Oprah have been chatting! Do you think she's going to bump you into her lineup of book picks?"

The crowd of literary luminaries gathered around Luke was five people deep on each side. It was a tight cluster, impermeable as a rugby scrum. His launch party had been under way for twenty minutes, and I hadn't spoken to him yet.

"Front page of *The New York Times Book Review*! That's really something!"

Luke's book had hit shelves exactly one week before and was already being lauded as one of the most exceptional novels of the era. Vivian, thrilled by its immediate success, had spared no expense in throwing together a suitably elegant book party at the National Arts Club on Gramercy Park. No quill-shaped pasties tonight.

I watched as David Remnick and Graydon Carter threw gentlemanly elbows to grab Luke's attention. You could practically hear Sara Nelson composing her next editor's letter for *Publishers Weekly* in her head. The response for Luke's book had far exceeded everyone's expectations—even mine, which were high.

"Claire!" a man's voice boomed from behind me.

"Jackson!" I gave him a huge hug, surprised and delighted to see him. It was hard to believe it had been a year since I'd been his assistant—it felt like ten, at least. "I didn't think you'd be able to make it! Luke said one of the grandkids was starring in the school play, and you wouldn't be able to get away."

"Alas, young Joshua's Hamlet was not to be. He's home in bed with what seems to be the world's worst flu. So I decided to hop on a flight. Big night for Luke! You did a wonderful job with his book, Claire. I was truly impressed. Didn't have to break out my red pen even once."

"Well, thank you. I learned from the best. But honestly, there wasn't much to do. The book was basically perfect when I first read it."

"Claire's being way too modest!" Luke popped up next to me, giving me a kiss on the cheek. I blushed.

"I see Mara," said Jackson, never one for subtlety. "I'm going to go say hello and leave the two of you alone."

"Can you believe this?" Luke said after Jackson headed off. It was the first time we'd seen each other since the wedding that wasn't, and I'd been nervous all day. "I can't believe all these people are here to celebrate my book. This could never have happened without you, Claire. Hang on, I have something for you—a little thank-you gift." He opened his jacket and pulled out a small, beautifully wrapped package.

"Luke, you really didn't have to—"

"Just open it."

I opened the silver wrapping paper slowly. Inside was a small, slim book. "My father's first collection," I whispered, tears immediately springing to my eyes. "Where'd you find it?"

"That's a long, really dull story for another night." He laughed, eyes twinkling. "But I thought you'd like it."

"Like it? I love— Thank you, Luke. It was really thoughtful of you. I, um—"

"Excuse me! Can I have everyone's attention!" Vivian clapped loudly on the microphone she'd grabbed from the jazz quartet playing in the corner. "Excuse me! People!"

The room fell silent, all eyes on her.

"This is obviously an exciting night for Grant Books. We're all very proud of Luke Mayville's success and talent. As some of you may know"—she lowered her eyes in false modesty—"I played quite a large role in discovering that talent. It's so gratifying, as a publisher, when you single-handedly raise someone out of, well, complete obscurity and help them share their gift with the world."

Vivian was taking "single-handed" credit for Luke's success? She hadn't even read the manuscript until the book was published!

"But there's another reason why tonight is momentous for Grant Books," Vivian continued. "I am very happy to announce that I am cutting loose from Mather-Hollinger. My company—Grant Enterprises—will be an independent, privately owned entity. I'm *delighted* that I'll no longer be constrained by Mather-Hollinger's ridiculous corporate bureaucracy. Grant Enterprises will not only continue and expand upon my record of success in the book world, but also be taking on TV and film projects. And I have no doubt that I will excel in those arenas just as I have with books."

I'd never hated Vivian more than in that moment. Here she was, on Luke's big night, first taking all the credit for his success and *then* stealing the spotlight from him.

And a separation from Mather-Hollinger? It was a horrible prospect. The company had done as little as possible to protect Vivian's employees from her abuse—but it was still better than nothing. I couldn't bear to think about how Vivian would behave under her own roof, left completely to her own devices.

"Wow," said Luke. "That's going to be interesting."

"That's going to be a catastrophe." My head hurt.

"Luke! Would you like to say something to your many fans?" Vivian purred over the microphone like a lounge singer. At first, Luke looked like he'd rather not—but then he seemed to shake off his discomfort, walking over to the microphone and taking it from Vivian. She kept her hand planted on his arm, batting her eyelashes and leaning in to give him a languorous double kiss.

"Thank you, Vivian. I really appreciate everyone being here tonight." There was a round of hearty applause, and my heart swelled with pride. "There's one person I really need to thank—one person who saw the book's potential and worked tirelessly to realize it. It's as much her book as mine. Claire Truman, my editor and friend—Claire, would you come up here, please?"

I stood frozen in my tracks as the sea of people parted.

"Come on, Claire," Luke repeated, waving me toward him. I reluctantly walked forward.

As I got closer, I saw that Vivian was shooting me a death glare, arms folded indignantly across her chest. Lulu was scowling from stage left, and Dawn looked on nervously from the front of the crowd. Only David flashed me an enthusiastic thumbs-up. "As I was saying, I wouldn't be standing in front of all of you tonight if it weren't for the hard work and careful eye of—"

I started to smile—but my eye was drawn back to Vivian, who let out a loud huff. "Sit the fuck *down*," she hissed at me. The microphone picked up her words and amplified them across the still hushed cocktail party.

My cheeks turned scarlet. Luke paused. I stood rooted in place.

"I said, sit down!" Vivian repeated in a louder voice. "You're embarrassing yourself, Claire. You played a small role in the book, fine, but he's giving you way too much credit. At least have the grace not to accept it." She smiled at the crowd apologetically, as if I were some wayward, greedy child whose appetite couldn't be controlled.

"Vivian," Luke said firmly, "Claire played a very *significant* role in—"

"It's okay," I said quietly, and Luke hung his head in frustration. I looked straight at Vivian, suddenly unafraid. I'd had the courage to put the brakes on my wedding—I could do this too. "This isn't my moment, Luke. It's yours. But it's also the last moment I'll be working at Grant Books. Vivian, I quit."

I walked briskly back to where I'd been standing. Stunned, the crowd remained parted, cleaving a path between me and Vivian. Half the faces stared at me, half stared at her. All we needed was a few tumbleweeds, some pistols, a saloon—and our showdown would be complete.

"Good riddance to bad rubbish," Vivian snorted, grabbing the mike out of Luke's hands. "You were in way over your head, Claire. You were a liability from day one. Those of you who might consider hiring Ms. Truman, consider yourselves warned!" Vivian threw back her mane of reddish blond hair and laughed villainously.

For a second, I was dying to scream back at her. I wouldn't let Vivian smear me in front of a crowd I respected! I'd call her a miserable bully—very few in the room would fault me for it.

But then I looked down. I was still holding Dad's book.

"Good-bye, Vivian," I said calmly, turning to head for the door.

I'd walked a few steps when I felt a hand on my shoulder.

"My card," said a top editor at Knopf whom I'd met earlier that night.

"Here's mine," said a senior editor next to him. "Call me, Claire."

As I headed for the door, almost every major publisher in the crowd extended his or her business card to me. I'd collected more than a dozen by the time I reached the hallway. I looked back at Luke. He was beaming. For that matter, so was I.

Twenty minutes later, at the office, I was frantically putting my files in order when two men in black from the HR department materialized in the doorway. It was after 10:00 p.m.

"Vivian thought you might come back here," said one of the goons, looking at me menacingly. "We came as soon as we got her call."

"You need to vacate the premises immediately," instructed the other.

"Fine. I just wanted to be sure my notes were clear, so that my authors won't be left in the lurch—"

"Immediately means *immediately*. You have two minutes to collect your personal items, and after that, the city police will be notified of your disruptive behavior and you will be escorted out of the office by armed guards."

I considered the fact that getting frog-walked out of the building would be the most fitting end to this chapter of my life. But then I dumped my Rolodex and extra shoes into a cardboard box and hurried to pack up. I'd hit my quota for ugliness. I just wanted to get out of here with my dignity intact.

The HR reps exchanged suspicious looks. "Enough stalling," one declared. "Time's up." They eyed the contents of my cardboard box, which I hoisted onto my hip. It was time to go.

Good-bye, conference room, site of so many of Vivian's egregious overshares.

Good-bye, conference room door, slammed every time Vivian flew into a rage.

Good-bye, coffeemaker that I relied on for life support. I think I'll miss you most of all.

"Move!" barked one of the guys.

"I don't know why you're still doing her bidding," I said. "Vivian's leaving Mather-Hollinger. She just announced it. Did she tell you *that* when she called?"

As I stood there buffeted on both sides by the men in black, the elevator doors closed shut on Grant Books. And not a moment too soon.

EPILOGUE

 TO HAVE AND TO HOLD

Glad you could make it," said Phil, opening the door to his apartment. "We've got a lot to celebrate!"

"Phil? You look like a completely different person!" I hadn't seen Phil in weeks, not since he'd been hired as a senior editor at Simon & Schuster. He'd lost at least fifteen pounds, and the bags under his eyes had miraculously disappeared. He looked no less than a decade younger.

"I feel a lot better, that's for sure. The stress of Grant Books had me blown up like a tick." Phil ushered me into his living room, where ten or so people sat clustered on couches and cushions. "Hey, everyone, this is Claire Truman. She just quit Grant Books last month." All the faces turned toward me, smiling warmly. A few were familiar from my early days at Grant, but the others I'd never seen before.

When Phil had called me last week to invite me to an ex-Grant support group meeting, I'd thought he was joking. A support group for former employees of Vivian Grant? The meetings, Phil explained, were a forum for airing the grizzliest, most painful memories—stories that anyone who hadn't experienced Vivian firsthand would think were exaggerations.

I'd hesitated to accept the invitation. I was still pretty shell-shocked, but I wasn't sure I needed to swap tales of woe with a bunch of strangers.

"I know it sounds a little weird," Phil had admitted, "but it's kind of like we're war buddies. All of us have shared the stories with our family and friends, and they've listened patiently, tried to understand. But they can't. You have to live it to understand it."

Phil hadn't lost his flair for the dramatic, that was for sure. Finally, though, I'd agreed to stop by. And looking around the crowded room, I found it strangely comforting to know that these people had done their time at Grant Books and lived to tell about it. They seemed well-adjusted now, but like me, they knew what it was like to be in the trenches with four buddies, take a quick break to go to the latrine, and return to find everything destroyed and their friends all gone. These people knew what it was like to work in a professional war zone, dodging the bullets flying out of Vivian's office, negotiating the hostile territory that encompassed Lulu and Graham. They'd been forced to carry out orders that they now shuddered to remember.

"Welcome to life on the outside, Claire," said a pretty woman in a sundress, "and congrats on getting out!"

"I'm Marvin," said the man on my left. "I used to be the art director at Grant Books, until one afternoon Vivian called me a 'fucking impotent she-man' in front of the entire staff. I just settled the lawsuit and bought an apartment on the Upper West Side with my girlfriend."

"I found out I was fired when my card key was deactivated," piped up a mousy brunette. "Someone from HR shipped some of my personal belongings home. All because I'd disagreed with Vivian's point of view during an editorial meeting."

"Oh, she loves doing that," her neighbor commented, "The unexpected card key thing? It's one of her favorite power plays."

An older man cleared his throat. "I was one of the few people who came to work for Vivian who had more than a decade of publishing experience. I'd worked at Random House for over six years, and Penguin before that. I lasted ten days at Grant Books. I've never seen anything like it, before or since."

"So how'd things go down, Claire?" asked Phil. "Was she livid that you'd quit?"

"I'm not sure, actually. David, my former assistant, quit the next day, and I haven't spoken to anyone else at the company. I really needed to clear my head."

"Well, you're lucky that she hasn't spun the reason for your departure in the gossip columns," muttered Mike Hudson, a young guy I recognized as a former marketing director at the imprint. "She told everyone I was addicted to crack and stealing from the marketing budget to feed my habit. Or something like that. The story itself didn't make any sense, and not a shred of it was true—but that didn't stop her."

Phil went into the kitchen and reappeared with a tray full of champagne flutes. "Well, I propose a toast!" he said cheerfully, passing the glasses around. "To Vivian finally getting what's been coming to her!"

"What do you mean?" I asked when he got to me with the tray.

"Didn't you read the *Daily News* this morning? Hang on, Linda bought ten copies, there must be one in here—ah, here you go." He pulled a paper out of a basket next to the couch. "Take a look."

AND THEN THERE WERE THREE

Publishing powerhouse Vivian Grant has now officially split her business from former parent company Mather-Hollinger, transplanting her new Grant Enterprises into a 20,000 sq. foot loft space in Tribeca and plastering her name on the side of the building, Trump-style. As reported last week, Grant hoped the independence would give her "more time to conquer the film and television worlds"—we hear you, Viv, the pesky thing about being a book publisher is that books take up *so* much of your day—but so far, the move has only spurred her former staff to reclaim *their* independence. Word is that all but two staff members walked out yesterday after a particularly epic Grant tantrum.

Who were the two loyal suckers—er, souls—who stuck by her side? One insider describes senior editor Lulu Price and editorial director Graham Fisher as "brainwashed cult members," while another says "they're as cruel as Vivian." In any case, Vivian Grant now has plenty of room to throw chairs—but far fewer minions to use as targets.

"I can't believe it," I shook my head, putting down the paper. "Dawn quit, too?"

"Yup. Apparently, she led the charge. I invited her tonight, but she still sounds pretty shaken. We'll get her to the next meeting."

"Good for Dawn." She'd finally hit her limit. "Jeez, can you imagine what it's like over there?" A shudder passed through my body despite the summer heat.

"They deserve each other," said Phil. "And come on, this is Vivian. Let's not kid ourselves too much. You know her evil genius will find some way to make buckets of money again, and she'll lure in a fresh crop of employees who don't know better. The cycle will start all over again. She's not out of the game."

Maybe, I thought to myself. Maybe Vivian would find some way to rise again, stronger than ever. Phil was right; she was a genius. Vivian had a unique ability to see opportunities that others didn't, her work ethic was insane, and even her egomania could be considered an asset in certain circumstances. She was beautiful, brilliant. She had everything going for her, really... and yet I'd never encountered anyone who exuded so much misery and anger. And that was the shame of it all. What if a woman as capable as Vivian was also able to treat her employees with some respect and decency? There'd be no stopping her.

"Anyway, enough about her," Phil said. "Tell me how you're doing, kid. How's the job search?"

"Some promising leads, but I'm just gathering information. This time around, I want to be sure I know exactly what I'm getting myself into before I commit." Fortunately, thanks to Mara, I had already managed to find David a great job at P and P. He was working with a well-respected senior editor there, and was happy and thriving in his new environment.

"And have you been in touch with Randall?"

"I have, actually. He's doing well. Taking things slow, trying to get out of the office a little more. He seems happier."

"I'm glad to hear it. You seem so much happier, too, Claire."

I *was* happy. I felt like myself again, which came as an incredible relief. The last month had been really great. For starters, I'd found a cute one-bedroom apartment in Williamsburg, which Bea had helped me transform into a charming little home. It wasn't grand, but it was mine—and the rent was pretty reasonable. Mom had come out to visit for a week, and the night before we'd christened the apartment with its first *Anne*-and-Cherry Garcia marathon.

This afternoon, before she had to leave for the airport, Mom and I had visited Lucille. Needless to say, I'd been nervous, despite Mom and Randall's reports that Lucille was recovering well from the wedding disappointment. But the visit had turned out to be shockingly enjoyable. If Lucille had some lingering hostility toward me, she hadn't shown it at all. She was all smiles as she ushered us in for tea, even congratulating me on "standing up to that hideous Grant woman."

Apparently, she'd been keeping busy since the wedding derailed. At Mom's urging, Lucille had agreed to team up with Mandy for wedding consultations—just part-time work, but it was keeping her occupied. As soon as we'd sat down, Lucille proudly showed off their plans for a lavish winter wedding in Palm Beach.

"I'm sorry I never thanked you for all the work you put into the wedding," I told Lucille. I'd been so preoccupied with my own struggles, I hadn't appreciated just how artistic and beautiful Lucille's vision had been. It wasn't my style, but her eye for detail was exquisite.

"You're welcome, dear," Lucille said, squeezing my hand. "I'd be happy to plan your next one."

No chance of that happening—but it was her way of saying that all was forgiven, and I appreciated it. Having Mom back in her life and embarking on a new career had brought out Lucille's spirit of magnanimity.

"Here's to changing our lives for the better!" Phil said, clinking his glass against mine and snapping me back to the party. "Of course, Claire, it will probably be a while before you're ready to start dating again."

"Oh yeah." I nodded solemnly.

"By the way, I got an interesting submission from a friend

of yours recently. Luke Mayville. His agent said you'd suggested he send his next manuscript my way, since his option with Grant Books is now obsolete. Well, he did—it's a partial, maybe five chapters at this point—and it's excellent. No surprise, given the success of his first book. Of course, we put an offer in immediately. We'll see if we can get Dominick to accept it"—Dominick Peters was the William Morris bulldog to whom I'd introduced Luke a few weeks earlier—"but hopefully he will. The offer was extremely generous."

"I've read the chapters. I knew you'd be a great editor for the job, Phil."

"Well, thanks. I really appreciate it. We all think Luke has a big career in front of him."

"Definitely," I agreed, glancing at my watch as subtly as possible. Eight-ten already. "Phil, I wish I could stay longer, but I've got to meet someone. I'd love to have you and Linda over for dinner sometime, now that I have a kitchen table." Bea and I had done an Ikea raid that weekend.

"We'd love that. Don't get to Brooklyn often enough anymore. Anytime."

I said my good-byes to the rest of the ex-Grant group, collected some more business cards, and slipped out the door. It was a warm night, and people were all over the streets. I walked the four blocks to Mimi's quickly, loving the feeling of summer air on my skin.

"Sorry I kept you waiting," I said, kissing Luke softly before settling in across the table from him.

"Worth the wait," he smiled.

"Luke! Claire! My favorite couple!" called out Mimi, charging toward the table. "Let me tell you what is special tonight."

As Mimi launched into her recitation, Luke reached over the table and took my hand. I couldn't seem to stop smiling when I was around him. Fortunately, it seemed mutual.

"You two," laughed Mimi after she'd finished. "My love birds!"

I sat back in my seat, excited for the night ahead of us. A whole new chapter of my life was beginning—and this time, I was writing it.

ACKNOWLEDGMENTS

I'm deeply grateful to Jamie Raab for taking this book under her wing. It's been a delight and privilege to work with Karen Kosztolnyik, my insightful, diplomatic editor. Rick Wolff's support and guidance—on this book and in general—have been a tremendous blessing. My agent, Daniel Greenberg, has been an outstanding ally, advocate, and reader. The entire team at Warner Books—especially Michele Bidelspach, Harvey-Jane Kowal, Lisa Sciambra, Anne Twomey, Heather Kilpatrick, and Jennifer Romanello—has been ace.

My heartfelt thanks to Marisa Brown, Mariah Chase, Dan Clark, Grace Clark, Kelly Collins, Stephanie Harris, David Kanuth, Carey Mangriotis, Elizabeth McGloin, Colleen McGuinness, Daria Natan, Ashley Phipps, Lindley Pless, Massy Tadjedin, Elisabeth Wild, Alexandra Wilkis, Andra Winokur-Newman, Chris Wolff, and Laura Zukerman. Most of all, John Loverro, whom I can't possibly thank enough.

As always, I'm indebted to my parents and grandparents for their unconditional support, inspiring example, and open door policy.